"POETIC, HAUNTI

A FRESH AND EXCITIN

A highly accomplished, down-to-eart... This one is long on love but surprisingly short on sentimentality."

—*Mobile Register*

"*Clay's Quilt* surprises us and rewards us sentence by sentence with the deep poetry of kinship. The book is so real it's painful to read in places, lit by a special knowledge and affection."

—Robert Morgan

"Stunning authenticity . . . Exquisitely crafted . . . House gets it right—from the dialect of characters with names such as Dreama and Cake to the details of this world in which the bond of family is stronger, almost, than gravity. . . . On nearly every page words are strung together with such electricity they almost make you weep. . . . Still, perhaps the most endearing quality of *Clay's Quilt* is its message, tactfully woven into the storytelling. It's a simple message, one we all ought to know by now: From death comes life. Following winter is spring. Even a lonesome heart can feel the spark of love."

—*Impact Weekly*

"Murder, music, coal dust, clairvoyance: all are part of the pattern of Clay Sizemore's life in Black Banks, Kentucky. And the thread is passion. . . . *Clay's Quilt* is stitched to last."

—George Ella Lyon

"A small gem . . . This is one of those rare treasures—a simple and beautifully told story that brings to life an unfamiliar world, and makes it as real as any you have ever known. . . . This is a deeply thoughtful and moving story not only of a boy's coming of age, but of a way of life that comes to seem as precious to the reader as it does to those who live it."

—*The Island Packet* (SC)

"A heartrending tale of one man's search for his identity and the corresponding struggle of a Kentucky community to hold on to its unique heritage."

—*Register-Pajaronian*

"Deftly written, replete with wisdom and remarkably light on sentimentality, this lovely novel makes plain the value of family."

—*Publishers Weekly*

"A treasure to be handed down from one reader to another."

—*BookPage*

"A lovely and accomplished literary debut."

—*Booklist*

CLAY'S QUILT

ALSO BY SILAS HOUSE

The Coal Tattoo
A Parchment of Leaves
Eli the Good
Same Sun Here
Southernmost

CLAY'S QUILT

a novel by Silas House

BLAIR

Cover design by Laura Williams
Interior design by Anne Winslow
Illustration on p. xi by Robert Cronan,
Lucidity Information Design, LLC

Blair is an imprint of Carolina Wren Press.

The mission of Blair/Carolina Wren Press is to seek out, nurture, and promote literary work by new and underrepresented writers.

We gratefully acknowledge the ongoing support of general operations by the Durham Arts Council's United Arts Fund.

ISBN: 978-1-94-946724-6

Library of Congress Control Number: 2020933682

For Cheyenne and Levi
I hope you dance

Blood and bone remember
surely as nerve and neuron.

—Jane Hicks, “Ancestral Home”

Foreword

by Tyler Childers

Not but three weeks ago, I was at an outdoor market in Amsterdam. As I was walking through the booths gawking at the trinkets and knickknacks, the city rang with bicycle bells and conversations I didn't have the slightest clue how to decipher. Then from a booth down the way, as if I had been offered a fraternal handshake or secret signal, I heard, "Now how much you asking for 'is bell rightchyar?" I looked over to see a man holding an old bell with a tractor as the handle.

I approached the man and told him I couldn't help but notice from his accent that he must be a foreigner. He looked me up and down over the top of his glasses, kind of confused, then smiled as he caught the joke within my own accent. He was from Bristol, Tennessee. Him and his woman had just got in that morning. I told him I was from east Kentucky and asked him how the weather was when he had lit out. Neither of us knew each other from Adam, but we understood each other better than anyone around us. For a minute, in the middle of that spiderweb of a canal town, I was close enough to home to be there by evening.

I have come to feel at ease in the identity I was given. Nonetheless, I had to come around to it. Too many teachers and mentors, with the best of intentions, had left me feeling my "east Kentucky-ness" was a thing that I'd need to be shed of in order to get further in this world. The further from home I got, the more I realized it was the only thing that would keep me pointed north. And the furthest I had got, at the time of my late teenage revelation, was Lexington. My, what a world of difference two hours and ten minutes can make.

As if I stood a chance of shaking it anyhow. You can take the boy out of Lawrence County, but who else would claim him? And what else could I be but a backslid Baptist honkytonker from Hickman Holler? Why would I look to be anything other? And if not for me being it, then who? In the words of Clay's Aunt Easter, "It's a good thing, being able to find your place in the world." A good and freeing thing indeed.

Clay's Quilt is the first novel from an author who has surely found his place and is ready to confidently walk the reader across its hills and hollers. It neither romanticizes nor apologizes so much as it allows us to witness four solid seasons in Crow County with Clay Sizemore. Through Clay's tight-knit network of family and friends, the outsider is given a glimpse of life within these hills and the spirit that settled them. For the young Appalachian writer searching for his or her own voice, it sits among the finest as an inspiration to take what is and shine it outward. Much like it did for myself ten years ago, eighteen and wanderin'.

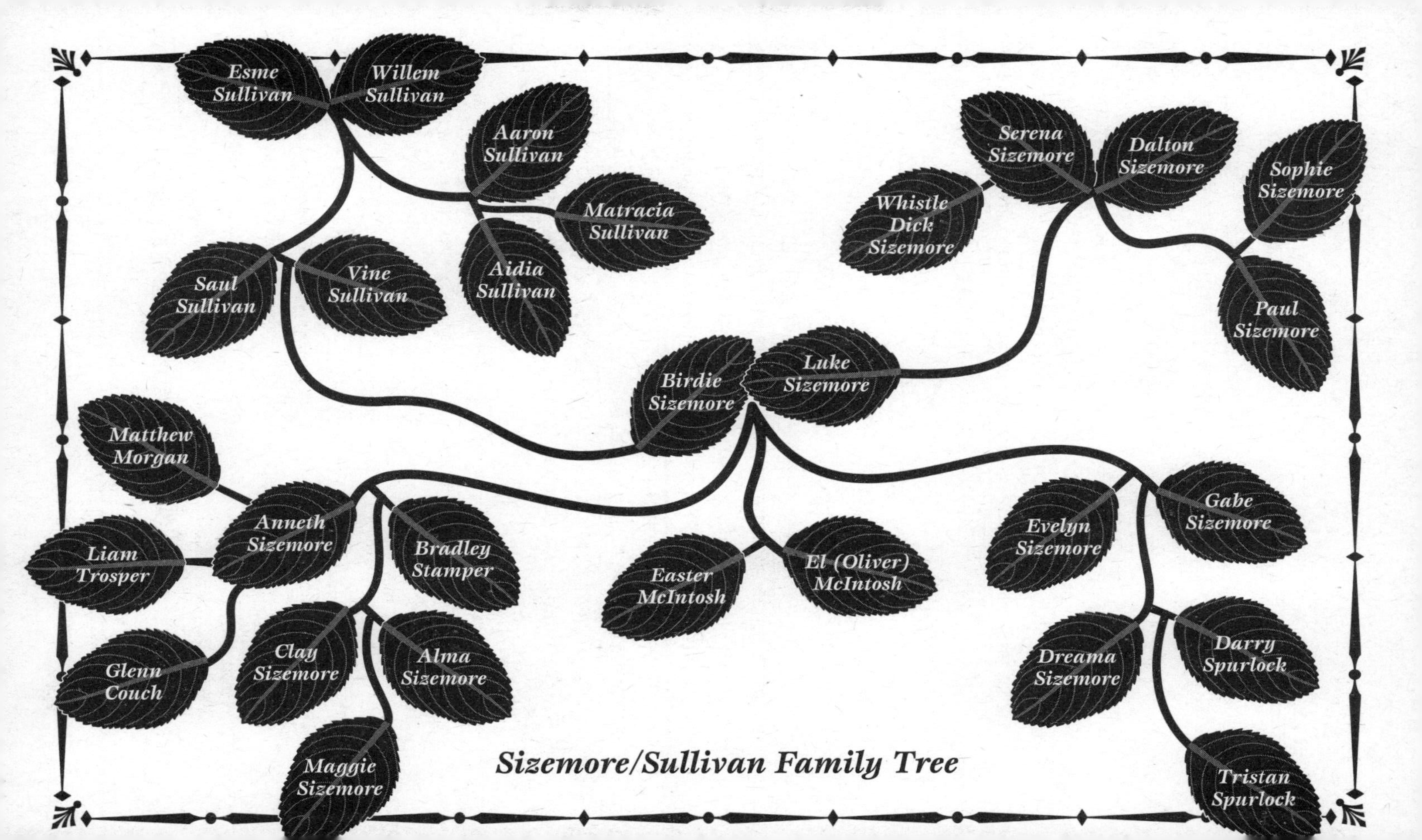
Esme Sullivan
Willem Sullivan
Aaron Sullivan
Matracia Sullivan
Aidia Sullivan
Saul Sullivan
Vine Sullivan
Serena Sizemore
Dalton Sizemore
Sophie Sizemore
Whistle Dick Sizemore
Paul Sizemore
Birdie Sizemore
Luke Sizemore
Matthew Morgan
Anneth Sizemore
Liam Trosper
Bradley Stamper
Glenn Couch
Clay Sizemore
Alma Sizemore
Maggie Sizemore
Easter McIntosh
El (Oliver) McIntosh
Evelyn Sizemore
Gabe Sizemore
Dreama Sizemore
Darry Spurlock
Tristan Spurlock
Sizemore/Sullivan Family Tree

CLAY'S QUILT

PROLOGUE

THEY WERE IN a car going over Buffalo Mountain, but the man driving was not Clay's father. The man was hunched over the steering wheel, peering out the frosted window with hard, gray eyes. The muscle in his jaw never relaxed, and he seemed to have an extra, square-shaped bone on the side of his face.

"No way we'll make it without getting killed," the man said. His lips were thin and white.

"We ain't got no choice but to try now," Clay's mother, Anneth, said. "We can't pull over and just set on the side of the road until it thaws."

Clay listened to the tires crunching through the snow and ice as they moved slowly on the winding road. It sounded as if they were driving on a highway made of broken glass. On one side of the road there rose a wall of cliffs, and on the other side was a wooden guardrail. It looked like the world dropped off after that.

They met a sharp curve and the steering wheel spun around in the man's hands. His elbows went high into the air as he tried to straighten the car. The two women in the back cried out "Oh Lord!" in unison as one was thrown atop the other to one side of the car. Anneth pressed her slender fingers deep into Clay's arms, and he wanted to scream, but then the car was righted on course. The man looked at Anneth as if it were her fault.

The women in the back had been carrying on all the way up the mountain, and now they laughed wildly at themselves for being scared. They acted like going over the crooked, ice-covered highway was the best time they had had in ages, and the man kept telling them to shut up. It seemed they lit one cigarette after another, so many that Clay couldn't tell if the mist swirling around in the cab of the car was from their smoking or their breathing.

The heater in the little car didn't work, and when one of the women hollered to the man to give it another try, the vents rattled and coughed, pushing out a chilling breeze. Clay could see his own breath clenching out silver in front of him until it made a white fist on the windshield. The man wiped the glass off every few minutes, and when he did, he let out a line of cusswords, all close and connected like a string of paper dolls.

Anneth exhaled loudly and said, "I'd appreciate it if you didn't cuss and go on like that in front of this child."

"Well, God almighty," the driver said. "I ain't never been in such a mess before in my life."

Clay knew that his mother was getting mad because a curl of her hair had suddenly fallen down between her eyes. She pushed it away roughly, but it fell back again.

"They ain't no use taking the Lord's name in vain. I never could stand to hear that word," she said. She patted Clay's hands and focused on the icy highway. "Sides, you ought to be praying instead of handling bad language."

"Yeah, you're a real saint, ain't you, Anneth Sizemore?" the man said, and a laugh seemed to catch in the back of his throat. He pulled his shoulders up in a way that signaled he was ready to stop talking. Clay watched him hold tightly to the steering wheel and look out at the road without blinking. He knew this man somehow, but couldn't figure how exactly, and he didn't feel right with him. He wished that his father had been driving them. He reconsidered and simply wished he could put a face to the word *daddy.* He was only four, but he had already noticed that most of his cousins had fathers, while his was never even spoken of. He wondered if his father would smell so strongly of aftershave, like this man, and have a box-bone in his cheek that tightened every few minutes. He started to ask his mother about this but didn't. He had so many questions. Today alone, he couldn't understand what all had gone on.

Clay looked out at the snow and wondered if the world had stopped. Maybe it had frozen, grown silver like the creek water around the edges of rocks. They had not met one car all the way over the mountain, and the few houses they passed looked empty. No tracks on the porches, no movement at the windows. Thin little breaths of black smoke slithered out of chimneys, as if the people had left the fires behind.

The windows frosted over again, and Anneth took the heel of her gloved hand and wiped off the passenger window so they could look out. The pines lining the road were bent low and pitiful, full of clotted ice and winking snow. Some of the trees had broken in two. Their limbs stuck out of the packed snow like jagged bones with damp, yellow ends bright against the whiteness. There was not so much sunshine as daylight, but the snow and ice twinkled anyway. The cliffs had frozen into huge boulders of ice where water had trickled down to make icicles.

"Look," Anneth said, "them icicles look like the faces of people we know."

She whispered into Clay's ear and pointed out daggers of ice. The one with the big belly looked like Gabe. One column of ice looked like a woman with wigged-up hair, just like his aunt Easter. There was even one that favored the president, who was on television all of the time. Clay put his hands inside hers. The blue leather gloves she had on were cold to his bare hands. He didn't move, though, and hoped the warmth of her fingers would seep down into his own.

"I need to get this baby some mitts," Anneth said, to no one in particular. The women were singing, and the driver was ignoring every one of them. "His little hands is plumb frostbit."

She undid the knot at her neck and slid the scarf around her collar with one quick jerk. The scarf was white, with fringes on each end. She shook out her hair and picked at it with one hand. The car was filled with the smell of strawberries. She always washed her hair in strawberry shampoo, except on Fridays, when she washed it with beer. She took his hands and lay the scarf out across her lap, then wound the scarf round and round his hands, like a bandage.

"I'm awful ashamed to have on gloves and my baby not," she said as she worked with the scarf. "There," she said. There was a fat white ball in Clay's lap where his arms should have met.

One of the women in the back put her chin on the top of the front seat. "I hain't never seen a vehicle that didn't have a heater *or* a radio. This beats it all to hell."

The man shot her a hateful look in the rearview mirror.

She fell back against her seat and began to sing "Me and Bobby McGee." The other woman joined in and they swayed back and forth with their arms wrapped around each other's necks. Their backs smoothed across the leather seat in rhythm with the windshield wipers. They snapped their fingers and cackled out between verses.

"Help us sing, Anneth!" one of them cried out. "I know you like Janis Joplin."

Anneth ignored them, but she hummed the song quietly to Clay, patting his arm to keep in tune.

The man said that he would never make it off the downhill side of the mountain without wrecking and killing them. There was more arguing over the fact that they couldn't pull over. They would surely freeze to death sitting on the side of the road. They were on top of the mountain now, far past the row of houses. There was nothing here but black trees and gray cliffs and mountains that stretched out below them. Everybody started talking at once, and it reminded Clay of the way the church house sounded just before the meeting started.

Clay looked over his mother's shoulder at the women. One of the women was looking at herself in a silver compact and patting the curls that fell down on either side of her face. She snapped the compact shut with a loud click and looked up at him happily.

"Don't worry, Clay," she said. "We'll make it off this mountain." He could see lipstick smudged across her straight white teeth.

The other woman stared blankly into space, and it took her a long moment to realize that Clay was studying her. She was beautiful, much younger than his mother, but as Clay looked at her, she aged before his eyes. Her face grew solid and tough, her skin like a persimmon. Her eyes looked made of water, her nose lengthened and thinned, and her mouth pinched together tightly. He caught a glimpse of what would never become of her, because she was killed that day, alongside his mother and the man driving the car.

The man's voice was suddenly harsh. "Well, I was good enough to take you over there, now dammit. I need to pull off and calm down some," he said loudly. "My nerves is shot all to hell."

"I'll never ask you to do nothing else for me, then," she said with disgust. "I ain't worried about myself—I have to get this baby home."

"Hellfire, I'd rather be home, too, but this road is a sight," he said. "You ought not got that child out in this. I'm pulling over, and that's all there is to it."

"Go on, then," Anneth shouted in a deep voice. She turned toward the window and didn't speak to him again.

"Let's just set here a few minutes and figure something out," the driver said.

The shoulder widened out and they could see the mountains spread out below. The white guardrail was wound about by dead vines that showed in brown places through the thick snow. The mountains looked like smudges of paint, rolling back to the horizon until they faded into one another in a misted-over heap.

Anneth wiped the icy window off once more and said, "Look how peaceful. Look at them mountains, how purple and still."

Clay knew that the mountains looked purple under that big, moving sky, but they didn't look still at all to him. They seemed to be breathing—rising so slowly, so carefully, that no one noticed but him. He watched them, concentrating the way he did when he was convinced a shadow had moved across his bedroom wall. It seemed to Clay that they rose and fell with a single pulse, as if the whole mountain chain was connected.

Everyone had grown silent looking out at the hills, and later this struck Clay as strange. They were all accustomed to seeing hills laid out before them, but there was something about this day, something about how silently the mountains lay beneath the snow.

It was so quiet that Clay was certain that the end of the world had come. Everybody on earth had been sucked up into the sky in the twinkling of an eye. He was used to hearing people talk about the End and the Twinkling of an Eye; his Aunt Easter constantly spoke of such things. She looked forward to the day when Jesus would part the clouds and come after His children.

"Rapture," she called it, and the word was always whispered. Easter said if you weren't saved, you'd be left behind.

He pressed against his mother and felt the warmth of her body spread out across his back. She ran her fingers through his hair and began to hum softly again. He could feel the purr of her lungs against his face. It was the same song the women had been singing. Clay knew it by heart. He'd watched his mother iron or wash dishes while she listened to that song. Sometimes she would snatch him up and dance around the room with him while the song was on the record player. She had sung every word then, singing especially loud when it got to the part about the Kentucky coal mines. The vibration in her chest was as comforting as rain on a tin roof, and he fought his sleep so that he could feel it. She must have thought he was asleep, too, because finally she took her hand from his head and stopped humming.

She pressed her face to the window, leaning her forehead against the cold glass. "I ain't never seen it so quiet on this mountain," she said.

That was the last thing Clay was aware of, but afterward, he sometimes dreamed of blood on the snow, blood so thick that it ran slow like syrup and lay in stripes across the whiteness, as if someone had dashed out a bucket of paint.

PART ONE

A CRAZY QUILT

• 1 •

CLAY SLID HIS blackened coveralls down his legs, jerked them off, and tossed the hard clump of clothing into the back of the truck. Coal dust twinkled on the metal of the truck bed. He put his work boots back on and pulled off his T-shirt, sailing it through the window and onto the floorboard. Already his chest was glistening with the sweat of July sun.

It was hot and white, and all up the hillsides, tangled trumpet vines wilted and thirsted. The blacktop of the parking lot glistened, so soft that it threatened to seep down the hillside. There was only the hint of a breeze and it felt as forced and tired as the heavy-footed men who made their way out of the coal mine.

The men laughed and loudly called out their good-byes. They climbed into their trucks, ground gears, and set out for home. They told Clay not to get too drunk this weekend, not to get into any fights when he went out honky-tonking. They loved it that every Monday he told them big tales about barroom brawls and drunken women while the men leaned against the black walls of the earth and took their lunch. They all liked Clay. They called him Baby-boy, since he was the youngest man on the crew.

They talked with cigarettes bobbing up and down in their mouths, feeling deep in their pockets for their keys. As Clay got into his truck, they all hollered out in singsong voices: "Bye-bye, now Baby-boy. Be good this weekend."

Clay wheeled his truck carefully down the steep incline of road that led to U.S. 25. Once off the company road and onto the highway, he shifted gears and laid rubber on the road, his tires issuing little barks. He passed two of the men who had gotten out before him. He laughed into his rearview mirror at the miners behind him, who gave him the finger and smiled with their teeth blazing white against their coal-dusted faces. He liked the way the ball of the gearshift felt, all cool and shiny, covered up in his fist. His big, rough hands slid over the steering wheel with ease as he sped down the road, shifting gears and pushing the gas all the way to the floor. He loved the rough purr of the engine and the smooth sound of tires humming sweetly on hot pavement. With one deliberate motion he clicked a cassette into his player, and Steve Earle started singing "I Ain't Ever Satisfied."

The road was long and curvy, making its way around jutting mountainsides where sandy cliffs dripped sulphur and parched gullies lay where creeks usually spilled down. Close to the company land, it was heavily wooded with straight white pines and scaly-barked hickories. As Clay passed houses, he could see into the yards, where husbands and wives worked side by side in the dusty gardens, hoeing out the weeds that seemed to grow even more rampant in the heat. Boys leaned into the mouths of their vehicles, grease smeared up their arms and across their faces, their tools lying silver and shining at their feet. Young wives swept the porch or sat in porch chairs breaking beans. At the Pentecostal church, the pastor was standing back to read the message he had just put on the large sign sitting on cinder blocks in the parking lot. It changed every Friday, and Clay loved to see what it would say each week. Today the sign read: MAN IS BORN TO TROUBLE, SURE AS THE SPARKS FLY UPWARD.

"Amen to that," Clay said aloud. The preacher always knew exactly what to say, as if he predicted Clay's moods and put the scriptures there just for him.

Clay maneuvered the truck around the curves while his fingers tapped on the steering wheel. He sang along without missing a word and felt around on the seat until he found his cigarettes. The Zippo fired, and the scent of new smoke and lighter fluid came to him, filling his lungs with the sensation of something that would cleanse him.

On one side of the road, the shoulder dropped off to a kudzu-covered slope that slid down to the river. In some places the river was so shallow that he could make out the small slate rocks lining its bed. The houses all sat on the other side of the water, with swinging bridges leading out to the shoulder of the road, where the people parked their cars. In one of the shoals, a mother in a denim skirt and faded blouse held the hand of her little daughter. They walked in the river, passing under blue shadows of sandbar willows. Their feet looked pink when they brought them out of the water to take a step. When the woman let go of the child's hand, the little girl fell heavily into the water. The woman laughed, bending over to look the child in the eye, and they began to splash each other. There was always something to remind Clay of his own mother.

The valley widened out somewhat and small businesses began to come into sight. He passed a green highway sign that read

BLACK BANKS just before he came up the last little hill and stopped at the red light where the highway became Main Street. There was a family-owned grocery store here, but a huge billboard on the mountain behind it told everyone to shop at the new supermarket in the shopping center. A new factory was out on the bypass now, and they were already building another lane on the highway that took travelers up to the Daniel Boone Parkway. A federal courthouse stood just up the street, and on the outskirts of town, rows of stores jutted from both sides of the Wal-Mart.

At the other edge of town, he sped up again and let the wind rush in to wash around the cab of the truck. The road grew wild again, following the path of the winding river beside it. His house sat between the road and the river, two stories, with the bottom half full of his landlord's storage. Clay sprinted up the wooden staircase and made his way across the high porch. Between the porch railings and the floor, ivy grew through the lattice like living cross-stitch.

He had rented the house when he was eighteen. On his eighteenth birthday, he had gone to the Altamont Mining offices and was hired on the spot. All his life, every boy he knew wanted to escape having to go down in the mines, but Clay thought it the most noble profession any man could have. As soon as he left the foreman's office, he had gone down into Black Banks and rented the house by the river. He had announced it over supper that evening, and Easter had cried until her eyes were red and swollen.

"Why in the world would you want to leave here? Why spend all that money on rent, and you just starting out in life? Don't make no sense. Is it one of us you running from?" she asked.

"I'm not running from nobody," he said. "I just want to see some more of the world."

Gabe laughed heartily, slapping the table. "I got news for you, buddy," he piped in. "Living on the other side of that little town ain't seeing nothing."

"That ain't what I mean." Clay wanted to see what it would be like to be on his own, but he also felt like there were too many ghosts there. Still, he couldn't have told them this. His family was one that didn't leave one another. They did everything together, warm in the knowledge that kin was nearby. Gabe and Easter were both torn all to pieces, and he was only moving ten miles away.

"A family should live right together," Easter said. She was being unusually hard-shelled about this, as she had always encouraged him to think for himself. "It ain't right."

"What if I was moving plumb across the country, or going into the service?"

"Army's different," Gabe told him. "Your people know you off doing for your country."

"Well, I need to do this. It's just for a little while."

Clay's house was so close to the water's edge that when the river rose in spring, the stilts under the porch stood right in the water. He liked the splash of the river and the night things that gathered there: katydids and crickets, frogs and cicadas. At night the smell of the river overtook his house. It smelled of everything it had passed on its way to him. It smelled of homes with families in them; of girls that sat in stiff chairs, painting their toenails and dreaming of far-off places; of boys who skipped rocks on the river's surface to break up moonlight. The river at night carried the scent of untamed mountains and long, cool fields where dew settled first and sunlight hit last in the mornings.

Clay pulled off his muddy boots and placed them beside the mat. On the porch, he slipped down his jeans and stood in his underwear a minute, stretching with bones popping. The air was momentarily cool against his bare skin. He ran his hand over his tight chest and felt the grit of coal dust on his palm.

He grabbed a beer from the refrigerator and stepped into the shower, using the hottest water he could stand. He let the water sting the top of his head while he drank the beer down. He crushed the can with one hand and sat it on the edge of the tub, then watched coal dust gather and disappear down the silver drain. He washed slowly, feeling the hot water open up his skin. He closed his eyes and let the water pound his face, tap at his eyelids. It was his birthday, and that always set him to thinking far too much.

EASTER RAN THE can opener around the top of the salmon can, drained it in a steady stream down the sink, cracked an egg, splashed it out across the fish, crushed up crackers in her pink hands, and cut up a whole onion, all in a matter of seconds. She mashed it all together with her hands, smoothing it and moving it around until she had a round patty that sizzled and popped when she slid it into the skillet full of hot grease. Steam rose as she took the lid off the potatoes. She moved the spatula under them fast, flipped them over, and replaced the lid.

Easter did everything quickly. She moved her arms fast and forcibly. When she wiped off a counter, she pushed down on the rag with her full strength.

She had devoted all of her time to her home since she finally quit her job at the school lunchroom last year. Sometimes, Easter walked slowly from room to room in her house, admiring what all she had. She ran her hands over the furniture, stroked a photograph, folded her arms and studied her home. Her granny used to say, "We've always been poor as Job's turkey and most likely always will be." Easter was amazed at how well they had all done for themselves.

Easter didn't like to leave her house, even to go into town. On Saturday night, she and El went to Black Banks to shop and always stopped at the Root Beer Stand for a foot-long and a peanut butter milkshake. Besides that, she hardly went anywhere but church. Easter was the lead singer there, and her voice was known throughout the county. People drove from all over to gather at the Free Creek Pentecostal Church on Saturday nights, when they had all-night singings. On Sunday nights, sinners that lived near the church sat out on their porches in the evening just so they could hear her voice float down the valley to them.

She had gotten up at daylight this morning and cooked El a big breakfast before he left for the road again. He was a truck driver for Appalachian Freight, gone for five-day stretches. As soon as he had lit out, she had lit into the house, cleaning it even though it didn't need it. Then she started in on Clay's favorite meal for his birthday.

Sometimes Easter looked at Clay and felt like lying down on her bed and crying her eyes out. He was just like his mother, up and down. Some of that was not good, in Easter's eyes. Anneth had been wild, maybe the wildest woman in Crow County, Kentucky. Easter could remember how people went on about Anneth, how she would sometimes come in at three or four o'clock in the morning, smelling of liquor, a cigarette always ruining her pretty hand.

Even when they were teenagers, still living at home with their granny, Easter would sometimes be awakened by the rumblings of cars pulling down into the holler. Anneth would stumble out of the car, singing a Brenda Lee song at the top of her lungs, and then stop halfway across the yard as the car made its way back out of Free Creek.

She'd yell, "Easter! Get up! Come out here and look at the moon. Ever-damn-body get up and look!"

Easter ran out to her, clad in her long flannel nightgown. Anneth pulled her up into her arms, holding her so tight that Easter feared she'd break her bones. She grabbed Easter's chin roughly and directed her face skyward. She whispered with sweet whiskey breath: "Look at it, Easter. I love a little slice of a moon, don't you? They way better than a full one."

"Let's go in, Anneth. You've woke the whole holler up."

Anneth laughed. "We ought to stay out here all night and study that," she said, staring at the sliver of moon. "That's church to me."

Anneth just liked to have a big time all of the time. Easter had always been the good girl, but she had never been jealous of Anneth. She had never gotten distraught when all the pretty boys went after her sister, never mad when Anneth refused to go to church.

Anneth used to beg her to have more fun, but Easter would say things like, "Just watching you is enough for me."

Anneth would fall back, her dress cool and thin against her milky thighs. "Easter, I don't want you to die and go to Heaven without having a little fun. The Lord forgives all things, honey. Live, sister!"

Easter had lived out her own sin through her sister, because God knows Anneth did enough of it for the both of them. She often asked herself how she could have been a Christian and condoned such actions. She loved it when Anneth threw back her head in laughter, letting all of her teeth show, her eyes clamped shut, hand pounding her red knees.

It didn't shock Easter when they came and told her that Anneth was dead. She was the only one Anneth never could surprise, despite how different they were. She had known that Anneth would not die naturally—somebody had to take a life like that. A person so full of life couldn't just up and die; a life like that had to be taken by force.

Anneth came to Easter sometimes, but Easter had told no one of this. One would think a spirit would come in quiet and solemn, but Anneth was the same in death as she had been in life. She came to Easter laughing, leaned up against a wall with her arms crossed and her bangs hanging down in her eyes. A lusty, ancient laugh, an open-book smile. She studied Easter, and her eyes grew misty with tears.

The first time Anneth came to her, not long after her death, she did speak. Easter was praying in the living room, something she did when the notion struck her. In the middle of her prayer, she sensed someone was standing behind her. When she turned, there was Anneth, smiling. Anneth said, "Live, girl."

Easter jumped up and ran toward her, knowing that she could not touch her, knowing that Anneth wasn't even real but was something that she was meant to see. Anneth said it again and Easter felt herself growing angry.

She yelled out, "This is the way I like my life, Anneth!" She closed her eyes, asking the Lord to take this image from her eyes. "This is too much. I don't have the strength for it. Take her."

Easter had seen spirits and known things since she was a little child. The Bible spoke against fortune-telling, but she could not deny what she saw in her dreams, what she sometimes witnessed right in her own house. She had lived with the spirits alone, telling no one of their company. When she was a child, they would come walking toward her in the corn. She caught glimpses of them dancing in the treetops. She had been forewarned of floods, deaths, births, and had never told anyone outright. Still, little hints proved to people that she had the sight, and they all respected her for it without mentioning it to her face.

Easter had been expecting Anneth lately. She hadn't come in a while, and Easter thought that it was about time.

• • •

As Clay sped down the crooked highway toward Free Creek, it was like he was driving back in time. If there had been mile markers on the side of the road, they would have clicked off the years instead of the miles: 1994 . . . 1982 . . . 1974. He slowed, turned right, and pulled down into Free Creek. He sang along with Dwight Yoakam and tried not to pay attention to the homesickness swirling around in his belly. He smashed out his cigarette in the full ashtray and sprayed a little cologne onto his neck so that Easter wouldn't be able to smell the tobacco. The truck bucked like a wild horse as it bounced across the old bridge set up on the huge boulders that lined the creek.

Free Creek was a narrow holler, really nothing more than an etched, packed-dirt road with a shallow white-water creek on one side and a row of houses on the other. On each side rose a great mountain, so steep and tall that when someone stood in the middle of the holler, they couldn't see to the top of either one. There were only about fifteen houses up there, and everybody knew everybody else. When Clay was little, newscasters boasted that the War on Poverty was being waged in those very mountains, but if the government had fought any battles close to Free Creek, no one in the holler heard the guns.

Clay drove slowly down the holler, silent in summer heat, and looked on Free Creek like it was a picture. When he thought about Free Creek, he always thought of long, cool evenings when you could hear the silver sound of men playing horseshoes and the redundant bounce of the boys playing basketball down on the road. The women hung out clothes, swatted children on the hind end, canned kraut in the shade. People worked in their gardens until dusk, played rummy on the porch, shouted out that supper was ready. The men worked all day and often came in drunk. The women sometimes threw their husband's clothes into the yard. There might be a fistfight or the firing of a pistol into the mountainside.

Nobody was out this evening, though. Clay cruised by the houses sitting close to the road, which were sealed up tight against the summer evening. It was suppertime, and nobody was outside. Far up on the mountain, two trailers sat side by side with all the windows open and box fans in their open doorways. That was how every house had survived when Clay was little, but now almost everybody had an air conditioner.

He pulled into Easter's short driveway, which was actually two sandy ditches amid the sparse grass. The house was built on the last little slope of the mountain, so that in a hard rain all the gravel washed out to the road. He sat in his truck for a long moment, studying the little house.

WMTG was blasting out of the radio sitting above the sink when he went in the back door. The Mosley Family was singing "Meeting in the Air" and Easter was singing along as loud as she could, patting her foot, and washing dishes. It was a fast gospel song, and she moved her hips around to the beat. He watched her, then surveyed the kitchen. The stove was crowded with steaming cookers and skillets.

He couldn't come to this house without remembering his mother's wake and funeral. There had been plenty of food then, too. Hams had been carved, potato salad and fried corn had been dipped out. There had been chicken dumplings and baked beans that were served warm, pork chops and fried chicken that were eaten cold and greasy, coconut cakes fit for a baby shower, and pies made from apple preserves usually saved for Christmas. All of those smells had not overtaken that of the casket in Easter's living room. It had been bought at the funeral home, made from fresh cedar. The smell had settled on people's clothes and crept into their mouths.

One woman had said that it was a shame Anneth had died in the winter, instead of summer, when so many good things could have been prepared right out of the garden. One of his mother's cousins had told how Anneth liked to walk out into the garden and pluck a tomato right from the vine. "She'd eat it while it was still warm from the sun, see," the woman had said. "She'd let the juice run right down her chin."

Clay stood now in Easter's kitchen and looked into the living room. He could almost see all of the people who had crowded in there that night. They had sat up all night with the body. When it was very late, the women had busied themselves with putting up the food. Outside, the men had stood around a rusted drum barrel—alive with a fire that sent up columns of sparks—and covertly passed around a pint of bourbon.

He had asked Easter to carry him to the casket so he could kiss his mother before going to bed. When she pulled back the net and bent over the casket, his mother's face had been shrouded in lavender shadows that made her high cheekbones more prominent, her stillness more noticeable. She had always been in motion, even while she slept. He had looked at her a long time, knowing that she was dead. He had known.

Easter had leaned over so he might reach her, and Clay kissed his mother on the cheek. Her skin had been so cold, like a piece of stone taken from a cliffside. When he had finally pulled away, he had buried his face in Easter's neck, sure that his lips were blue.

"Lord God," he said, announcing himself. "You've cooked enough for an army."

Easter looked over her shoulder and smiled, then lowered the volume on the radio. "It's bout time you got up here. Only way I can get you up here anymore is to cook you a big supper." She rinsed the last dish and wiped her hands.

"I been working double shifts and laying round the house. Been too hot to do much." Clay watched her move around the kitchen as she loaded a plate full of food. The long hair she had worn in a bun during his childhood was gone. Even though she was a Pentecostal, Easter decided long ago that her hair wasn't going to get her into Heaven, so she went and got a shoulder-length permanent. She was still a pretty woman with big-boned hands and dark eyes. Clay hadn't seen her in a pair of pants or shorts his whole life.

"Cake stayed with me three nights this week," Clay said. "Can't do much when he's up the house. I called you bout ever night, though."

Easter laughed. "I know you got your own life. What's Cake doing staying up your house? Him and Harold into it again?"

"Why yeah. Them two stay into it."

"I guess you still laying at that club, too," she said. "Partying and carrying on."

"Ah, not as much as I used to," he said, and shoved his hands deep into his pockets, fiddling with his change.

"Well, good," she said. "I hope that's the truth."

Easter ripped off a piece of foil and covered a plate of food, then handed it out to Clay. He knew it was for his uncle.

"Here, take this to Gabe. He's got a big crew over there gambling, so I know he won't come eat with us. Tell Dreama to come on before it gets cold."

Clay opened the back door to his uncle's double-wide, and the cold indoor air rushed out. Gabe sat at the table with two men, a bottle of Jim Beam and the deck of cards between them. The air conditioner sat in the dining room window, ruffling the short hair of the men, and Don Williams sang softly from the stereo. Gabe shuffled the deck of cards several times before Clay crossed the kitchen and set down his plate.

"Hidy, stranger. I've bout forgot what you looked like," Gabe said.

"I was here a week ago."

"Too long," Gabe said. "But it's been bout too hot to get out."

"That's the damn truth," one of the men offered. The other one said, "You're exactly right."

"Boys, if I'd knowed you all was over here, I'd brought you all a plate, too," Clay lied.

"Hell, Clay, we fixing to get drunk. Have too much food in your belly and it'll eat your liquor up. You going out tonight?"

"Naw, we'll probably go up the Hilltop tomorrow night, though."

Gabe dealt the cards, and the men stared at their hands. There was a long silence before Gabe said, "Your birthday today, ain't it?"

"That's right."

"Look there," Gabe said, and nodded to the edge of the table, where a small leather holster lay.

Clay picked it up and reached in to find a little pistol.

Gabe grinned. "Happy birthday, then."

Clay ran his fingers down the warm handle, stroking the cold silver of the barrel. Even if he didn't set much store by hunting, he loved guns. He loved their cool solidity in his hand. "I been dead for a pearl-handled pistol," he said. "It's a twenty-two, hain't it?"

"Yeah. Snub-nose. That was your granddaddy's. I took it to the gun shop and had that new handle put on it, though. Don't go packing it in no honky-tonk just cause it's little. Little gun like that'll get a man kilt."

The men laughed drunkenly.

Gabe wanted to get back to his card game. "Go on, now, buddy."

Clay held the gun on his palm for a long time. He turned it over and over again without saying a word.

"Where's Dreama at?" Clay asked.

"Back in that bedroom, only place she ever is." Gabe didn't take his eyes from his cards. "Might as well not even live with me, cause she sure as hell ain't no company, always locked up in that room."

The double-wide was the kind of clean that only a bachelor and his eighteen-year-old daughter could achieve: it appeared to be clean only because things had been pushed behind other things. A new, obese sectional couch sat in a U in the living room, a tall Pioneer stereo system had several dozen loose cassette tapes stacked haphazardly inside the glass, a gun rack on the paneled wall held the rifles and shotguns. On the walls were pictures of Dreama and Clay in various states of growing up, blown-up snapshots of Anneth that they had had made after her death. A framed picture of Gabe and Dreama with OLAN MILLS stamped in silver in the corner. There were no photographs of Dreama's mother in the house; she had left when Dreama was just a few months old, and Gabe wouldn't even speak of her. There were a few pictures from Home Interiors that Lolie, Gabe's girlfriend, had put on the walls to make the place look more homey.

Clay could remember so many nights spent here, so many nights when he had been awakened by men singing Loretta Lynn songs, stumbling up to the back door to buy a pint of whiskey or a half case of Blue Ribbon. Easter had raised him, but he had lived at Gabe's. Sometimes Gabe would tell the men to hush, that he had children in the house. Other times Gabe would invite them on in and they would play poker and get drunk. Gabe loved to drink, and he loved to have a big crowd around all the time. When he had a party, people came from everywhere to attend.

Several times Easter had burst in to grab up Clay and Dreama, her voice thunder when she shouted that Gabe was going to kill himself drinking and drive everyone else crazy in the meantime. But when Easter was gone to tent meetings or revivals—where people hardly ever brought children—he and Dreama were allowed to stay right in the party crowd. Clay sat in Gabe's lap while they played quarter bounce or five-card draw.

The women sat on the couches and smoked long cigarettes, playing 45s on the stereo. They would all sing together on songs like "Harper Valley P.T.A." and "Love Is a Rose" in wild, laughing choruses with their bottles held high. They danced by themselves to anything by Bob Seger, but called the men in to twirl them around when Tom Jones sang "Say You'll Stay until Tomorrow." It was like that—scratchy records, smoke-filled rooms, cussing men, the bing of a quarter being bounced off the table and into a shot glass.

Usually Clay and Dreama tired of watching the party and sat outside long into the night. They waded in the black water of the creek until Lolie came out to call them back. Sometimes the people who came brought their own children, and they all played hide-and-seek or *Star Wars* in the blue-dark yard. They sneaked cigarettes from unwatched packs and smoked on the creek bank. Dreama would put on talent shows, and she always won by applause when she put on a blond wig left behind by her mother and danced across the porch, pantomiming Dolly Parton singing "Old Flames (Can't Hold a Candle to You)." They would catch the lightning bugs that came up out of the laurels lining the creek and then put them into mason jars or wear them as glow rings on their fingers. Clay and Dreama climbed trees or lay back on damp grass, talking about how they would be when they grew up.

All of the people would stay all night, and on Sunday mornings Clay would awake to find sleeping bodies strewed throughout the house—two or three on the couch, more on mattresses Gabe had dragged out of the closet, people lying right in the hallway.

Clay walked down the hallway toward Dreama's room. He paused at the closed door of his old bedroom, even going so far as to put his hand on the cold knob. He knew it was just an empty room now, occupied by nothing more than a bed with no headboard. The bed was kept in there so people who stayed and partied would have a soft place to fall. It wasn't his room anymore.

He went to Dreama's bedroom door and opened it without knocking. She sat on the edge of her bed, painting her fingernails in slow, careful strokes.

"Clay!" she squalled, and ran to him. "I'm glad you finally here. You might as well live in Lexington as over in Black Banks—I feel like you a hundred miles away."

She hugged him around the neck, holding her hands out in the air behind his head to keep the polish out of his hair.

"What've you been up to?"

"Nothing much. Going out with Darry, cleaning up after Daddy and all them drunks that lay here practically every night of the week nowadays. I run some of them off the other night. I swear, them men are scared to death of me, and I can't understand it. They'd stare down death if somebody was holding a pistol between their eyes, but when I come running down the hallway and tell them they're too loud, they scatter."

He laughed. "Come on," he said. "Easter's got supper ready."

"D'you bring Daddy something to eat?" she asked.

"Yeah, come on before it gets cold."

Across the yard, Dreama hung on to his arm and talked about how she hated working at Hardee's and how she couldn't stand the thought of school starting back, since she had graduated last May. She couldn't find a thing worth reading and hadn't been to the movies in ages. Dreama had long, black hair that slapped her back when she jerked her head around and blue eyes so bright that you could see them coming down a dark road. The annual Heritage Festival had held a look-alike contest last autumn, and Dreama had won for borrowing some girl's prom hoopskirt and looking just like Vivien Leigh.

"And Clay," she said, catching his arm before he could go in the back door. "They's something I've got to talk to you about."

"What is it?"

"Just don't set and jaw with Easter all day and don't be in no big rush to run off." She glanced down to his hands, where he was still clutching the .22.

"And put that pistol up," she said. "Easter sees that and she'll die stone-hammer dead over Daddy giving you a gun."

• 2 •

THERE IS A COOL that sometimes comes down over the mountains in the evening. The day slips away slowly, so quietly and secretly that no one really notices until it is gone. The peach light stands like steam along the horizon, changing the shape of things. Night does not come quickly, does not even give a hint of its coming, and for a while, there is just the cool, when there is no night and no day, only time, stretched out like ice. No clocks ticking away the minutes, no movement of the earth, nothing growing or changing.

And the cool comes down, peaceful and soft. Mist seeps out of the jagged cliffs. The breeze picks up a bit, stirring the mist in a slow, graceful dance through the trees, dampening thirsty leaves. No night sounds are heard. A lone bird hollers somewhere, far up on the mountain, and its lonesome sound cracks the stillness. The creek slips over old rocks.

It was an evening like that.

Easter wiped her hands off on the dry dishcloth and spread it over the shiny wall dividing the sink. "Let's go out on the porch," she said. "It's too pretty an evening to be setting in the house."

The porch was long and cool, as if the air of last autumn was stored within its little space. Dreama and Easter sat on the padded glider, and Clay positioned himself up on the railing. The worst thing about coming up to Easter's to eat was that he couldn't smoke a cigarette after supper. His mouth watered for one, but he couldn't stand to smoke in front of her.

Easter exhaled loudly, like someone who had spent a long day at work. Clay watched as her thin body settled into the deep cushions and she lay her head back against the wall to close her eyes. Lately he had noticed the gray at her temples, the thinness of the skin at her wrists, and the pale blue of her veins there.

"Summer won't be here much longer," Easter said. "We in for bad weather this fall. Smell wet days right in the night air."

"I love the fall. Fall clothes is so much prettier than any other time," Dreama said, swinging her legs.

"It's pretty, but too lonesome a time for me," Easter said. "Fall makes you think of old times, somehow."

Dreama was not anxious to hear an old tale. She jumped up out of the glider and kicked the bottom of Clay's boot. "Clay, let's walk up in the holler fore it gets dark," she said, and widened her eyes, nodding toward the road.

"Won't you let me set and talk to Easter while my food settles?"

"Go on with her, Clay," Easter said, and waved them away. "I just want to set here and rest."

They walked up the holler road, past the rows of houses and the gardens that grew close to the road. The corn looked black in the waning light. People were making their way out onto their porches to watch night set in, and they all waved and called out to Dreama and Clay. As soon as they were out of Easter's watchful eye, Clay fired up a Marlboro.

He paused where the road forked and looked up toward the family graveyard, sucking hard on his cigarette.

"You want to go up to the graveyard?" Dreama asked, watching him. "You ain't been in a while."

"Not this evening."

"Let's go on the old path, then," Dreama said. "We ain't been to the cedar together in forever."

They crossed the bridge and went up on the path into the mountain that faced the row of houses. Tiny bunches of bluebells grew in clumps on one side, and the other side was a straight cliff that supported a forest of pine trees that leaned over and peeked at those who walked below. At the end of the path stood a huge, domineering cedar. Within its shadow, the fragrance of its wood covered their clothes, just like the scent of his mother's lacquered casket had. Beneath the ancient tree sat a long, wide boulder that had bowls worn in it from years of children's rumps. The tree and rock were directly in front of Easter's house, about level with the roof, and Clay couldn't count the hours they had spent playing here, watching everything go on at the houses without anyone knowing they could see. This had been their secret place, the one place the adults never intruded on.

The rock was still warm from the sun, and Clay kept his hand on it, stroking it like a woman's back, when he sat down. "I'm gonna smoke another'n," he said, and lit a new cigarette off the burning filter of his last. "I been dying for one the last two hours."

"You'll really want one when I get done talking to you, my opinion," Dreama said. She stood in front of him with her arms folded. Behind her, Clay could see Easter through the thick trees, walking around her porch, picking dead petals off her hanging plants.

"I *know* you ain't pregnant," Clay said, finally hearing what she had said.

"Lord no," she said. "But I swear, I dread telling this to you. They's something you got to promise me before I tell it. Please don't start giving me advice and trying to change my mind, all right? My mind is set on this and there ain't no way I'm changing it."

"Hellfire, Dreama, what is it? Tell me." He hated the way she dragged out every little thing. When she won that look-alike contest, she had spun round and round in her hoopskirt, saying, "Why, fiddle-dee-dee!" over and over, until the announcer had to force her off the lunchroom stage.

Dreama ran her eyes up the damp cliffs behind them, as if she was seeing them for the first time. Then she looked right at Clay. "Well, me and Darry's fixing to get married."

Clay stood and hooked his thumbs into his belt loops. "Dreama, you're just eighteen year old."

"I know, Clay, but I love him." Dreama did not strike Clay as a child when she spoke, although he had always seen her as one before. He started to say that she wasn't old enough to know what love was, but he knew that he didn't believe that.

"You've got your whole life to get married. Why now? You always wanted to go to college. Don't be like everbody else."

"No, I always wanted to marry Darry Spurlock, and you know I did. I've been crazy over him since the seventh grade. Me and him's done talked about college and he wants me to go. I never would've left here to go, no way. I'll go up the community college and get in their nursing program."

"Shit, that's what everbody says. It's hard enough to get

through school, period, much less be a married woman and go. I guarantee you'll never go."

"Well, I will. Mark my words. Even if I don't, it won't be the end of the world. You can't have it all, Clay, and this is what I want most. I want to be with Darry."

"See, you already talking like school ain't important. Don't do this, Dreama. Don't ask for a hard life, cause that's all you'll get with Darry Spurlock."

Dreama laughed. She kicked the dirt at her feet and sat down on the rock.

"You just don't understand. I want something real and solid, Clay. I want something I can say is mine."

"That ain't no reason to get married."

"That's what love is, Clay. It ain't about getting away from Daddy or having a change. I told you first thing, I love him. Don't you understand that?"

"Naw, I guess I don't. Not when you just graduated from high school and got everthing laid out in front of you, I don't. What's the big rush?"

Dreama stood up beside Clay, weaving her arm through his. Darkness had descended over the valley, and they stood there a long time without speaking, listening to the night sounds fill the holler. The sound of the creek's rushing water seemed to have intensified with the darkness.

He could tell that Dreama was thinking too hard; she was trying to get her words just right, and her face announced this as plainly as if she were running her finger down the pages of a dictionary.

"Clay, I can feel this right in my stomach, and I know it's real. I can't throw it away. If things was different for you, you might be able to see my point."

"What do you mean?"

"You ain't never been in love, Clay. You don't know what it feels like."

"No," he said, "according to you all, I just stay drunk and don't want nothing else but that." He felt a wave of jealousy wash over him, but he did not know where it had come from. He jerked his arm away from her and went back to the tree, standing so close to it that its strong scent nearly sickened him.

"I never said nothing like that," Dreama said, and put her hand on his arm again. "Clay, what is it?"

"Nothing," he answered. The swelling clamor of the creek nearly overtook his words. "Go on back to the house."

"Are you that mad over me and Darry?"

"It ain't you," he said. "It's me. I just want to set here, by myself."

She left without a word, and he did not look up to see her go down the old path and fade into the gathering shadows. When he finally looked up, he could just barely make out her figure moving down the road, going back toward Easter's house. He imagined the way she looked: her long hair swinging back and forth, her small ankles beneath her skirt. He wanted to run through the tangle of brush and brier between himself and the road, splash through the loud creek, and run to catch up with her. He wanted to pull her around and hold her close to him without saying a word, but he didn't. He stood by the cedar and let night seep in around him.

Clay and Easter had sat up so late talking that he stayed the night. He hadn't stayed over in a long while and was surprised by how familiar the bed was to him. The sheets smelled the same; the shadows on the wall moved in the same jagged patterns. The sound of the creek came through his open window and made him think that he was still a child and that time had not moved forward at all.

He awoke early the next morning. He was surprised to see that he had risen before Easter, who usually got up at the crack of daylight. He moved carefully out of the house so he would not wake her, and put on his boots on the back stoop. The morning hit him like two handfuls of cold water. The white mist easing off the mountain was burning away quickly in the new light of day, and the dew sparkled in the grass like bits of glass. He breathed deeply and shook his head side to side in satisfaction.

Without knowing why, he walked down to the mouth of the holler, where he could stand on the bridge and look back at the houses lining the road and hanging from the mountainsides. He looked at the sleeping houses, the scratch of road, the noisy creek. He planned to stare at them so long that he would burn this picture into his head, the way you can do with the sun when its image is left imprinted on the tops of your eyelids. He didn't know why he felt the need to do this; when he had moved to town, he had felt as if he was escaping this place.

Almost to the bridge, he heard a little voice call out: "Aye! What're you doing up so early?"

He looked to the porch of his great-uncle Paul's house, where Paul's wife, Sophie, was standing on the porch in her housecoat. Their house was a big, forbidding one with black shutters and a long porch built on painted cinder blocks. It seemed to be the matriarch of all the others.

Sophie was so small that Clay wondered if her bones were hollow, like a bird's, and she looked even smaller on the high, wide porch. Even now her hair was already up in the perfect, church-ready bun she had worn as long as he could remember. Her glasses caught sunlight and glinted out across the yard.

Once Clay got up the steep steps to the swinging door on the porch, he saw that his aunt Sophie was smoking a cigarette.

"What are you doing, Aunt Sophie?" Clay said, not hiding his surprise.

She glanced at the cigarette, took one long last draw, and threw it into a coffee can that sat on the porch rail. She laughed mischievously. "Didn't you know I smoked, Clay?"

"Lord, no. I never would've thought that."

"Well, I let you see me. Only two or three people know. It's such a pretty morning, I wanted to share a secret with somebody." She eyed him curiously and realized he needed an explanation.

"I smoked before I started going to church. When I got saved, I tried my best to quit, but I couldn't. My mommy bout killed me, said if I was really saved, the Lord would take such a craving away. I bout backslid over it, because Mommy and Paul and everbody took such a fit over it. So, I started having me one of the morning, before anybody was up, and one at night when everbody was in the house. I sacrificed a lot of satisfaction for the Lord, I'll tell you that much." Sophie's laugh was soft and polite, yet uncontained, like a kitten coughing. "Well, do you think I'm a bad sinner?"

"Why, no," Clay answered. "I don't see eye to eye with the church telling people how to serve the Lord."

"A person should go by their heart. That's what I believe." She put her hand atop his. "It's good to see you."

She held the front door open, motioning to Clay to go on in. He pulled off his boots and left them on the welcome mat.

Sophie went into the bedroom. "Paul's in the living room. Go on in there while I put me on some clothes," she hollered. "I'm going to cook us a big breakfast."

Clay found his great-uncle sitting at his quilting frame, where Paul was making a king-size quilt that filled up the whole room.

The curtains and sheers had been thrown back so that the white sunlight lit the whole room in a cool glow, as bright as new snow. Paul sat in a stiff ladder-back chair and fished needle and thread up through the fabric without even noticing Clay.

"What kind of quilt is that?"

"One to keep you warm." Paul smiled and peered over his glasses to see who the visitor was. "Why, Clay! I can't believe you've come to see your poor old uncle. You've bout quit me, buddy. Remember how you used to come up here?"

"Yeah."

Paul paused and straightened a hem. "This here is a crazy quilt, buddy."

"Why's it called that?" Clay asked. Paul was a man who loved to answer questions.

"I reckon because it's just scraps and whatever pieces you can get. It's a poor man's quilt, I guess," he said, watching the quilt. "They don't go by no real design. It's all up to the quilter. Ain't the best-looking quilt there is, but I like em."

Clay watched the needle and thread, the scraps of fabric pulling into one another, separate one second and a part of a whole the next. Clay had spent many evenings here, watching Paul make the quilts. Paul would take the scraps out and lay them on the bed, like pieces of a jigsaw puzzle that had to be fitted together perfectly. Clay had loved to watch the needle and thread go in, out, up, and through.

The scraps sat in a half-bushel basket on the coffee table, where Paul could reach over easily and pick them up. Clay moved to the couch and picked up one of the triangles of fabric. With his eyes closed, he ran his thumb over the strange landscape. He felt geography and history beneath his fingertips.

"Clay?" Paul asked. Clay handed him the scrap and watched as Paul worked it into the sea of color and shape.

"You the only man I ever knowed of to quilt," Clay said, without thinking.

Paul secured the piece in place and laughed after a long pause. "Men nowadays wouldn't pick up a needle if ever shirt they had was without a button. When I's growing up, a man was more liable to quilt than a woman. That's a fact. People forget where they come from, though."

"That's how Paul got me, by quilting," Aunt Sophie said, coming out of the bedroom. She wore an apron over her skirt. "I know that's the only reason my mommy let me marry him. Mommy never had liked Paul, and one evening he brung a big Wedding Ring quilt in, while we was courting, and spread it out on the couch beside Mommy. She bragged on it a sight. When he said he'd made it, she accused him of lying. She finally believed him, though, and that night she said, 'That's the one, Sophie.' " She laughed her kitten cough and disappeared into the kitchen.

"I was thinking bout your mommy right then, while I was stitching that piece," Paul said. He pointed to a bright turquoise square crowded with small, yellow flowers.

"She was a good hand to quilt, but she couldn't hardly stand setting still that long. Anneth couldn't stay in the house to save her life, and the only way she'd quilt is if we set the rack up outside. One summer, me and her and Sophie made the awfullest big quilt you ever seen, and we had a time with Anneth. She could stitch the best ever was, but she wasn't worth a dime when it come to the colors. Only thing she'd use was bright colors. A quilt needs some browns and grays to even it all out, but she wanted ever quilt to look like a big field of flowers. She'd dig through rag piles to find all the wild colors."

Paul held the needle still for a moment and looked off into space, as if he had to pause to let his mind wander back through time. Finally, he said: "That bright patch there made me think of her."

Clay waited as long as he could without prodding further, but Paul didn't say a word. Silence ate up the room, broken only by grease popping in the kitchen. "Tell me something else about her," he said in a near whisper.

"Well, let me tell you something I done to her and Easter one Christmas."

Clay nodded and Paul cackled out laughing. He had to calm himself to start the story.

"We had the biggest time ever was. All the men got wild drunk on Christmas Eve—them that didn't go to church—and we'd let off big powder kegs and fire shotguns way up in the night. We'd stand on the porch and hold Roman candles. We'd set up all night and either play the radio or have somebody there that could play the banjo or a fiddle. The women usually laid down and left all of us up, but Anneth snuck and got back up.

"She wasn't but bout fifteen year old, but we's all drunk, and we decided to let her drink a little with us. She always fit right in with us men, anyway. Well, that gal drunk like you never seen the beat of. She set right up with us.

"Anyway, the next morning, Anneth had to get up and help Easter and them women cook the Christmas dinner. Easter was running all over that kitchen, working like she was fighting a fire, and Anneth was just dragging behind her, barely able to walk. Hung over, you see. Easter was griping on her a sight for being so slow, and they was both standing at the kitchen sink, cutting up a big hen to fry. Well, I took a big mule and rode it right in the back door. I was real easy with him, real slow, and they never even heard me, they was in such a big fizz arguing and working. Now, I never knowed of Easter to be scared of nothing in her life, but when she felt that big mule's breath on her neck and turned around eyeball to eyeball with it, she liked to died. She passed slick out." Paul burst out laughing, holding both big hands against his belly. He closed his eyes and leaned his head far back, barely able to catch his breath. "Aye Lord, that liked to tickled me to death."

"What about Mommy?" Clay asked. "What'd she do?"

"Oh, that never even phased Anneth. She just started laughing and liked to never hushed. That's how Anneth was," Paul answered, and started laughing again.

Clay laughed, too, but only partly at the story.

"Scoot up here, now, Clay," Paul said. "Watch here."

Paul told him everything about quilting, things he would never remember, but he savored each word as if they were lost verses of Scripture. He watched the needles, and the pieces of cloth, and his uncle's brown eyes. Paul hummed and never blinked. He had big, confident hands. The needle seemed very thin between his square-tipped fingers. Paul worked the pieces in slowly.

Clay wished that he could piece the story of his mother together in the same way. He might find scraps of her life, stitch them together, and have a whole that he could pull up to his neck and feel warm beneath. Someday he might be able to fit all of his questions together and work needle and thread between them and the answers. If he did, he would take two corners in his hands, snap the whole out onto the good air, and let it sail down smooth and easy to settle on the ground. It would be a story made up of scraps, but that was all he had.

• 3 •

Dreama's wedding took place on a cold, dreary day. A thin rain fell upon Free Creek. It was slow and quiet, falling straight down without the company of wind or black thunderheads; instead it brought along a gray, swirling sky that seemed to shift and wrap itself around the edges of the horizon. It smelled fresh and damp, like clothes that have been left out on the line after the dew has fallen.

A rain like that brought spirits with it. The translucent sky gave off the hint of otherworldliness. The rain was so cold and the sky so dark that it looked like a scene from the past, either in another time or in another world.

Beneath the pelting rain, the Free Creek Pentecostal Church sat up on the hillside at the mouth of the holler as if it were keeping watch over the houses and people below. It was an old church, but it looked just the same as it had when it was built in 1917. The people who had raised the roof were stern-faced and rough, and they had all held firmly to the belief that buildings were meant to be sturdy, not beautiful. The exterior of the church looked suitable for a funeral, but not the place for a wedding. Still, Dreama wouldn't even have thought of being married anywhere else.

Dreama was in the baptistery dressing room, standing in front of the full-length mirror and about to cry. Easter was bent behind her, trying to fasten the two dozen pearl buttons that ran down the back of her wedding dress.

"I knowed it would rain on my wedding!" Dreama moaned. "It never rains on nobody's wedding. Nobody's. I knowed it would on mine."

"This rain hain't hurting nothing," Easter said. "Be glad for the rain; the Lord sent it."

Easter struggled with the buttons, which were supposed to squeeze through loops that weren't half big enough. Against her will, she gave up. She was far too nervous to be irritated.

"Geneva, come do this," she yelled to Dreama's cousin.

Dreama looked at the ceiling and tried to hold still for Geneva. "Where's Clay at, Easter?" she asked. "Bring him in here to me."

"Clay can't come back in here, Dreama. Not in the dressing room." Easter stood at the small stained-glass window on the outside wall of the room, watching the colors of the glass grow distorted in the streams of rain that ran down it. Imprinted in the glass were the words 1 CORINTHIANS 13, which Easter thought was fitting, since the room served as a dressing room for brides just as often as for people getting ready for their baptisms. Used to be everybody got baptized in the river, which Easter thought was so much prettier, but now they only did that in the summer. In the winter they used the baptism tank behind the pulpit, which had warm water and a painted mural of a blue river behind it.

"Lord God, Geneva, have you got em buttoned?" Dreama asked. "Now I'm bout to pee."

"Well, you'll just have to hold it, Dreama Marie," Easter said. She felt anxious and sweaty, the way she sometimes felt just before something was revealed to her. She was aware of the possessed rain outside and hoped that Anneth wouldn't appear today. Not today.

"Get Clay in here," Dreama said, and stomped her little foot. "I ain't seen him all day and I want to see him once more before I do this."

Easter shook her head and ran her hand down the side of Dreama's heart-shaped face. "If you wasn't so pretty, I could refuse you. Geneva, run out there and see if you can find Clay."

Dreama twirled around with her arms out to her sides. "Easter, do I look a sight?"

"No, baby. You the prettiest thing I ever seen," Easter said.

"Lord have mercy," Dreama said loudly, and pinched her cheeks for more color. "If I had a cigarette, I'd fire it right up, I'm so nervous, and I don't even smoke."

"Don't talk about smoking in the church house, Dreama Marie."

From the sanctuary they could hear the sound of the fiddler playing "When You Say Nothing at All." Ever since Dreama watched Princess Diana get married on television, she had dreamed of having violins play Pachelbel's Canon in D at her wedding, but she had finally settled for a fiddler playing old mountain ballads and country songs. Everybody else said it was crazy not to have a pianist, but this was the one thing Dreama stood firm on.

"Clay's coming," Geneva announced, rushing back in. "He looks so good I wish he wasn't my cousin."

Dreama had made Darry go and personally ask Clay to be his

best man. Darry had complained that his brother ought to have this honor, but Dreama had cried and pouted. She had reminded Darry that his own brother had run off to Jellico, Tennessee, and gotten married by a justice of the peace in an IGA and he hadn't even asked Darry to go and be a witness. Darry had gone to Clay's, where they sat out on the back porch and drank three or four beers, watching the river flow by, and Darry had shuffled his feet before asking Clay what he thought about being his best man. Dreama had always wanted them to be friends and was always trying to push them together.

When Clay came in, Dreama cried out like she hadn't seen him in ages. Seeing her in her wedding gown, Clay felt like crying. Memories encircled him, poking their fingers in his ribs. He never would have guessed that things would turn out like they had, that Dreama would fall in love so quick and so hard and get married before he even had a real girlfriend. Looking at Dreama, Clay felt very old.

Dreama pushed him back to the corner of the room, where no one could hear them talking. She straightened his bow tie and picked lint off his jacket, never meeting his eyes. "I'm fixing to get married now," she said, sadly.

"I know it."

"Well, I don't know if I'm doing the right thing, Clay. I'm afraid."

"If you love him, that's all that matters."

She stared into his green eyes, which were framed by the coal dust that no miner could get out of his lashes. She nodded.

"I know why you got so upset at me, that day up at the cedar," Dreama said. "I didn't mean to hurt your feelings. I never knowed you had any intentions of even wanting to have something serious."

"I never did," he lied. "It's all right."

The bridesmaids all crowded in front of the mirror, pinning their wide-brimmed hats atop their heads. When they caught a glimpse of Clay leaving, they all turned to watch him go. His eyes settled on Easter.

"This is the best-looking bunch of women I ever seen," he said loudly.

"You damn straight," Geneva said, and Easter nearly passed out from hearing such a word uttered within the walls of the church.

CLAY WALKED BACK into the sanctuary and down the aisle toward the foyer. The pews were full, and Clay nodded to everyone as he passed. There were people Easter went to church with sitting right beside people Gabe got wild drunk with, which made Clay smile to himself. There were aunts who told him how good-looking he was and asked why he wasn't married yet. There were uncles who knew perfectly well that Clay didn't hunt but continued to ask him when he was going to go squirrel hunting with them.

In the foyer, Darry was leaning up against the wall, green-faced and red-eyed. None of them had lain down until six that morning because Gabe wouldn't let them. Gabe got wilder than any of them and ended up on a crying drunk that half of them didn't even remember. They all got up at ten in order to get ready for the wedding, and that was when everyone realized it had been pure foolishness to have a bachelor party the night before the wedding.

"I hope you don't get up there and puke when you're supposed to say 'I do,'" Clay told Darry.

"I've never got sick yet. I'm tired, though."

Clay felt awkward when he couldn't find anything else to say. He had known Darry all of his life, but for whatever reason, he had never even considered being friends with him. Darry talked slow and easy, choosing his words carefully, and Clay liked that about him, but he had never been able to like him. Weddings always made people feel closer—especially the men—but that was about as far as it went between Darry and Clay. They had been pushed together by the ceremony, and afterward they would just nod to each other when they met and not be able to hold a whole conversation. They stood side by side, waiting for the wedding to begin, and didn't say another word.

Clay stood and looked out at the crowd, remembering all the Sundays Easter had brought him and Dreama to church here. He recalled the way Pastor Morgan's voice had shaken the church, as did the heavy thumping of his fists upon the podium. Clay had often wondered if God had a voice as powerful as the preacher's. Sometimes the preacher would pull off his suit coat and let it fly through the air to land wherever it might. The singing gave Clay visible chill bumps, and he had been mesmerized by the women who spoke in unknown tongues and shouted, often falling onto the floor and shaking until someone spread a towel over their legs so that their skirts wouldn't ride up and shame them. More than once he had witnessed Easter rising from her place at the piano midsong to take off running down the aisles, hollering, with her hands raised over her head. Once she had shouted and danced so hard that her hair had fallen out of its pins and she had broken one of the short heels off her shoes.

He remembered the Sunday school classes he had attended downstairs, where it had always smelled of chalk and damp books. He had memorized the verses and the books of the Bible in order: Matthew, Mark, Luke, and John. Clay never had felt really close to God inside the church, not the way he did when he could see the creek running over the rocks and the mist coming down off the mountain. By the time he was about thirteen, he began to realize that God didn't just live inside this old church house, even though the preacher called it God's house every chance he got. One Sunday, in the middle of the morning meeting, Clay told Easter he had to go to the toilet, but instead he left the church. He walked up into Free Creek and up the mountain. He ran quickly along the white path until he reached the big cedar tree and then sat on the rock ledge with his knees pulled up to his chest.

He closed his eyes and felt God floating all around him. He felt His presence burning into the trees, popping on the air.

No sooner than he found salvation, he heard Easter. "What do you mean, up and leaving during the preaching? You lied to me, right in the church house," she said, her voice nearly as loud as Pastor Morgan's.

"I don't know. I felt cramped up."

"You've got to learn the ways of the Lord, Clay. I've got to give that to you. I'm the only one will."

"I like it better right here," he said. He wanted to say, *This is where God lives,* but he knew Easter would probably say that was blasphemy. She was always worried about people blaspheming since this was the only sin that God would not forgive. He couldn't think of anything else to say, so he told her, "I believe in God."

"Well, I sure hope so," she said. She clutched her purse in front of her and didn't move. "But you have to congregate with other Christians, honey. You've got to let your light shine."

"Why can't I shine it right here?"

Easter fretted her eyebrows together. "You going to be just like your mommy."

He kept going to church with Easter. He felt the fire of the Holy Ghost run up and down the back of his neck, he clapped and sang along to songs like "The Good Old Gospel Ship" and "Ain't No Grave Gonna Hold My Body Down," but it wasn't the same feeling that came to him when he was on the mountain, alone. That was where he prayed. On the mountain, he was able to recognize the Lord hanging in the trees, blowing against his face.

Clay heard the first strains of one of his favorite songs, and he was brought back to the present. When he turned to look past the pews crowded with everyone he knew, he saw a girl he had never seen, stepping up on the altar. She brought a fiddle up to her face and began playing "Midnight on the Water."

He had barely gotten to size up the fiddler before Darry nudged him and said it was time they walked on up to the altar. Even after they were situated in front of the congregation, he couldn't help looking to his side, where she was playing.

The girl's eyes were closed tightly, as if she felt every note of the music flow through her. He liked the straight way she stood, the careful placement of her feet. He watched the way she moved, her body bending forward slightly with each changing note, her hair swaying softly behind her, the curve of her cheek against the cool wood of the fiddle. She concentrated on the cries of her fiddle, making sure each one came out correct and full of pain. When she finished, she stepped to the side of the altar pews without even looking out over the audience.

Anita Whitaker went to the altar and began singing "Love Can Build a Bridge," and the bridesmaids began their walk up the aisle. When Dreama appeared in the foyer on Gabe's arm, the fiddler stood and broke into a rousing version of the "Wedding March," and then everyone jumped up and looked toward the back of the church.

Clay looked at the fiddler, though. Still she did not open her eyes but sawed away at the instrument like a man determined to cut down an oak. She let her hair fall into her face, her knuckles white. The music seemed to flow right out of her skin. He felt dizzy from the beauty of her fiddling and swallowed hard. Even after she had stopped playing and the ceremony began, he watched her. He didn't even notice when one of the candles in the tall, brass candelabra fizzled out with a hiss, foretelling infidelities, and a little murmur rose up from the crowd.

Dreama and Darry tangled around each other for a long, sensuous kiss, and the preacher introduced them as man and wife.

Darry and Dreama walked quickly back down the aisle as the fiddler launched into a fast, celebratory song that Clay had never heard before.

The reception was held across the road in the fellowship hall. Everyone settled into their seats while Dreama and Darry went about shoving wedding cake into each other's mouths and twisting their arms awkwardly together to drink their punch. Clay sat down beside Easter, who had taken her seat at the very back of the room. She was gray-faced and looked as if she had walked wearily into the building and fallen into the first chair she had seen.

"We're supposed to be up front," he said. "Dreama will kill us."

"I know it," Easter answered. She did not meet his eyes and seemed to be looking at nothing at all. Suddenly, she seemed very old.

"What's wrong?" Clay asked.

"It's just come to me," she said, as if she was out of breath. "Dreama's carrying a baby."

When he turned in his seat, he saw the fiddler, standing straight-backed in a coat that was too heavy for the season.

"Are you Dreama's brother?" she asked.

"No, I'm her first cousin, but I might as well be. We was raised up together." He could smell the strong, fresh scent of Coast soap easing out of her skin.

"Well, can you tell her that I need to go on and leave? She said I didn't need to play at the reception. I hate to run off, but I've got to go."

"Why yeah, I'll tell her," Clay said. "Did she already pay you?"

"You all don't owe me nothing," she said. "It was such a pretty wedding that they ain't no way I could charge for playing. It was my pleasure."

Clay patted his back pocket for his billfold, then realized it was in his tuxedo jacket. "Here," he said, and shoved a twenty-dollar bill into her slender hand. "At least take this, for gas up here."

"No," she said, pushing the money away with a half-smile. "I don't want it. Swear I don't."

"Are you a friend of hers?"

"Naw, I had a little paper on the bulletin board at the community college, saying 'Fiddler for Hire,' and she called me," she said, and laughed as if she was embarrassed. "This is the first time I ever played for strangers."

"Well, you'll never make no money this way."

"That's all right. We'll see you all later. Tell Dreama I said congratulations."

He watched her skipping across the puddles of the parking lot, her fiddle case clutched tightly in her hand. She got into her car and plowed off through the rain as if she was running away from something.

• 4 •

CLAY AND CAKE were headed to the Hilltop Club. The night was warm and well lit by a bright rind of a moon, but there was a scent to the air that signaled autumn approaching. Clay had rolled down all of the windows, and the wind came into the cab of his truck to swirl about roughly. Steve Miller was singing on the radio.

Cake patted the dashboard to the beat of the music and took long hits on a joint. Clay didn't hunger for pot, and he definitely didn't feel like it tonight. The aroma of marijuana was sickeningly sweet and tangy as it met the damp, warm air.

"You want to cruise through town before we head up to the club?" Clay asked.

"Why yeah," Cake answered, after singing the entirety of a verse. "We do every Saturday night. Why would we change it now?"

Clay drove on, leaning this way and that with each curve of

the road. They drove into town, where the stores were all closed and lit up like many-windowed boxes stacked along Main Street. The town itself was closed, as nothing stayed open past dark, but the streets were filled with slow, rumbling cars crowded with people who waved and hollered to Clay and Cake. They knew by the cars who they were passing, without even glancing at their faces. They went on up to the shopping center, where people sat on their car hoods beneath signs that ordered NO LOITERING. People were dancing beside their open car doors or sitting on the tailgates of trucks, swinging their legs and yelling to everyone that passed. Cake burst out of the truck window, half his body extended into the air, and screamed for everybody to go up to the Hilltop with them.

The Hilltop Club sat nestled halfway up Town Mountain, a wide-shouldered wall above Black Banks. As they climbed the steep grade, they could see the whole town spread out below them. There were so many lights and zooming cars that it almost looked like a big city. Across the bowl that held the town, another mountain rose up to support the hospital, which you could pick out by the marble statue of Jesus with his arms stretched out in front: the white figure was so lit up that it could be seen for miles.

In the parking lot, Clay turned off the truck and sat breathing in the good air for a minute while Cake primped. It was such a beautiful night that Clay considered asking Cake if it would be all right with him if they just went driving around, but he knew this would have been foolish talk to Cake. Cake had waited all week, thinking of nothing but Saturday night while he worked at the gas station, and there was nothing he would rather do than party. Besides, Clay liked being dressed up and having somewhere to go, liked knowing that he could walk into the club and know everyone there, that he could hold up a dollar bill and have a cold beer delivered to him. They could hear the beat of the music rolling across the blacktop, and already he felt like dancing.

"How I look?" Cake asked. He had on a black bowling shirt, tight black Levi's, and shiny black boots. He brushed his hair again and studied himself in the visor mirror.

"You look all right," Clay said.

"Just all right? You mean I don't look damn good?"

"You look good, Cake," Clay said. Cake knew exactly how good-looking he was, and his vanity annoyed Clay. They went through this every time they went somewhere.

"Well, hell, why didn't you say that instead of just 'all right'? Now I feel like I look awful." Cake fished down into Clay's glove box and pulled out a small bottle of cologne. He sprayed it all over his shirt and, with a maniacal grin, squirted two sprays onto his crotch.

"Shit-fire, Cake. Now we gonna smell just alike."

Cake laughed and climbed out of the truck. Cake didn't give a damn about anything on a party night. As long as he was having a good time, nothing mattered. Some Saturday nights, when they fought and the bouncers had to pull Cake away with his boot heels dragging, he would laugh like a lunatic while blood poured from his lip.

"All right, let's see who goes home with the best-looking woman tonight," Cake said, strutting across the lot.

"Who are you, John Travolta? I can't remember many nights you took somebody home with you."

"I'm picky, I guess."

As soon as they opened the door to the honky-tonk, cigarette smoke burst out onto the crisp night air like a translucent fist being unclenched. They paid their way and walked into the spell Evangeline was casting over the audience with her husky voice.

The music churned about them. Evangeline was singing "Don't Ask Me No Questions" while she danced across the stage. She smoked a cigarette and took sips from her bourbon and Pepsi as she sang.

The honky-tonk was full. They had to push their way through to get to their table. Every small wooden table was crowded with more chairs than it could accommodate, and people stood against the walls like a line of police guards. People threw their heads back in laughter, women sat on men's laps, people downed shots of liquor and blew the fire off their jellybeans before throwing the drinks down their throats. The dance floor was filled with people, hunched and swaying beneath the huge stage, where Evangeline strutted back and forth.

Everyone spoke to Clay and Cake as they made their way through the club, so that it took them five minutes to cross the short distance to their table. The table was marked by a piece of notebook paper that read RESERVED. Cake wadded up the piece of paper and threw it onto the floor.

As soon as they sat down, their waitress arrived to put napkins and a bowl of pretzels on their table. She also sat two longneck beers and two shots of whiskey before them.

"I seen you all coming in," Roe explained, "so I went ahead and set you all up. I know what my boys order."

Cake paid her and added a hefty tip. "Go ahead and bring us a fifth of Jim Beam," he said.

"I'll do it." Roe nodded and parted the crowd.

Cake danced in his seat and squalled out loudly to let everyone know they had arrived. He swallowed the shot of whiskey without chasing it. Clay downed his own shot and felt the fire of bourbon scorch his throat. He looked out over the crowd and watched Evangeline as she finished the song and took a long swallow from her cup. Cool air rolled off the dance floor, and the place was filled with the scent of liquor and beer and a hundred different perfumes. Clay felt a strange sense of dissatisfaction that he couldn't actually name, and looking around, he suddenly felt that most of the people around him looked pathetic.

"Man, I love this song," Cake said, jumping up. "I've got to dance."

Cake faded off to the strains of "Night Moves," hunting for somebody to dance with.

When Roe came back, she sat right down at the table with Clay. She shook a cigarette out of his pack and lit it. "What're you up to, Clay?"

"Nary thing, Roe. Gonna try and get drunk."

"What's wrong? You don't seem like yourself tonight."

"Ah, I don't know. I feel kind of lonesome tonight."

"Well, you in the wrong place, then," she said with a wheezing laugh. "People don't come to honky-tonks to be lonesome."

"People don't go nowhere to be lonesome, do they?" he asked, and smiled.

Roe laughed loudly as she got up. "Naw, I don't reckon they do. I don't see what a good-looking boy like you is doing lonely, though. I don't understand it."

"Well, I don't neither," Clay said.

Roe ran her finger through the air. "Look around, then. They's plenty of women here, and most of em would give their eyeteeth to have you."

"There ain't nobody here I'd have," he said. "Don't want nothing you can find at a honky-tonk."

"When you get ready to settle down, where you need to go and find you a woman is the church house, buddy," Roe said.

Clay felt like saying, "You're one to talk," but he didn't. Roe had worked at the Hilltop for the past twenty years and wound up just as drunk as everybody else by the time the club closed, since she took a sip out of everybody's glass—just like she bummed a smoke out of everybody's pack. She was a good old girl, though.

BEFORE LONG, CLAY and Cake's table was crowded with drunks. Geneva and her husband, Goody, were there, along with several other people that they always partied with. They were all intent on getting wild drunk tonight, and they were well on their way. They talked loudly, yelling back and forth over the music. They drank from the same bottles and lit one another's cigarettes. They had been drunk together so many times that if they were not related, they felt like it.

Cake poured Clay another shot and slid it across the table. "Drink up, brother!" he hollered. "Let's get knee-walking drunk tonight."

Clay threw his head back and swallowed the liquor. Half the bottle was gone, and he was already feeling the dull electricity coursing through him. Liquor did not make him stumble or stutter, did not make him meaner or louder, but seemed to prod his jumpy spirit. When he got drunk he wanted to jump up and down, hollering to tell everybody that they ought to enjoy life more.

Geneva was obviously drunk, as her consumption of beer had been pepped up by several Xanax. When Evangeline and her band began to play "Cherry Bomb," Geneva bolted out of her seat and grabbed hold of Clay's arm, pulling him up. She danced through the crowd toward the dance floor, turning round and round, snapping her fingers and twisting her hips until Clay caught up with her and they began to swim around the floor.

Geneva was a good dancer not only because of how well she

moved but because of the cool, serious look on her face. She seemed completely absorbed in the music, unaware of her dancing partner or her surroundings. She shut her eyes or looked at the floor, holding her mouth in a firm, straight line with her top lip stuck out hard above the bottom one. Clay followed her in perfect stride, moving his body in all different directions and managing to keep in sync with the music.

When the song ended, Geneva and Clay hugged and she said, "Thanks, baby," loudly into his ear. Clay put his hand into the small of her back and began to stroll across the dance floor, but she stopped.

"Wait," Geneva said. "Let's see what they gonna play next."

Evangeline took her time between songs. She drifted across the stage to grab her cup of whiskey from a wooden stool and emptied it of all contents. She held the cup up in the air until Roe scrambled up to the stage and took it to be refilled. Evangeline lit a cigarette and breathed smoke out through her nose as she conferred with the lead guitarists. Finally, she made her way back to the microphone. The band strummed softly behind her, tuning their guitars.

"We going to do one of your-all's favorites, now. How bout a little 'Blue Moon of Kentucky'?" The crowd roared with applause and high squalls. "Wait a minute, now. Wait. Tonight it'll be the real thing. My little baby sister is going to come up here and play the fiddle for us." The applause intensified with more clapping and whistling. Roe brought Evangeline another cup of whiskey. She breathed loudly into the microphone and winked at Roe.

She looked offstage and yelled, "Alma, get up here, now."

Evangeline's sister, Alma, walked slowly up the steps and onto the stage. She carried her fiddle and its bow in one hand. She waved as she made her way across the big stage while everyone whistled and clapped, but she didn't look up, as if she was afraid she might misstep and fall right in front of everybody.

"If you don't know her, this is my little sis, Alma," Evangeline said. "And she can play that sumbitch like nothing you ever seen."

Even with all the bourbon coursing through him, Clay knew that she was the same fiddler from Dreama's wedding. He could tell by the way she moved.

He thought she was beautiful but didn't know exactly why. She was dressed modestly—unlike most of the women there—in a long, black skirt with a slit and a white, ruffle-collared shirt that was open by only one button. She wore black flats and black hose, and her hair fell in a wild auburn blur down to her waist. There was something about her face that struck him as out of place. She looked like somebody from another time. Her face was smooth and made up of soft, rounded curves, but it was interesting in the same way older people's faces are: there seemed to be a story in her eyes that was waiting to be told. She pulled her sleeves up, threw her hair to the side, and positioned the fiddle on her shoulder. When she put her chin onto the cool wood, Clay felt a start run all through him.

The band was silent behind her, and the crowd was paying reverence, too. Fiddlers were not common fixtures at the Hilltop, and everybody was quietly excited. Either that or Clay was simply unaware of any sound other than that of the bow first touching the strings of the old fiddle. She began the song slowly, the strains high and mourning. She was a part of the music, her face a peaceful hillside. Her eyes were clenched tightly shut, and she swayed softly, so slowly that it was barely noticeable. She reminded Clay of tall grass in a slight breeze. The sad voice of the fiddle filled the building. Evangeline began to sing the slow first verse of the song, and it seemed that her voice and that of the fiddler were in perfect harmony, like two sisters ought to be.

When the prelude was finished, Alma launched into the song fast and furious. One long leg burst out of the slit in her skirt, and her foot stomped on the stage. Her head and shoulders moved back and forth wildly, her hair swinging behind her like a fiery sheet hung out to dry. She began to move around the stage, and it seemed to Clay that she didn't really mean to start pacing—it seemed as if she was forced to. The music had control of her.

Geneva had begun to clog, and when she noticed that Clay was still staring up at the stage, she slapped him hard on the arm. He began to dance with her, but still he didn't take his eyes from Alma. Everyone churned around them, feet stomping, skirts slicing through the air. People hollered out and kept their arms limp at their sides, careful not to let their eyes follow their feet. Shoes and boots clicked and beat on the wooden floor.

Evangeline leaned back into the song, letting her voice rip from far down inside her. Clay half-expected her to break into tongues as she sang about being a cuckold. Alma also seemed to be taken by a higher power and moved around the stage with the slit in her skirt sneaking higher up on her leg, her body writhing with each cry of the fiddle. Clay decided right then and there that he wanted to know her. He wanted to hold her hand flat in his palm and look for the red lines the strings of the fiddle had left across her fingers. He imagined her fingertips would be hot as coals, and he longed to put his cool mouth around them.

When the song was over, Alma tapped the strings lightly and bent at the waist for a quick bow. The club was filled with the roar of applause. Geneva held her hands high over her head as she clapped.

"Damn, she could play," Geneva said.

When they got back to the table, everybody was still clapping. The band was noisily making its way offstage, taking their first break of the night. The canned music kicked on, and people raced back to the dance floor to do a line dance. Clay and Geneva, exhausted by the clogging, fell into their seats, taking great gulps of air. Cake slid another shot of liquor across the table, but Clay ignored it as he gathered his breath and senses.

As soon as he saw Roe coming through the crowd, he motioned her over.

"What is it, sugar?" Roe asked, balancing a full tray of beer over her head.

"Who is that fiddler?" Clay asked quietly.

"She's Evangeline's sister—"

"I know that. Do you know her?"

"Met her tonight, before we opened. Real sweet, from what I seen of her. Why, you wanting to meet her?" She laughed before he could answer. "I'll see what I can do."

Clay was unaware of anyone else at his table as he watched Roe deliver the beer and then go over to where Alma sat. He couldn't see her table from where he was, but he knew she was over there.

Geneva dipped a napkin into a glass of water and squeezed it so that streams ran down into her blouse, then wiped the sweat off her brow. "Anybody bout to pee?" she asked, looking around at the girls crowding the table. "I danced so hard it's a thousand wonders it didn't run right down my leg."

All the women left the table, and Goody and Cake scooted across the chairs until they sat next to Clay.

"What'd you all think about that fiddler?" Clay asked. "She was a doll, I thought."

"She could play that fiddle, but she wasn't all that to look at," Cake said.

"She looked good to me," Goody said in his slow, careful drawl. "Had a nice little ass on her."

Cake cackled loudly and swatted Goody on the back. His heavy hand cracked against Goody's leather jacket like a man's face being slapped.

Roe appeared at Clay's shoulder, breathing as if she had just climbed the mountain up to the Hilltop. "She won't come over to your table. Said if you want to talk to her, you'd have to come over there."

Clay nodded and took the shot of bourbon that Cake had offered him ten minutes before.

Roe grabbed his arm roughly and set her face close to his. "Now go over there, Clay Sizemore. Talk to her. No use in being lonesome."

"I will, soon's I get me a sup of beer." He grabbed Goody's ice-cold Miller and drank half of it straight down.

Alma was sitting at a small, round table pushed up against the stage. Evangeline sat with her, smoking a long cigarette and waving it around in the air as she talked. Alma listened intently without an expression on her face. Before he could reach the table, Evangeline threw her head back in wild laughter.

"Hey, Evangeline," Clay said, and both women looked up as if startled by his sudden presence. Evangeline studied Clay for a long second. She was half-drunk and had snorted so much coke that she might as well have worn the powder on her nose.

"Well, hidy, Clay. I bout didn't know you. What're you up to?"

"I come over to talk to your little sister, here."

"Well, hell, there she sets, son," Evangeline said, and roared with laughter again. "Talk away. You don't need my permission."

"Hidy," Alma said, and nodded.

"This here is Clay Sizemore," Evangeline said dramatically.

Evangeline gathered up her cup and cigarettes and pushed her chair back so hard that it fell backward. She laughed loudly, looking at the chair as if it had fallen from the sky. "Hey, you all want to hear anything special?" she asked.

"I'd like to hear a good two-step," Clay answered.

"You got it, then," Evangeline said, winking, and walked away.

Clay looked at Alma. "You know we met before, don't you? At Dreama Sizemore's wedding? Well, she's a Spurlock now. Dreama that married Darry Spurlock."

Alma squinted her eyes at him, as if she could not see him clearly. "That is right. You tried to pay me."

The band began playing the first strains of "Heart Full of Love." A huge speaker hung over their table, so Clay had to lean forward and yell out, "Well, you want to dance this one with me?"

"I ain't much of a dancer," she screamed.

"I don't care. Come on. I love this song."

He put his hand out, and she hesitated before giving hers to him. He had been right, imagining her hands. They were as hot as freshly stoked coals. On the dance floor, he put one hand on her waist and took her hand as they began to two-step. The song was a fast two-step, but calm and easy. Clay moved his hand up to the small of her back, where the soft fabric was cool and thin. He could feel her muscles moving there, hard and flat in the palm of his hand. They danced well together, their feet and hips moving in exact time. Alma looked over his shoulder without moving her face, like someone watching a movie and waiting for something to happen.

"You ought to play that fiddle up here more often," he said, for lack of anything better to say.

"I wouldn'tve done that a-tall if Evangeline hadn't begged so. I ain't much on playing in front of a crowd. Your cousin's wedding was the first time I ever played anywhere besides on the front porch, or my bedroom."

"You're lying," he said.

"No, I swear. That was the very first time, and tonight was the second."

"Well, I seen your first two performances, then," Clay said.

They danced silently for a moment, and Clay breathed her in. He could still smell the Coast soap on her. She smelled clean and soft and made him picture the ocean.

"Your breath smells good," Alma said suddenly, and laughed with embarrassment. "I love to smell whiskey and cigarette smoke mixed up together."

He laughed too loudly, not knowing what to make of her.

"I mean it. You prob'ly think I'm crazy, but I love that smell."

"Where you from? I hadn't never seen you before the wedding, and we look bout the same age. Why didn't we go to high school together?"

"We live plumb up on Victory," she answered. Victory was at the farthest edge of the county, so far away that the students there were bused to school in neighboring Laurel County. Victory was famous for being a strictly religious town, populated solely by members of the same church. Clay knew that Evangeline was the daughter of the well-known Mosley Family and suddenly realized that this meant Alma was, too. He wondered what their father would do if he knew both of his girls were gracing the stage of a place like the Hilltop.

"You still live at home, with your people?" he asked.

"Naw, I live with Evangeline right now."

The song ended, and Clay realized that he hadn't heard one word Evangeline had sung. He wondered how he and Alma had moved so gracefully around the dance floor, when they had both seemed to live that moment outside of the music.

Alma let her hand drop out of his. "Thanks for the dance. It was nice."

"Save another'n for me?" he asked, and heard himself sounding desperate.

"I don't know," she said. "I better not."

"You be up here next weekend?"

"I sure don't know," she said, and started walking away. "Thanks for the dance."

Alma moved away and faded into the crowd, not waiting for him to walk her back to her table. When he finally stopped looking for her, he realized that he was standing in the middle of an empty dance floor.

• 5 •

BACK AT HOME, Clay shoved a John Mellencamp CD into the stereo and began moving around the room to the beat. He closed his eyes, moved up and down, bent his knees, shook his hips, jerked his head to and fro with the rhythm. His arms moved all around him, his sock feet finding their way easily around the kitchen floor.

Clay was filled with a wild blood that he was always conscious of; he sometimes felt it pulsing through his veins with such fire that he thought it might burst from the tips of his fingers. Maybe it was the mixture of his Irish and Cherokee blood. He was sure of one thing—he came from a long line of lively people. He knew enough about his mother to be sure that she had been one of the wildest women in the untamed tangles of Crow County.

He danced two or three songs straight through before falling heavily onto the couch beside Cake. Cake had been watching him with a half-grin on his face, and only now did he cackle out in his wild madman's laugh.

"I believe you drunk," Cake said.

"Naw, just high on life," Clay replied, and patted his shirt pocket for his cigarettes. "I was wild until we went through that roadblock. That sobered me up right quick. You still drunk, though."

Cake laughed again, that high, piercing laugh that people either found charming or annoying. "That's right."

Goody had dropped them off at Clay's house but wouldn't come in because Geneva was so drunk that he had had to pack her out of the Hilltop with her mouth lolled open and her skirt hiked up to show her panties. Clay had hoped for a big party to develop after they left the club, as it usually did, but it seemed that everybody had gone their own way tonight. It was just him and Cake.

"I got *you* knee-walking drunk, son," Clay said. "You ought to go lay down."

"Naw, I'm fixing to go over there and make us some breakfast." Cake stood up and unbuttoned his jeans, letting them drop down about his ankles. He kicked his leg furiously until the jeans glided across the hardwood floor and into the middle of the living room. He stood in his long shirt and boxer shorts. "Them damn Levi's come one ace of killing me tonight," he said. "Too frigging tight."

Clay lay back on the couch and watched Cake as he made his way into the kitchen to cook them some breakfast. Cake put on a pot of coffee, opened a can of biscuits, and slid them into the oven, then fried baloney and eggs.

"You want to make gravy?" Cake asked with his back to Clay. "You always say mine is like mush."

"Naw, we can do without it tonight."

Cake got the biscuits out of the oven and let the pan slap onto the counter. They fished some beer from the refrigerator and went out onto the porch to eat. They ate silently, listening to the music that came out of the house and mingled with the song of the river below. The night had turned cool and damp.

"Best part of the meal," Cake said, lighting a cigarette after he had placed his emptied plate on the floor beside his chair. His voice echoed out across the river.

"I can't get that fiddler out of my head," Clay said suddenly.

"What fiddler?"

"That girl that played up the Hilltop tonight. Evangeline's sister. I know you ain't too drunk to remember her."

"Can't get her out of your head?" Cake laughed sarcastically. "Lately you been wanting to get a woman so bad that you'd be crazy over the first one you come into contact with."

Clay thought Cake might be right, but he didn't say so. "She could play that fiddle, couldn't she?"

"That's for damn sure. She could play that thing like Charlie Daniels or somebody."

"No, it was more than that. It wasn't just the music, but that look on her face. You could tell she felt that music. You know, like when some people sing a song, you can see right on them that they feel ever word of it," Clay said. "I don't know. They was just something about her. She just killed me."

"You danced with her, didn't you?" Cake asked. "Why didn't you ask her out?"

"I tried to, but she didn't seem that interested."

"Well, all I can tell you is that if she made that big an impression on you, you ought to try and get her. That sounds like something real to me. Nobody ain't never made me feel thataway."

"Let's go lay down," Clay said. "I'm killed."

"I ain't nary bit sleepy," Cake said, "but I'll lay down and talk to you awhile."

They had slept with each other all of their lives. They climbed into the bed and smoked, with an ashtray sitting between them. Before long, Cake faded off to sleep, but Clay sat up in bed wide awake until morning.

CLAY AND CAKE were connected by their mothers. Easter had said that Anneth was the only friend that Cake's mother, Marguerite, had ever had since she arrived on Free Creek.

Cake's father, Harold, had met Marguerite in Baton Rouge, where he'd spent three weeks after his tour was over in Vietnam. They had known each other only fifteen days when they were married by a justice of the peace. Two days after they were married, Harold brought her home to Free Creek.

Everybody in the holler had made their way up to Harold's house to welcome him back from the war and get a look at his new wife, including Easter and Anneth. Harold was as red-faced and deceptively jovial as ever, the men all pumping his hand and the women hugging him while they told him of the many prayers they had sent up for him while he was overseas.

Harold's new wife had sat on the couch, hugging herself, looking as if she would pass out any second. Her eyes had darted all over the room, not settling on anyone. She hadn't known what to make of these people and jumped with a start each time they spoke in their loud voices. She didn't say a word unless she was spoken to first, and even then her replies came out in short, whispery tones, so that everyone had to ask her to repeat herself. People distrusted and disliked her right away.

Even Easter was put off by her. In fact, she was frightened by her. On that first day, Easter saw that everyone else had begun to shun Marguerite because of her doe-eyed silence, so she sat down on the couch beside her and pulled Marguerite's hair out of her collar.

Easter told her what she told every other person she was meeting for the first time: "You'll have to go to church with me sometime. What religion are your people?"

Marguerite touched her hair where Easter had straightened it and didn't look up. "They're Catholic," she said, quietly, "but I'm not."

"Well, what religion are you?" Easter asked innocently.

"None at all," Marguerite said.

Easter had never heard such talk in her life. Even Anneth said she was a Pentecostal when asked by a stranger, knowing that sinners as well as the saved had a chosen denomination. Easter was dumbfounded. All this could possibly mean, Easter reasoned, was that Marguerite was an atheist. This had upset her so badly that Easter got hold of Anneth's arm and made her leave with her right then. She vowed never to talk to Marguerite again.

After that first day, nobody went around Marguerite. All the women in the holler went to the grocery together, sat out on the porch together, hollered to one another across their yards as they hung out clothes, but they never asked Marguerite to do anything. It made it all the worse that Marguerite didn't seem to care. She sat out on her porch alone and read books all day while Harold was off at the mines. She read with wet washcloths on her forehead and never even looked up when Easter passed on the road. The women stood in their yards and talked about her. They said that her house must have been a hog pen, since she never did anything but read. They certainly did not have time for such entertainment. They had never even seen her making a fuss over her little baby, Cake. She was probably crazy.

Their suspicions were heightened the day she took a fit in her yard. It was spring, and she was sitting on her porch, reading, with Cake in a bassinet beside her. Everybody was outside and they all saw what happened.

They had long since gotten past the point of watching her, but when she threw her book onto the wooden planks of the porch, they were all startled enough to look up to her house. The book hit the floor with the amplified sound of a wall falling down, and as soon as it did, the baby started wailing. Marguerite tumbled down the porch steps and fell into the sandy yard, where she convulsed and kicked at the tufts of grass about her, holding her hands around her neck as if she were choking herself.

Anneth and Easter were in Easter's front yard, planting spring flowers. They couldn't see Marguerite's yard from there, but they could hear the other women shouting. They both ran up the dusty road and found a group of women standing at the edge of Marguerite's yard, their fingers curled around the old fence. The women had stood there while Marguerite writhed, her eyes rolled back in her head. She looked as if she were fighting an invisible ghost that was trying to strangle the life out of her.

Anneth pushed through the women and ran into the yard. She took Marguerite's bony shoulders in her hands and shook her as hard as she could. Marguerite's hair, which she always wore pinned up, tumbled down to tremble around her face and brush the dust. Anneth shook her so hard that she expected to shake Marguerite's eyes back down to their proper place. Finally, Marguerite made a low, coughing sound, as if her mouth was full of dirt. She fell into Anneth's arms and breathed in great gulps of air. She looked up at Anneth with such a pathetic mixture of thanks and bewilderment that Anneth had decided right then and there to befriend her.

"What is it, honey?" Anneth asked. "What in the hell's wrong with you?"

"I'm smothering," she coughed out. Her face was covered in dirt, and one tear rolled out to make a long, crooked line down her cheek. She held on to Anneth tightly, digging her fingernails into her arms. She reminded Anneth of a child, with her little, breakable hands and those pale eyes, big and round as dollar coins.

"These mountains are smothering me to death," Marguerite said. "Too close."

Anneth laughed heartily. "Well, you might as well get used to em. They're here to stay."

After that, Anneth had made it a point to go see Marguerite every chance she got. Marguerite was smart and she seemed so exotic. Marguerite had shelves and shelves of books and received a new one every month in the mail. She had a whole milk crate full of classical records, and when she played them, she would move her hands around in the air like two white doves floating in front of her. The wild violins of Paganini made chills run up the backs of Anneth's legs.

Anneth sat on the floor going through the records while Marguerite played them and moved her hands around, telling the life stories of each composer.

They went for long walks together, climbing the mountain that stood behind Easter's house. They talked and looked at the trees while they each packed their babies on their hips. Marguerite taught Anneth how to press autumn leaves between sheets of wax paper, and Anneth told her about the old tradition of finding a four-leaf clover and putting it in the Bible when a child was born to ensure good luck throughout the child's life.

No one understood this friendship. They couldn't see why Anneth, who loved to drink and run wild all weekend, would want to spend time with Marguerite, whose face was as flat and featureless as her personality. Easter was especially upset.

"I don't understand you," Anneth said. "Why would I want to slight her? She's good to me."

"There's just something about that woman," Easter said.

"Maybe she is a little strange, but I like that. Just because she don't claim no sort of religion, you think she's a devil. That don't make a lick of sense."

"It ain't just that," Easter said. "That first day I met her, when I touched her hand, I didn't feel a thing. I can't explain it. It was like touching a dead person."

Anneth threw her head back and laughed, slapped her bare knee. "That's why you don't like her, because you can't read her. You believe somebody is without a soul just because you can't see into it."

Easter didn't say a word, which let Anneth know she was insulted.

"Don't you feel sorry for her?" Anneth asked.

"Why?"

"My God, I feel sorry for anybody that's married to Harold Singleton. He's the ugliest, stupidest man I ever knowed," Anneth said. "She's all alone, miles away from her home."

When Anneth was killed, Marguerite actually did lose her mind at first. She broke every dish in the house and, when she realized what she had done, gathered up all the pieces in a paper bag, which she hid underneath her bed. Only when Harold came home from the mines did she see that her hands were cut and bleeding. As soon as Harold came in and told her to get ready to go down to Easter's for the wake, she straightened herself as if she had flicked a switch. She put on makeup and her brightest dress and walked down the holler holding on to Harold's hand.

Marguerite walked straight-backed to the coffin. Everyone

watched, as she seemed changed, a different woman. It was as if some of Anneth's immense strength had been pumped into her. She leaned down and took hold of Anneth's hand, mouthed a short prayer, and walked out. At the door, Easter took both of Marguerite's bandaged hands into her own.

"She thought so much of you," Easter said.

"Thank you," Marguerite said, and for the first time that any of them could see, she smiled.

Later, when Clay came up to play or stay the night with Cake, Marguerite dropped whatever she was doing to sink down on the floor and sit with him until Cake asked her to leave them alone. She would bring out her milk crate of records and wipe them with a damp cloth, handling them as if they were a priceless set of dishes that would be ruined if one was broken. Every time Clay came to the house, she dragged out the records, waiting for the day he would ask about them.

When he finally asked to hear some of the albums, she told him to play whatever he wanted. He picked the records at random, choosing an album more for the cover than anything else. He grew fond of Mozart, Bach, Paganini. From then on, every time he came, he wanted to hear them. This was the only place he knew of to hear such music, and it gave him a guilty thrill to listen to it. Cake and Dreama rolled their eyes and laughed when he played the records. They made jokes while he played the foreign music, and ended up running outside to play without him.

Marguerite would sit and hold a glass of iced tea with a paper towel around it while Clay sorted through the albums. She directed him to set the needle to a certain groove and sometimes closed her eyes while the music played, the way Clay had seen some people do when they were savoring an especially good piece of corn bread.

"That is Johann Sebastian Bach, my mother's favorite

composer," Marguerite said. She chose her words very carefully, so that even in conversation she sounded as if she were reciting a poem. "That is the Air, from the Suite in D Major. We played it at my mother's funeral. When I hear it, I picture her and the way she looked when we would go to the ocean."

Clay hardly ever spoke when he was alone with Marguerite. He loved to sit and listen to her, watch the way she cast her eyes down slowly at a thought she didn't announce, the way she moved her hands around in front of herself when he played something she liked.

He held up a record cover and tried to pronounce the name of the composer.

"That is Niccolò Paganini," Marguerite said. "There is a piece on there that your mother loved. It's called 'La Campanella.' She'd turn that up as loud as it would go and dance around the living room."

Clay ran his firm, flat hand across the record album. It felt very cold.

"You may have that, if you promise to take very good care of it."

Clay couldn't believe his good fortune. He didn't protest, as he had been taught to do when offered a sudden gift, but jumped up and hugged Marguerite around the neck. She laughed nervously. She wasn't used to being touched. "Don't tell anyone I've given it to you," she said.

He put the record on and counted the correct number of grooves until he came to "La Campanella." Neither of them spoke as the music filled the room, encircling them like ghosts. Clay looked at the floor, picturing his mother dancing round and round.

When the song ended, Marguerite brushed Clay's bangs back off his forehead. Her movements were like water, so full of grace and ceremony that they looked practiced. She ran her hand down the side of his face and put two fingers beneath his chin so that she could look into his eyes. Clay felt strange, almost uncomfortable, and wondered what she was looking for. They both jumped with a start when Cake ran into the room. Cake stopped suddenly, the smile fading from his face as if it had been wiped away. Clay knew that Marguerite had never touched Cake in such a good, secretive way.

• 6 •

ALMA WAS STILL at the honky-tonk. It was almost four o'clock in the morning, but Evangeline would not leave. As soon as the crowd had cleared out after the club closed at two, Evangeline had come straight off the stage, taken five shots of liquor, and gone up to the deejay's booth to put on a seemingly endless tape.

Now she was dancing in the middle of the dance floor by herself. She convulsed around the floor barefoot, with her eyes tightly shut, dancing as fast as she could to "Hot Legs." One of the bouncers, Frankie, sat in a chair at the edge of the dance floor, watching as Evangeline twisted and shook. He smiled as though he knew something nobody else did, believing that she was dancing just for him, and each time she came near, he reached out for her, hoping she would finally collapse, exhausted, into his arms.

Alma sat at the bar, slowly nursing a Dr Pepper, and watched her sister. This was the way it had been ever since she had moved in with Evangeline a month ago.

Roe came out of the back room and went behind the bar, splashing Seagram's 7 and 7UP into a glass. "You want one, honey?" Roe asked. "Seven and Seven. It's what Patsy Cline drunk."

"No, thanks," Alma said, and nodded toward Evangeline. "I've got to get her out of here."

"She does that ever once in a while," Roe said. "I usually just leave and tell her to lock up on her way out. Frankie always takes care of her."

"I'll bet he does."

Roe sat down at the bar and began counting her tips. The counter was covered with greasy dollar bills and shiny quarters. "Hey, I seen you dancing with Clay Sizemore tonight," she said. "If I was you, I'd latch onto him."

Alma smiled without taking her eyes off Evangeline, who had sat down on Frankie's lap and was taking the cigarette from his mouth to take long, exaggerated draws. "He seemed nice, but nothing'll ever come of that."

"Why not? He's the best feller ever was."

"I'm married," Alma said.

Evangeline fell out of Frankie's lap and onto the dance floor. She lay on her back, clutching her belly while she laughed. Alma left her bar stool with a loud sigh.

"Come on, Evangeline." She spat her words out over the loud music. "This is ridiculous."

"Oh, baby, don't be mad at me," Evangeline said, and sat up. She ran one hand down the side of Alma's face. "I'm just drunk is all."

"Frankie, help me get her out to the car. Come on, now. I've set here long as I'm going to."

They walked her out of the club and across the parking lot

to the car. Alma got into the car and started it up while Frankie stuffed Evangeline into the backseat. "Turn on the radio, by God!" Evangeline hollered, lying down.

Frankie put the seat back up and started to get in up front.

"What do you think you're doing?" Alma asked. She put her arm across the passenger seat so he couldn't sit down.

"I'm going home with you all. I stay up Evangeline's all the time."

"Not no more. I stay with her now."

"Well, how in the hell am I supposed to get home?" He shoved his hands deep into his pockets.

"I don't know, and I don't give a shit. I don't like you, and you ain't getting in this car."

She shifted into drive and took off with the door open. She peeled out of the parking lot and almost lost control of the wheel in the deep gravel. The steering wheel spun around between her fingers and she bolted upright in her seat as the car straightened out. The door slammed closed heavily as she turned onto the road and started down the mountain.

"Turn that radio on, by God, I said!" Evangeline screamed again, as Alma turned onto the ramp to Daniel Boone Parkway toward home. Alma snapped on the volume, and the radio blared country music so loudly that the words of the song seemed to run together.

The parkway was deserted, and Alma felt like screaming, screaming even louder than the radio. She rolled down her window to let some of the music flow out onto the cool air.

She flew down the highway, and suddenly the image of her father appeared on the windshield. She pictured him at home, down on his knees beside his bed, praying aloud with tears streaming down his face. He was crying over his two daughters, who he was certain were going to hell. Anytime she heard from him, he said: "And your blood will be on my hands. The Bible says so."

Their family was the most popular gospel group in the mountains. Everyone had heard of the Singing Mosley Family, and everyone loved and respected them. Being in a gospel group was second only to being a preacher.

Evangeline had been the lead singer until she was sixteen years old. Back then, Evangeline would barely get out the first verse of a song before people rose to their feet crying and praising the Lord. Evangeline's voice stirred up emotions in people, made all of their feelings spill out on their faces. It wasn't long before Evangeline started moving her hips a little too much as she sang. Their father thought she was too wild with her tambourines, often beating them so hard that her palm went right through the covers.

Alma could remember the night Evangeline left the singing group—and childhood—behind. They were at the Lost Fork Full Gospel Church, and Evangeline was taking control of the crowd. People were running up and down the aisles, screaming out in tongues, falling onto the altar to pray. Alma watched as Evangeline's eyes fell on a boy in the audience. The boy was sitting slumped over in his seat, turning something over in his hands. He was the only person present who didn't seem to be under Evangeline's spell, and she must have liked that. He had curly brown hair, and eyes as green as water. As soon as the singing was over and the preaching began, Evangeline slipped out of her seat and walked down the aisle, looking at the boy in such a manner that he knew he better follow her out. She didn't come home until the next morning, and when she did, Thomas met her at the door with a belt. She jerked it out of his hand before he had a chance to use it and slammed her bedroom door.

Now Evangeline sometimes dragged their old tapes and albums out and laughed at their hairstyles or late-1970s clothes.

"God, can you believe we wore such shitty things?" she would ask Alma. "We look like the frigging Partridge Family."

Alma had never been more than a backup singer in the group, since the family blood had given her the talent to play the fiddle. Fiddle music was not acceptable in church. Long ago, people had considered the fiddle an instrument of the devil, but even now the wild, eerie screams of its strings were too much for a church crowd. Her father hadn't forbidden it, but she had known better than to want to play her fiddle in church. She had resigned herself to singing harmony at an early age, but she hadn't done that for very long. Instead, she had sold tapes at the back door when church was over.

Alma used to sit in church and watch the way her parents and brother and sisters moved people and wish that she could do such a thing. She couldn't remember a time when she didn't feel guilty about something, and she had spent much of her childhood wishing she could move people to receive the Holy Ghost, fall to their knees in prayer, or burst out crying. She loved watching her brother's long white fingers race up and down the piano, loved the bump of her father's guitar, the exciting tingle of her sisters' tambourines, the symphony of all their voices coming into one and hovering over a congregation like the Holy Spirit itself.

Evangeline stirred in the backseat and rose up quickly, putting her chin on the back of the front seat. Alma capped her fingernails around the metal stub of the volume control and turned it down.

"Where we at?" Evangeline asked.

"Fixing to get off the parkway and onto the curvy road. You ain't going to get sick, are you?"

"Hell no." She fell back down into the seat. "Turn that radio back up. I can't hear it."

Tears came into Alma's eyes, but not on account of Evangeline. She was still thinking of her daddy. For the last month, she had been replaying over and over in her head the last time she had seen him. She felt as if he could cast the spell of guilt and send it out over distance or time.

Thomas Mosley was a big, square man with a voice as huge as his presence. She always likened his voice to the low, distant rumbling of thunder before a summer storm, the kind of thunder that shook the ground. He was not so much a fanatical Christian as he was incurably old-fashioned. Religion wasn't his problem—he merely used it to make his rules seem sensible and moral. He was famous within the family for distorting the Bible to make his points clear. It came as no surprise to Alma when he cursed and disowned her on the announcement of her divorce.

Alma had gone to him in the middle of the night. Her face was black and blue from the blows of her husband's fists, but she still felt at fault. Her lip was swollen, the blackened blood hard and smeared on her chin. Denzel's handprints were on her arms. She could still hear every word her husband had said to her. The words were far worse than the strikes. When she got to the door, she fell onto the porch and waited for someone to come out. She was barely able to hold her arm up in order to rap lightly on the screen door. Suddenly her father appeared, as if he had materialized out of the air.

"Help me up," she said, and extended her hand.

"Alma, what's happened to you?" he thundered.

"Denzel's happened to me."

Thomas put her on the couch and rushed into the kitchen, where he wet a rag. He wiped the blood from her chin without saying a word.

"I told you he had hit me before," she said. Minutes before, she had barely been able to speak, but upon seeing her father, anger had bubbled within her. Her father had introduced her to Denzel, had pushed him on her. Denzel had been a young deacon at the Victory church, and every girl in the congregation had been after him. As soon as Alma married him, Denzel had quit going to church. "Now look, Daddy. Do you believe me now?"

"What did you do?"

"Nothing!" she screamed. "What's the difference, anyway? Look at me." She was aware of her mother and brother entering the room.

"Why would he do this to you?" her mother asked, her voice full of tears.

"Because I live." She could taste blood in her mouth, as thick and black as used oil. "I have to quit him. I can't live a life like this. I won't."

"Hush now," Thomas said, rubbing her hand. "The Lord takes care of all things. Divorce ain't the answer to everything. You have to work through this. You can't just give up on your marriage."

"I'll be giving up if I stay with him. One of these days he'll kill me."

"What you all need is to get back in church," Thomas said. After a few minutes, he got up slowly, quietly, and went outside. She hoped that he was going to kill Denzel. That was what she wanted. She tried to rise up off the couch to go with him.

"Lay down now. You will leave him, no matter what your daddy says," her mother whispered. "You get out of there as fast as you can. There ain't no changing a man like that. I've seen it before."

When Alma awoke the next morning, her mother was still there with her, rubbing her back in a perfect circle. Her father was sitting across the room, propped up in his chair and staring out the window. He had not slept, but from his expression, she knew that he had not changed his mind, either.

"Daddy, I'm leaving him," she said weakly. "I don't care if it makes your singing group look bad or nothing else. Why in God's name would you want me to stay with him?"

He said nothing.

WHEN SHE WAS SURE Evangeline had passed out, she felt around in her purse until she found her Jean Ritchie tape and pushed it in. Jean had not even gotten out the first verse before Evangeline put her face up between the seats again and muttered, "Alma. Pull over."

"You ain't getting sick, are you?" Alma asked, turning down the volume again.

"Yeah," Evangeline said, her mouth already filling up. "I sure am."

Alma pulled to the side of the road and held Evangeline's hair back while her sister vomited. Evangeline sat right down on the shoulder of the road and told Alma to leave her alone for a minute. Alma stood at the open door and looked up at the black mountain towering beside the road. The cliffs stood dark and solemn and made the silence more noticeable. There was no sound except the redundant bell signaling that the door had been left open. The stars were spread out as if spilled, and the moon was a smudged spot of gray on the black sky. The tears that had lingered in her eyes began to spill, although she didn't have a clue as to where they might have come from. After what she had been through in the past two months, she couldn't see how she even had any tears left, but they fell fast and straight down.

• 7 •

Easter awoke to whispering—low, cool whispers like the wind off a falling leaf. When she opened her eyes, there was no one, nothing. It took a moment for her eyes to adjust, and in that space of time, she felt a slight breeze in the room, like the barely noticeable wind of someone's leaving. An image came to her mind: a woman quickly, gracefully leaving the room, clad in a dress made of silver winter air.

She had expected to wake up to someone there with her. Anneth, perhaps. She had been troubled by dreams of her sister all night long—dreams in which Anneth did not laugh, did not throw her head back, did not show her beautiful, straight teeth and red lips. They had been dreams of Anneth coming to her as she would have looked if she had lived to be very old. Her beauty had faded, changed into a different kind of loveliness, the kind that only very old women possess: the shadow of a lost hourglass figure, a widening of the hips, a silvering of the hair. In the dreams, Anneth had tried to speak, but her mouth had been clotted with dirt, and it had trembled out to fall on the floor. The dirt had looked as dark and rich as chocolate, good enough to eat.

Easter often lay in bed feeling that someone was standing over her. But this morning it had been different: short, lisped whispers, like the comforting voice of seduction. The feeling of dread was all around her. Something was going to happen. She knew that as soon as she felt someone leave the room—the quiet, straight vacuum of air following someone out. She felt the dread seep into her body, moving slow as kudzu.

She looked at the clock and realized that she had never slept this late on a Sunday morning. It was well past eight o'clock, and as soon as she saw this, it seemed that the room was filled with morning, although it had been light for well over an hour. Beams of sunshine came in like thick planks of whitened lumber, slanting through the window and onto the floor. She heard the sounds of the new day: birds in the tree next to her bedroom window, roosters crowing far up in the holler, cars starting. She threw back her warm bedcovers and climbed out of the bed quickly, ashamed. Her grandmother had been a firm believer in not wasting any part of daylight, and she had ingrained this habit into Easter.

She sat back down on the bed, as if someone had pushed her back. She fell into the soft mattress heavily with the springs screeching under her. Her knees felt weak and her palms broke out in a cold sweat, the way her hands did when she was traveling a long distance in a car. She started to call out for her husband, El, who was most likely already up and drinking his coffee on the front porch, but then she didn't.

She sat there for a long moment, her head swimming from rising and sitting so quickly. She tried to remember the whispers and was frustrated that she couldn't. It was the most annoying thing, just like trying to remember a dream. She put her face into her damp hands and scolded herself silently. Maybe she wasn't really a seer at all—maybe she was merely overimaginative. Or crazy. She sometimes wondered if she didn't make herself believe that she was cursed to see what others could not. Doomed to hear whispers when nobody was there.

She wondered if it could all stem from when she was just a child and had stood in the cornfield, listening to the pluck of a dulcimer far up on the mountain.

She had never heard such a sweet sound. She dropped her hoe and began running up the row of corn. The plants were thick and tall and green. Their sharp leaves sliced at her face, but she didn't feel the paper cuts they left on her cheeks. She ran through the corn, intent on running all the way up the mountain until she saw who was playing that music. She wanted to see whose magic fingers could make such a beautiful noise.

She almost ran right into the man. He was tall and slender, with black hair and coal-black eyes. Black birds flew off in a noisy frenzy. The dulcimer's song intensified. He had a face that was toughened by sun, work, and age. She could hear his footfalls in the tender soil, could hear the swish of air as he pushed the corn leaves out of his face. His lips moved, and she felt that she was meant to know what he was saying, but she could not decipher it.

She tore through the cornfield. She was not able to call out. All she could make move were her legs, and when she finally found her grandmother, bent over the hoe, she ran into her long brown skirts and held tightly onto her leg. Her grandmother pulled away, dropped to her knees, and put her hands on both sides of Easter's face.

"Didn't you see the man? Didn't you hear that dulcimer?"

Easter asked in a pleading voice. It seemed that her grandmother's face was made out of the earth she put the hoe into. Her eyes, blue as prized marbles, were always watery, but Easter finally realized her grandmother was about to cry.

"It's a sign," the old woman said, and it seemed that her voice was full of dirt, too. "Don't fret. It's something God has gived you."

A week later her grandfather had died, killed in the little mine that he had burrowed out behind their house to haul his own coal. Easter had watched as they carried him out, his body crumbled and broken, looking just like a cornhusk doll.

A superstitious old woman had told Easter she had the sight, and she had believed it from then on. Maybe that was the reason she had carried this curse with her all of her life.

She tired of waiting for anything to happen and left her bedroom to get herself some coffee. El had left her a half pot, and she poured a cup and stepped out onto the back porch to get a breath of morning. As soon as she stepped out, she saw the box lying on the top step. She recognized the box; she could remember the day it had been delivered to their grandmother. It had originally carried a huge family Bible, but Anneth had claimed it as a child and put all of her mementos within it. Easter hadn't seen the box in ages, probably since she was a teenager, and could not understand where it had come from. She stood quickly and walked around the corner of the house, imagining that she might see someone leaving her yard. There was no one to be seen.

Only Marguerite would have had something of Anneth's, and only she would have left it in such a mysterious way.

She sat down on the top step beside the box and lifted the lid. She leafed through its contents. These were her sister's possessions —the things she had really cherished, although they were strange sorts of things to keep. Old napkins and matchbooks, a whole pack of unopened cigarettes. Carnival pictures, beads, newspaper clippings. There was a small Gideons Bible, which fell open to a marked verse. There were sketches that Anneth had drawn, postcards, catalog receipts.

At the bottom, Easter found two envelopes. One was addressed to her, and the other was to Clay. She ripped the first envelope open.

> Dear Easter,
>
> I know if anything ever happens to me, you'll find this old box. I want Clay to have it. I've wrote him a long letter to try and explain everything to him, but what he don't understand, I know you'll be able to answer. Don't keep no secrets from him. I don't know how to tell him who I am, but maybe you will be able to. I love you, sister.
>
> Yours,
> Anneth

El appeared in the doorway, coffee cup in hand. "Easter? What in the world you doing? I figured you was getting ready for church."

"I ain't going to church this morning," she said.

"What's that box?"

"It's something of Anneth's. I've just found it." She closed her eyes and put the letter against her lips. The paper was so soft and white that it looked as if the letter had been written this very morning. She expected it to smell like Anneth, but it carried only the tangy scent of old ink.

"What do you mean, you hain't going to church? You've got to lead the singing."

"I'm not going, I said. Just go on without me." She shoved everything back into the box and closed the lid gently. "I just want to stay home. I believe I'll cook a big meal and tell everbody to come up and eat."

"All right, then," El said.

When he left, she could see him walking all the way up the road, up to where the church sat, at the mouth of the holler. Sometimes she wondered if she went to church simply to try to purge herself of past mistakes. Some people made her out to be a saint, but she had done plenty of wrong in her life. She trembled all over, looking at that church, sitting on the hillside just like a solemn judge.

ALMA WAS LEAVING her attorney's office on Main Street when she heard someone playing "Sweet Old World" by Lucinda Williams in a car waiting at the stoplight.

She let the office door close quietly behind her and looked out into the street. It was Clay Sizemore. Evangeline had been kidding her about him ever since she had danced with him at the Hilltop, but she had put him out of her mind. There was no use even thinking about a man right now. Sometimes she wondered if she'd ever want to be with a man again.

She couldn't help watching him, though. She liked the way he sang along to the song, his arm stretched out across the back of the seat while he waited for the light to change. He moved around a bit while he sang, not caring who saw him. His face was covered with coal dust. He nodded his head and tapped one thumb against the steering wheel to the beat of the music.

God, he was good-looking. And she had always believed that you could tell a lot about a person by looking at the albums they had. She had been wrong about this only once: part of the reason she had decided to marry Denzel was the simple fact that he liked Bill Monroe when everybody else was listening to Bruce Springsteen.

She wished the light would change so Clay would go on. Her car was sitting down the street, and if she moved past the lawyer's door, Clay would catch sight of her. If she kept standing there, he would eventually notice her, too. She was suddenly glad that she was dressed up. She held her purse before her with both hands and began to feel around for her keys, even though they were lying right on top of her billfold. There was no use even thinking about somebody like Clay, no matter how nice-looking he was, or how confident he had been when he strolled across the dance floor to ask her to dance, or what kind of music he liked.

Still, she looked up at him again. When she did, he caught her eye.

He lifted a hand to wave and smiled widely. She nodded and started to walk on toward her car, hoping he would go on, but he wheeled into the empty space along the sidewalk. A little sign stood there that read NO PARKING ANYTIME.

"Hidy, Alma," he said, after turning down his radio. "You remember me?"

She put her purse strap on her shoulder and studied his face for a moment without a change of expression. After a moment of stalling, she said, "Why yeah, you're Clay."

"I've been hoping to see you ever since we danced up at the Hilltop."

She ran her car keys through her fingers, and their clinking seemed very loud despite the traffic that was sailing by.

"I've tried calling up Evangeline's, to get up with you. You all don't never stay home," he said. She noticed his eyes were outlined with coal dust. They were green as unripe acorns, and the whites of them were bright against his black face. "What've you been up to?"

"Not a thing," she said. "You doing all right?"

"Be a lot better if I could get you to go out with me sometime," Clay said. He stared her in the eye. She silently bet herself that he was an expert at asking girls out on dates. He had probably had half the girls in Crow County.

"I don't guess so, Clay," she said. She should have told him that she was still married, that she had only just now started the divorce procedure. She should have told him that Denzel would go wild if he even saw her talking to a man. But she couldn't make those words come out of her mouth.

"Aw, come on, now," he said. He smiled, showing teeth that were very straight and white. "We don't have to go honky-tonking. Go out to eat? Or to a movie over in London?"

"I better not, Clay." She couldn't make herself say no, plain and simple. She wanted to tell him good-bye and walk on to her car, but instead she said, "That's my favorite song you was playing."

"Yeah, that's a great one. I love all Lucinda's songs." He reached for a box of cigarettes that lay on the dashboard, but apparently thought better of it and didn't pick them up. "Let me come get you Saturday evening. We'll just go riding around or something."

A little breeze kicked down the street and lifted her hair. The air was cold and smelled of autumn. She stood there, leaning down so she could look into the truck.

"It's good of you to ask, but I can't," she said. She looked up the street, trying to get away from his eyes. The breeze blew her hair into her face and she brushed it away. She kept her fingers behind her ear so the locks wouldn't blow out again. "I better get going."

"Well, you can think about it," Clay said. "Be nice to just ride around and listen to good music all night, wouldn't it?"

She smiled at that and walked away. She was aware of him watching her through his rearview mirror as she slid into her car and started it up. He sat there until she had pulled out onto the street and driven by him.

• 8 •

AUTUMN SETTLED ITSELF down over the land like a colorful skirt. Dusk came earlier and touched the leaves with sharp breath. The hills were filled with the smoke from smoldering patches of forest fires. When the season finally overtook the mountains, so complete in its work that the trees were nearly black in their nakedness, Clay and Alma met again.

During the first full moon of October, the Heritage Festival invaded Black Banks. A large carnival came in on rumbling rigs and campers, converting Main Street and its tributaries into rows of tall neon rides, concession stands, and barker games. The people of Crow County set up booths of their own, offering everything from chicken dumpling plates to peanut butter fudge. High school clubs manned hot dog stands and dunking booths, the ROTC handed out army stickers and told wild, beautiful lies to sophomore boys outfitted in Eastland shoes and thin mustaches.

Cherokees came up from the reservation to display their pottery and shirts bearing the seal of their nation. Festival chasers offered booths of junk and impulse buys. Large Pentecostal women hung their best quilts on high clotheslines, and the Mennonites sold hand-dyed fabrics and breads.

Music was the main draw of the festival, and the chamber of commerce enlisted local musicians to stroll through the crowd playing their instruments of choice. Nashville hopefuls sat on street corners and picked, the open guitar cases at their feet lined with a few quarters that they had supplied themselves. Stages were set up all over town.

The main stage—which was actually the long, wide porch of the courthouse—was now being dominated by Evangeline and her band, the Revolvers. That was where Clay went as soon as he and Cake got to the festival. He figured he'd be able to find Alma there. He had been thinking about her ever since he had seen her on Main Street. He had tried to call her several times but was always greeted by Evangeline's answering machine, which announced: "You know what to do. Leave a message." He had done just that but had never received a reply. Every time he had called, he had pictured Alma standing right beside the phone, probably rolling her eyes when she heard his voice.

Evangeline moved all over the stage, dancing and singing, her skirt swishing about her knees, her head thrown back. The people were yelling out, whistling, singing along; they were in awe of her, like a swarm of dazed bees under the spell of a bee-charmer. The band began to strum a soft acoustic set while Evangeline paused to take a long drink from her cup of whiskey.

"We gonna change the pace a little right now," Evangeline breathed into the microphone. She had brought the cup with her and took another long swallow. "Since this is the Heritage Festival, we gonna do a real old song that come over from Ireland. This is one of my favorites, called 'Barbara Allen.' "

It was a song that all of the people knew, a song that their parents had sung to them and that they had sung to their own children, but Evangeline transformed it into her own: the tragic look on her face made the song seem new and exotic. She sang every word perfectly, singularly. Her voice seemed to stream out over the whole town and overtake everything in its path. Her steady song went down and mingled with the music of the well-lit carousel and the chatter of the people browsing the booths, and farther down to mix with the subtle song of the river that had given the town its name.

> Slowly, slowly she got up
> And slowly she went nigher
> And all she said when she got there
> Was "Young man, I think you're dying."

People began to dance. Lovers, mothers and their young sons, old married couples. Main Street was filled with dancers who stamped softly on a ground that was becoming decorated with the first fallen leaves of autumn. Clay looked about anxiously for Alma, but he saw her nowhere. He watched the dancers and felt a tightness in his stomach. He saw married couples much younger than him, some of them dancing while the girl held a baby right on her hip, and an older couple, who still seemed in love after all these years. He doubted love like that would ever come for him.

> "Oh, yes, I'm sick, I'm very sick
> I hear the death-wind howling
> No better no better I never shall be
> If I can't have Barbry Allen."

Cake lit a cigarette and sighed heavily. "This song kills me," he said. "It's too damn depressing."

Clay did not reply because he could not take his eyes from Evangeline, who looked as if she was crying and trying her best to conceal it.

"You might as well forget that fiddler, buddy," Cake said. "She ain't even here."

"She's here somewhere. I guarantee that," he said. "I bet she's one of them musicians they hire to walk around and play." Clay wanted to keep walking through the crowd, to look for her, but somehow he thought this would not be right. The whole crowd was transfixed by this ancient song, and he felt it would have been disrespectful to move among them. It would have been like digging into the food while someone was right in the middle of saying the supper blessing.

> She was on her sad way home
> She seen the hearse come rolling
> "Lay down lay down his corpse of clay
> So I might look upon him."

When the last notes of the music drifted away and Evangeline's voice was overtaken by the river's music, the people took their arms from one another, the moon went back into the clouds, and the microphone issued a long screech. Evangeline announced a break, and taped music came on.

Clay watched as the band and Evangeline went off the side of the courthouse porch and back into a large tent.

"I'm going to find out where she is. I'm tired of just thinking about her," Clay said. "You going with me?"

"No," Cake said, dropping his cigarette and smashing it out with his boot heel. "I'm going down to the carnival."

He took off through the crowd while the people hollered out for the band to come back. "E-vang-line! E-vang-line!" the people chanted.

He found Alma standing at the entrance to the handicrafts booths. She was wearing a heavy wool dress suit, the black bright against her pale skin, her face peaceful and intent on her music. She held the instrument with the palm of her hand touching the neck of the fiddle, and her little finger stood out from her hand in a permanent crook. Her eyes were closed, but her lips had the hint of a smile on them.

She was playing an old song, something that Clay's Irish ancestors might have played as they danced about these mountains celebrating their newfound freedoms. Clay felt close to each pluck of the fiddle, wondering how many among the generations before him had heard those same notes. The music lifted and fell, was quiet, then loud, the notes rising and rising, only to fall low. Was he entranced by her, or by the music?

People walked by slowly or stood near her, as if she were a mechanical contraption some theme-park scientist had dreamed up. She did look too beautiful to be real, Clay thought. He saw something in her face that was sad and alive at the same time, which alarmed him and made all of his sensations begin to move at once. He could feel them surging through him like juices. Alma's face was out of place in this world—it was from another time, like the face of a young woman who stared out at you from a picture taken during some horrific period in history, looking tired and lovely, noble and slightly broken, all at the same time. It was not just her face or her hair or her body, but the way she moved, the way her eyebrows fretted together as she played the higher notes on the old fiddle. The slight bend at her knees, the graceful flow of her neck, the easy slide of her arm—everything about her seemed to be a part of the music, as if the fiddle were the one in charge. She seemed possessed by the song.

When the song ended, there was soft clapping and people walked on in to see the quilts and pottery. But Clay remained, and when she finally let out a long breath, took the fiddle down, and lifted her head, he was looking her straight in the eye.

"Hey," Clay said.

She met his eyes only briefly before looking down at her fiddle. "Hidy, Clay," she said.

"I've been looking for you."

She smiled politely. "Aye, do you know what time it is? I forgot my watch."

"It's close to eight-thirty, I guess."

"The chamber hired me to move around and play until eight. When I start playing, time flies by." She stepped into the booth behind them and spoke to a Cherokee girl with hair that swept the ground: "You care to hand me my fiddle case?"

"Well, it's about half an hour until the next big concert," he said when she had gotten her case. "I been wanting to ride some rides, but I ain't got nobody to ride with me. You want to?"

"I guess I ought to go on up to the main stage." She spoke softly, so quietly that it seemed she was afraid someone might hear her talking to him. She took up her black case and put the fiddle down into it carefully. "I'm supposed to meet Evangeline up there."

"Can't I walk up there with you?"

She smiled softly again, fastening the top button on her jacket. "I guess."

They walked along quietly for a few minutes. Clay eyed the moon as it floated in and out of view in the big October sky. He was trying to think of something to say.

"You play the best fiddle ever was," he said, looking at her, but she would not meet his eyes.

"You told me that up at the Hilltop."

Clay shoved his hands deep into his pockets. "No, this was different—that song you were playing back there. That's real fiddle music, where the fiddle is all that matters. Up there at the Hilltop, you was just entertaining, adding to the band's music. That song back there is what the fiddle was meant to play."

"That's right." She eyed him for a long second, as if she was trying to figure out if he had really meant what he had just said or if he had rehearsed it.

They were nearing the carnival, and a hundred loud sounds echoed down to them: teenage girls screaming on the rides, music thumping from up on the hill, men calling out for people to play games, Tilt-A-Whirls screeching, the eerie, hokey music of the merry-go-round. As they slipped into the crowd, Alma moved among the people like a vapor, easing through the churning mess without ever having to stop or ask to be pardoned. He followed behind closely, straining to keep up, and he felt that he ought to grab her hand or touch the small of her back to help guide her through this confusion, even though she was having a much easier time than he was.

When she turned to give him a small, half-mouthed smile, he blurted out, "Let's at least ride the Ferris wheel, since we up here."

She could not hear him over the hundreds of people and the blur of music and machinery, so he had to repeat himself, and in doing so, he must have looked either very pitiful or very sincere, because Alma went against what her head told her to do, and she told him all right. He rushed to a booth to buy them two tickets and they walked together toward the neon-lit wheel. They stepped onto it without a word, the ride operator eyeing them suspiciously as he chewed an hours-old sucker stick. The wheel had nearly reached the top before either of them said a word.

"If I come to the festival without riding the Ferris wheel, I feel like I ain't even been," Clay told her, holding on to the steel bar in front of him with white knuckles shining.

She exhaled loudly, as if calming herself. "Lord God, I ain't been on a carnival ride since I was a little child, and I had to sneak then."

"Sneak?"

"Don't you know who my people are? You've heard of the Singing Mosleys, ain't you? Well, my daddy thought coming to the carnival was a sin. He called it a 'worldly place.' Anything besides church was a worldly place in his book. And after I left home, I sure never got to go nowhere—" She broke off and let out a little yelp as the wheel swooshed down quickly, tickling their stomachs as it sped up.

"How come?" Clay asked, and she looked at him as if she had no idea what he meant. "Why didn't you go nowhere after you moved out of your daddy's?"

"You don't know a thing about me, do you?" she asked, looking at him with a pleasant smile. "I figured everbody up the Hilltop had filled you in on my story, as good as they all know Evangeline."

"I don't know a thing. What is there to know?"

She didn't reply. The Ferris wheel stopped just as their car came to the top, and the whole town was spread out below them. Neon rides swirled round and round. The river showed itself in sparks where light broke apart on its waves. Above it all, the moon floated across the sky like a silver coin, throwing its thick light on the mountains that held the town like a bowl in their hands. A cool breeze came up and smoothed Alma's hair back, and she seemed to be concentrating on that good air and where it had been.

"It's cold, ain't it?" Clay said. "I don't know why they have this festival so late in the year, when its nigh about winter."

"With all the festivals around here, I guess this is the only time they can have it," she answered, seeming to be glad for small talk. The Ferris wheel car shifted as they began to move again. It advanced, then stopped, then went down again as people were let off of cars below them.

"Look," Clay blurted. "I was wanting to ask you if we could go out this weekend, or sometime."

"I can't, Clay," she said, without a moment's hesitation.

"Well, hell," he said, and instantly caught himself. It had been drilled into his head that he should never cuss in front of a woman he didn't know. "Why can't you?"

"I'm married." She looked straight into his eyes as the wheel dropped another notch. She seemed to be waiting for a wild reaction.

Clay didn't have a thing to say. The nausea of true disappointment spread down through his body. He had never even thought of this possibility. He glanced down to her hand on the steel bar, but he saw no sign of a wedding band or any ring at all. He didn't speak, only looked at her as if there were something else she should say.

Alma pushed her hair back out of her face and looked down toward the carnival lights again, perhaps watching for that breeze to come back up and wash over her. "We're separated right now. I mean, I've filed for my divorce and everthing, but it still ain't a good idea. If he found out, it's untelling what he'd do." She laughed good-naturedly, like they were old friends. "Besides, what's a good-looking boy like you want with somebody that had done been married?"

"That wouldn't matter a bit to me," he said, and made his tone so serious that she couldn't have doubted him. He was suddenly even more conscious of her, and of how close he sat beside her. "Things like that don't matter. The past is the past."

"It's good to think that way."

"You look to me like you need to get out and live a little, to tell you the honest God's truth."

"Well, you sure pick up on things. I ain't been living in a long time."

"I don't care how many times you been married," he said. "I've got my eye on you."

She laughed again, and he bet himself that she was thinking how it would be to let him show her how to be alive again. He wondered if there had been a time in her life when she had felt like playing the fiddle until her fingers bled, sitting up all night to talk about big dreams. That's what he wanted to do with her.

"Well, nobody ain't never told me that. If you got your eye on me, I guess I don't have much of a choice."

The Ferris wheel dropped once more and they found themselves on the balcony. The little leather-skinned man opened their car roughly and eyed them carefully as he chewed on his stick. Their shoes rang out on the metal steps leading back to the street. At the base of the Ferris wheel, they stood facing each other, like two teenagers who had just had their first date and didn't know whether they ought to kiss or just say good night. Alma glanced at the ground and thought for a second.

"I'll ride into town with Evangeline on Saturday night, and you can pick me up at the Hilltop," she said. "About eight."

"That'll be real good," Clay said, smiling widely.

"I'm gonna go on up and meet Evangeline. I'll see you," Alma said, and disappeared into the huge crowd that was beginning to leave the midway. They were all headed toward the courthouse for the big concert. He stood for a moment, hands in pockets, trying to pick her out among the mass, then began walking back toward Main Street, thinking he would never find Cake.

When he got back to the courthouse, there were twice as many people. It seemed that everybody in Crow County was there. The ground was covered with handmade quilts and folding chairs. People picked at funnel cakes and craned their necks to see if Evangeline had come back out on the stage yet. Children ran up and down the street, hollering and laughing. Teenagers stood in clumps, smoking and looking about anxiously so their parents wouldn't catch them.

All at once, the big speakers began pumping out a recorded version of "Foggy Mountain Breakdown" and a group of young girls in skirts and ribbons ran out onto the courtyard and began stomping away on pieces of plywood that had been laid on the ground. The children twirled and threw their legs as the crowd pulsated in front of them, clapping and squalling. Clay looked around once more for Cake, who was probably behind the courthouse smoking a joint with somebody he had run into. Out of the swimming crowd, Dreama and Geneva burst through, laughing and hollering to him. Dreama was four months pregnant and already in maternity clothes, but she grabbed his hand and they began clogging as others moved back to clear a dance floor or joined in themselves.

"MARRIED?" CAKE SAID loudly, not looking up. He was taking pinches of pot up out of a sandwich bag and putting them into a folded rolling paper. "Son, you are plumb crazy. I'm crazy, and even I won't fool with a married woman—"

"Separated, I said," Clay shot back. They were flying down the highway toward Clay's house. "She's done filed for divorce and everthing. It ain't like she's happy and living with him and fixing to bear him a youngun."

Cake looked over at Clay and tried not to laugh as he licked the cigarette paper and began to roll the joint up between his forefingers and thumbs. He stuck both ends into his mouth to smooth them out and rolled his fingers over the middle of the joint again. Cake didn't even need the interior light on—he was an expert at rolling joints in a speeding vehicle. "You are crazier than hell, buddy. You sure are."

Clay reached into his cassette case and found a tape to slide into the player. Tom Petty began singing "You Don't Know How It Feels," and Clay sang along loudly.

"My favorite song. You gonna burn this with me?" Cake asked, sliding the joint under Clay's nose. Clay shook his head no.

"Come on, man. You ain't got stoned with me in forever. What's your glitch?"

"Fire it up, then, if you're gonna whine all night," Clay said, and took in the pot hard and slow.

"So you in love, after seeing her three times?" Cake asked.

"Hell no, but I want to get to know her." He picked a piece of marijuana from between his front teeth and realized that the song had ended. He fumbled around on the seat and put in a Bob Dylan tape. A strumming guitar and a high-pitched harmonica filled the truck as "You're Gonna Make Me Lonesome When You Go" came on.

"I ain't met too many people in my life that intrigued me. She does," Clay said.

"Intrigued?" Cake cackled, already stoned. "When'd you start using that word? I personally think that you are *intrigued* more by that fiddle she plays than by her. You've loved a fiddle all your life and now you just think it'd be cooler than hell to go with somebody who can play it."

"Now I know you're fried. You've started philosophizing," Clay said, holding the joint out from his mouth without taking a draw. The joint had shrunk too small to hold, and he set it in the ashtray and beat his hands against the steering wheel to the circling music of the guitar.

Cake suddenly pulled himself up to sit on the window frame, leaning out the window and letting the cold air beat against him. He squalled out, hollering as loudly as he could to the passing trees, to the night sky, then slid back into the truck just as Clay pulled into his driveway.

They made their place on the porch, the music from inside flowing past them and spilling out over the river and the little valley beyond. Clay brought out a liter of Dr Pepper and a jar of pickled baloney, which they ate while Cake rolled another joint.

"So brother's in love," Cake said in a sliding, drawn-out voice. "Do you believe in love at first sight?"

"First of all, I ain't in love. Why you keep bringing this up?"

"Just answer the question, damn you."

"Naw," Clay said. "I don't believe in it. I believe in feeling a connection to people, right off the bat. Like a spiritual connection, or something. You know. Some people you're just drawed to, without an explanation. I feel that way over you."

"Whoa, now, boy," Cake said, and laughed uncomfortably.

"You know what I mean. If I hadn't knowed you all my life and I met you now, I'd feel something. They's more between us than just growing up together. They's something spiritual there."

"Spiritual," Cake said, savoring each syllable of the word. "So that's how you feel over this Alma? A *spiritual* connection?"

"Yeah, I do."

Cake licked the gum across the top of the cigarette paper and rolled up another joint. He held it up close to Clay's eyes. "See there, the perfect camel."

"That's right," Clay said.

"Hey, I read that there was no such thing as true love for our generation."

"You read?" Clay laughed. "You ain't read nothing since high school."

"Well, I seen it on some show. They was talking about our generation and said we was all in too big a hurry for love."

"That's the stupidest thing I ever heard tell of." He was stoned, just off the little bit he had smoked, and he felt like talking all night. "People don't know nothing bout our generation. Even we don't. You can't analyze a generation until they're old, anyway. D'you think people in the sixties knowed what kind of history they was living through?"

"Hell no!" Cake shouted, like a member of a church congregation crying out an amen to egg on the preacher. He lit the joint and it crackled loudly. "That's right, brother. Preach it like it is," Cake screamed to the night.

He jumped out of his chair and did a little dance around the porch before lying down on the cold wooden floorboards of the porch. The cold sank through his shirt and ran icy fingers up and down his back. "Come down here. We'll smoke and study the sky."

Clay pulled off his shirt. He lay down on the porch floor beside Cake. When his bare back touched the chilled floorboards, he jumped and shuddered, but then it felt good. He put his arms behind his head and looked up at the stars. The tape inside had ended, and now there was no music except that of the river, silky and calm. A little breeze stirred the trees, which brushed together like a girl's prom skirt. There were not many stars, and the sky was so black that it seemed a thick, misty blue. Clay felt like reaching up and giving the velvety texture a good stir.

"Reckon our mommies ever got high together?" Cake asked.

"Guess we'll never know," Clay answered.

"It'd be a lot cooler for them if they had," Cake said, and they both lay there laughing for a long time afterward, feeling like they were a part of the autumn air.

• 9 •

THE EXTINGUISHED CANDLE at Dreama's wedding told true: when Dreama was six months pregnant, a woman called to calmly and methodically tell her that she was having an affair with Darry. Darry erupted in screams of denial—and that was all Dreama needed to confirm her suspicions.

"You're lying," Dreama told him. "Any fool could read it in your eyes."

Darry cursed and raved, adamant in his denial. Dreama knew that he was alarmed by her coolness. He was stunned by Dreama's calm, easy tone and clear-eyed, straight face. She stood before him without a hint of emotion. It was as if she had just stood up in class and read a poem and was waiting for her teacher to tell her she could sit down again. She enjoyed seeing him so taken aback. He fell to his knees and begged her to believe him. He was not about to admit to his infidelity, and his denial was pathetic.

"I never went out on you, Dreama!" he hollered.

She didn't flinch, although the people across the road surely must have heard. "You're lying," Dreama said. "You went out on me, and me carrying your baby."

He stood up and grabbed the ashtray from the coffee table. He threw it against the wall and it shattered. When it did, his face seemed to cave in on itself, and he came toward her with his hands in front of him as if he meant to stroke her face. His eyes were wet.

"Crocodile tears," Dreama said, folding her arms across her chest.

He fell onto the couch in exhaustion, crying, and finally stumbled out of the house and into his truck. Dreama stood in the door to make sure he was leaving.

"I'll still see my baby!" he yelled. He paused, as if he was trying to figure out if this sounded like he was admitting to the affair. "You won't take that from me, will you, Dreama?"

Dreama shut the door gently, her face hidden behind the lace curtains. Through them, she watched him tear out of the driveway and leave black marks all the way down the road before he shifted gears and rode on across the mountain. Dreama saw the neighbors out on the porch, watching, and then looked back to the road, as if he might still be there. She could hear his truck for a long time as its motor echoed off the cliffs.

The December sky was black with square clouds, and rain fell thin and straight. Birds flew away in a great racket.

Dreama felt clean and free of obstacles. She saw everything that she would do; it was all lined up for her, and she knew she could carry it through, though cold, tiny beads of sweat had collected on her forehead. She wiped them away with the back of her hand and went to the telephone.

"Clay," she said, smoothing her hand over her belly, "come get me right now. I'm leaving Darry."

WHEN CLAY GOT TO Pushback Gap, he found Dreama sitting in the yard in the downpour. She had packed everything she needed into three old suitcases. She sat on one upright case, and the other two lay helter-skelter on the porch steps.

"Just put them in the back," she said, handing over the suitcases. The rain intensified with every second. "The rain won't hurt em."

"You'll be dead with a cold, Dreama," Clay said, once they were both in the truck. He turned the heater on high, shaking his head. "Pregnant and setting out in the rain."

"Let's just leave here, Clay. Please. Get me out of here." She fixed her eyes on the little house, as if she would never see it again.

Clay backed out onto the highway and started down Pushback Gap. Large coal trucks boomed over the wet, winding road, seeming to slide around the blacktop curves on two wheels. The rain fell harder and harder. They drove about a mile without speaking.

"This girl called me this morning," Dreama began. "Just as soon as Darry had left for work. I was fixing me some French toast, since Darry never eats breakfast and I was starved to death. Well, as soon as he left, I was fixing the toast and the phone rung. This girl asked for Darry, and I said, 'This is his wife. Who is this?' When I said that, it was dead silent for a whole minute, but I wasn't about to hang up and she wouldn't either. So I waited, and finally I said, 'What do you want with my husband?' And she just told me. She was so cold about it. She said: 'Don't you know I'm F-ing your man?' She used the F word to me. At first, it got me so bad that I didn't know what to do. I knowed she was telling me the truth. Even using that kind of language, she sounded so honest. She sounded like she loved telling me about it, but she sounded honest, too. I knowed it was true. She said, 'I didn't know he was married.' And that seemed to hurt worse than what she had first said. I just hung up." Dreama let out a long breath. "Give me a cigarette, Clay."

"Hell no. You're pregnant."

"Shit. I'm just so nervous, now that I'm talking about it. But I can't cry to save my life, Clay. While I was waiting for you, I sat there and tried my damnedest to work up some tears, and I couldn't. I almost feel a relief. And I don't know why, because before today I never thought of Darry going out on me. We've only been married four months. And I love him, I really do. I'll never get over him."

"If you love him like that, you can forgive him."

"No," she said quietly, facing the window. The rain ran down the window in long, liquid fingers. Through the glass, the mountains seemed to tremble and the houses grew squat, then tall. Thunder rumbled overhead and lightning lit up the whole sky, making everything appear angular and in silhouette. They came to the four-way stop, and Clay asked if she wanted to go home with him or to go to Free Creek.

"I guess I'd better go stay with Daddy. He'll die if I don't."

"Dreama, I don't know what to say," Clay said.

"I don't want you to say nothing to me. I know what's going through your head: *I told you, Dreama. I said you all was too young, to wait. I tried telling you.* If I hadn't married him, I'd never been happy, though . . ."

"I don't care about that now, Dreama. I'm just worried over what will become of you, and the baby."

"Well, I ain't taking him back. I'll tell you that right now. I'll get a divorce, have my baby. Easter will help me with it. And then I'll start going to the community college and I'll make something out of myself. I am not going back with Darry Spurlock. Mark my words."

"If I see him, I'll stomp his ass," Clay said, turning into Free Creek. When Dreama didn't protest, he thought perhaps it truly was over between her and Darry.

"There's something I been dying to tell you, but I don't think this is exactly the right time," Clay said, turning the radio completely off. It had been playing quietly the whole trip.

"No, go ahead. I'm serious, I ain't upset about Darry right now. Tell me anything."

He should have just waited until they got to Easter's. If it hadn't been for the rain, they could have walked up the trail to their tree and their rock bench. All this was so hard to say.

"Well, I'm going out with somebody, and I like her," he blurted out, and instantly felt foolish.

"Dammit, Clay," Dreama said angrily. "How long has this been going on? You never talk to me no more. You have plumb quit me since I got married. We used to be best of friends, and now I call and call and you're never home and you never foot my doorstep—"

"We've been through all of this before, Dreama."

"I don't know why you've growed so distant from me. It kills my soul. I remember you not being able to sleep and coming into my room at three in the morning, making me get up and talk to you." Her eyes were wet now, but still she did not cry.

"Anyway, I'm telling you now. Just hush and listen. We've only been out once, but I swear, I've went crazy over her."

"God almighty. You sound plumb eat up with it. Who is it?"

"Alma Asher."

"Clay, that girl's married." Her tone was guarded, quiet. She hated to hurt his feelings.

"She's fixing to divorce. I know all about it. How did you know?"

"I talked to her a little when I called her to play the fiddle at my wedding. We got to talking. Honey, you don't need somebody like that."

"Like what? Just because she's been married?" he said. "I swear, Dreama, there is just something there that I can't explain, that I never knowed of before."

"I know exactly what you're talking about, Clay," Dreama replied. "That's how I always felt over Darry, too."

WHEN CLAY AND Dreama got to Free Creek, the rain was coming down so hard that Clay could barely see to make it into Gabe's driveway. Already the creek was raging, and water poured down off the cliffs. The new gravel of Easter's and Gabe's drives had washed out into the road again.

Gabe was drunk when they got there, since it was past six o'clock on a Friday evening. He looked from Dreama's suitcases to her face and seemed to gather what had happened. Three of his friends were sitting at the kitchen table, playing quarter bounce and smoking one cigarette after another. Gabe pushed his chair back from the table and jumped up. "I'll kill that sumbitch over hurting you," he said. "Get my pistol!"

The men got up without a word and left, like scared children, as Gabe ranted.

"Lord God, Daddy, quit acting like a fool," Dreama said, dropping heavily onto the couch. "You hain't shooting nobody and you know it."

"Clay, if you don't stomp that boy, I'll stomp you," Gabe said, wild-eyed.

Dreama laughed shortly and then turned on him. In the most hateful voice she could muster, she said, "You ought to have been stomped, then. Mommy told me you went out on her the whole time she was big with me."

Gabe settled back into his chair and didn't say a word.

"I'm craving some macaroni and tomatoes," she called out, as if there had been no harsh words spoken.

"They ought to be some Creamettes in the cabinet," Gabe said.

Dreama got up and turned on the stereo. It was as if nothing had ever happened, as if she had never gotten married or pregnant or left her husband. She went into the kitchen, where she started slamming cabinet doors and rattling pans. "Ain't you going to set down, Clay?"

"I'll be back in a little while. I'm going over to see Easter."

EASTER WAS WATCHING the *Renfro Valley Barn Dance* when Clay went in. The Osborne Brothers were playing an old standard and everybody in the audience was clapping and looking right at the camera.

"Ain't El home yet?" Clay said, coming into the living room.

"No. He just called me from Pittsburgh. They's a big storm up there and he won't be in till tomorrow. He said that was the awfullest town to drive in he'd ever seen, anyway."

"Why don't you go with him sometime, see a little of the world?"

Easter laughed to herself. "Lord God, Clay. You couldn't pay me enough money to hop in one of them big trucks."

She took the remote up off the table and held it straight in front of her, as if she was unaccustomed to using it, and flicked off the television.

"You heard bout Darry and Dreama?"

"Yeah," he said. "I brung her home from Pushback Gap."

Easter looked away, to the windows. The winter rain beat against the windows like someone tapping their fingernails on the glass. He recalled the night before his mother's funeral. He had stood at that window, watching his cousins play on the frozen road. Most of the snow had melted, and the remainder of it lay in stripes across the yard, although the mountainside was still covered. He had been urged to go out and play, too, but had refused.

"Listen to that rain. It'd be a good time to sleep, with that beating on the roof," Clay said.

Easter was studying him carefully, running her eyes over his face, so obviously, so carefully, that she might as well have put her hands to his face to study it, like a blind person might do.

"What is it?" Clay asked softly, as if they were both listening for something.

"I heard tell you was going out with that fiddler played at Dreama's wedding. Cake tole me."

"She's Thomas Mosley's girl—you know, the Singing Mosley Family. You have tapes by them."

Easter's face brightened and she sat up on the edge of the couch.

"She goes to church!"

"Naw, she don't claim to be saved. But she's a good person, Easter, she ain't wild or nothing."

"I've heard tell of her!" Easter fretted her brows together. "She's the one that has made such a fool out of her daddy. I heard he was the best man ever was, and she was running wild all over the country and singing in clubs."

"That's her sister, that's Evangeline. This is Alma I'm going with. You'll love her better'n anything, Easter, I know you will."

"Well, you bring her up here to see me," Easter said, and

settled back in her seat. She put one hand atop the other in her lap, the way people did when they had their photographs taken. She studied her hands for a minute, as if inspecting her fingers for cleanliness. "But I can't figure her not going to church with a daddy like that. When are you ever going to settle down and go to church? I worry myself to death over you."

"Easter, let's not talk about this right now. I just don't believe that way. I can't make myself believe the way you do. And I won't be no hypocrite."

They sat for a moment and listened to the rain. Easter studied her hands, and Clay went into the kitchen to fix them both a cup of coffee. When he came back, Easter was standing at the window, watching the rain. It was beating hard, and little puddles full of ringlets stood in the yard.

"Clay," Easter said suddenly, with her back to him. "They's something I have to show you . . . and I don't know how."

"What is it?" he asked.

Easter went down the hall and came back with the large Bible box. She set it on the ottoman in front of Clay and sat back down on the edge of the couch, her hands folded again, as if in repentance. "I just found it, Clay, day before yesterday. I should have went straight and called you, but I just couldn't bring myself to. Your mommy left all this stuff for you. There's a letter in there with your name on it. I didn't open it."

Clay pulled the box up onto his lap and ran his palm over the top of the box. Pictures of flowers, cut from seed packs and magazines, were taped all over the lid.

"The box was your great-granny's. She ordered a Bible that come in it, and Anneth always loved that box better'n anything. She taped them flower pictures on there when she was little."

Clay kept rubbing his hands over the box lid, suddenly dreading to open it. Staring down at the box, he quietly asked, "Where'd you find it?"

"I found it laying on the back porch. Somebody brought it here," she said. "It had to be Marguerite. She's the only one who would've had such a thing."

Easter drank from her steaming cup and then held it in both hands atop her legs. Her eyes were studying him intently again, seeming to outline every feature of his face, trying to etch it perfectly in her memory. "Just open your letter," she said. "You can go through the box later, when you're by yourself."

He knew Easter would not say another word, and there would be only the sound of the rain. He knew that every time he heard that sound from now on, he would look back on this and smell the old notebook paper of the letter he was now opening. He would feel the soft, almost damp paper under his fingers and see her beautiful, curved handwriting.

My Baby,

Tonight I intend to write about my life and my joys and my mistakes. I am writing a letter to your aunt Easter and to you, baby—to the two people closest to my heart. You are little as I write this. You're sleeping on the pallet across the room from me, all little hands and pided skin. I've been watching you sleep tonight, and it is such a pretty sleep, Clay, a sleep that only a child could have on a dark, lonesome night like this. Someday, though, you will read this and know of me. I hope you can find it in your heart to forgive me for the things that I done wrong and to love me more for the things that I done right.

I have to set all this down to paper tonight because I feel like I'm going to bust from keeping it all in me. I want to get all the words down as right as I can and explain myself good. I know that I am about to die. Your aunt Easter, she has always been able to see things. She'd always know when somebody was going to get killed in a wreck or when a big tide was coming or something like that. But me, I always knowed things just about me. Like when I was pregnant with you, I knowed the minute it happened. I just set right up in bed and said, "I'm pregnant." And now it has come to me that I'm fixing to die. I don't know when—soon, though.

This morning I woke up before daylight, before anything, in that time when there is no day and no night. I went outside in my gown. The air went through the cloth and touched my skin, like water, and the ground felt so soft and new beneath my feet—I imagined that was the way the earth felt at the beginning of time. I went on up the mountain and walked the steep trail without taking one breath. I came to the clearing on the mountain's top, where the yellow and purple flowers bend their heads. This is your favorite place, Clay. I pack you there on my hip all the time and lean over so you can put your face to the flowers. You breathe them in and laugh. Someday you will be big enough to go see them flowers by yourself, and maybe you will remember me best there, because we spent many a time there. This morning, though, I just stood there and breathed in the sweet air and waited. Directly the day broke, and the far reaches of the sky become purple and streaked with new sun. It has always amazed me how silent the sunrise is. It is such a beautiful thing that I always expected a great noise to come with it. All the land seemed to open up below me as the morning fog burned away, and I felt like I could see for miles and miles.

It was awful strange. I could feel the dew from the flowers' mouths and it wet the backs of my legs. I could hear the birds begin to sing up there in the trees, welcoming in the day, and it seemed like I could smell each cool leaf on every tree. But there was more than that. I could hear people far down in the valley as they went into their kitchens sleepy-eyed. I could hear women lay bacon into skillets where the grease set to popping and bubbling. I could taste vapors come up out of the mines on the edge of town and smell the bedcovers that had just been rolled back. I took long, deep breaths of the air and felt dizzy from it, like it was something that could make me drunk if I had too much of it.

I have heard tell of this. I have always heard people say that when your senses become like this, you are about to die. Plus I have a great burden on me, like a rock laying overtop my lungs. This is a sign of death, and I feel it all through me. I cannot deny that it is coming for me. I told Easter, this evening when I came back down off the mountain. She says this is foolish talk, but I read in her eyes that it is not. She said, Anneth, you are only thirty-four year old, girl. What do you mean talking death?

But I know it is true and this is why I have some things to tell you.

I never have been like other women, Clay. I've never let anybody get the best of me. There ain't no use letting people do you wrong in this life, baby, and just because I'm a woman don't mean they're going to. I have been known to outdrink a man and go dancing until daylight. I'm not ashamed of that. I'm not ashamed of anything about myself, because that's the way I was made. I am telling you this because I am a honest woman, too. That is one thing that anybody can testify to. People around here have always talked about me, talked about how wild I was. I don't blame them for talking—I am wild, but half of what they say is probably lies. You know that my mommy was full of

Cherokee blood and from this I have always been filled up with life. When I was little I can remember being so full of wanting more that I thought I might blow up if I didn't do something. A person so full of everything is never satisfied, though, and because of that, I have made a lot of mistakes in my life. But who hasn't?

These are the things that you will hear about me and maybe wonder about when you get big, so I want to be the one to tell you the facts. I have no secrets. I'm an open book.

Clay, I have been married three times. Now, a lot of people around here would say this is the worst thing ever was. But it ain't. There are way worse things, baby. I divorced my first husband because I didn't love him no more. We were married six months, and as soon as I married him I realized I couldn't even stand to eat at the same table with him. He made me sick to be close to. It's just one of them things that happen, that we can't control. I know in my heart of hearts that it's a much worse sin to live with somebody you don't love than it is to divorce them. Then I was married again for two years to a man who had another woman the whole time I was with him. I wouldn't about to take that off of no man. So I quit him and that was that. Then I married Glenn, who has been the only daddy you have ever knowed, since I was with him from the time you was inside me until you was three year old. But Glenn is not your daddy, and don't ever let anybody tell you that he is. I was pregnant when I married Glenn, and he knowed that, but he promised to treat you just like his own and raise you up the best he could. Soon as you was born, he went back on his promises. He wanted you to have his last name, but I refused, I wanted you to take my family name.

He always was jealous of you and that is why I am fixing to leave him. He is mean to you. Jealous of you, and one day I will have to pack up and leave him.

Now I'll tell you what I know about your daddy. This is the hardest part for me, the part you will have the awfullest time understanding. Before you was born, I just had divorced my second husband and I worked at the Depot Cafe. I run that little restaurant by myself. I was always meeting people because it was right there at the train depot and people was all the time getting off the train and coming in there to wait out the next one. One day a man come in there, and when I seen him I just about fell over. I cannot say what made me so crazy about him. Like all other things, it was just something that happened or was maybe meant to be. He was the prettiest man I had ever seen, that's for certain. His hands was what struck me the hardest. His fingers was big and straight, long and smooth, like somebody that ought to pick a guitar. His voice seemed to pour out of his mouth so calm and easy that it could smooth out your whole day. His name was Bradley Stamper, and he was from over in Laurel County. He was on his way to Ashland by train, going off to Vietnam. Back then soldiers was always coming through Black Banks on their way to Ashland. That's where they got sent to Vietnam from. He had some people up Ashland and was going up there to stay a couple of nights before he left. Soon as we met, I knowed I had to keep him with me as long as I could. It is too complicated to explain here without writing a book, Clay, but it is a feeling that someday I hope you will know of. I started talking to him that day and it was all just perfect, like I had just throwed a bunch of food into a pot and it had turned out the best soup ever was. Now,

I'm not simple enough to believe in love at first sight, but there was something there. The first night we met, we went for a ride. I had a little Falcon that I loved to drive, and I was always going off on long drives in that little car. We drove and drove, all the way to Virginia. When we crossed the state line, we pulled over on the side of the road atop this mountain and stood there and looked back at Kentucky. For a long time we stood there and watched everything below us. That is a hard thing to come by, comfortable silences between two people, especially two people who have only just met. Way over to our left we could see a strip mine. The mountain's top had been completely cut off and the sides looked like a big scar on the face of the earth. Your daddy studied this strip mine for a long time and finally said he couldn't understand doing that. As God is my witness, I believe that is when I fell in love with him. I had never met a man like that before. Seeing him look at the land like that just about killed me.

We spent two whole days together. We never slept or eat a bite. We met around four o'clock on a Thursday afternoon and he left me about six on a Saturday evening. In them two days, I felt like I knew him better than anybody in the world, and I told him everything about myself. Don't ever think I had a one-night stand and this is how you come into this world. That's not how it was.

He left on the train, but I wouldn't go to the depot with him. I had a room in the back of the restaurant made up for when I wanted to stay in town, and I just laid in that bed back there and cried and cried. I never had cried over a man in my life. I could hear the train pulling away and I just squalled into the pillow. I knowed I would never see him again and that I would never get over him. But he had his papers to serve his country, and there was nothing he could do about it. Love is the last thing that can stop a war.

By the time I couldn't hear the train no more, I quit crying and put my hands on my belly. That's when I knowed I was carrying you.

He sent me one letter from over there, but I don't have it for you. After you was born, I never could find that letter. I know I didn't misplace it. It just disappeared, gone like a ghost had snuck in and took it away. So the only thing of his that I have to leave you is this little silver medallion that he give to me that morning he left. It says "Saint Christopher Protect Us" on it. When I was having you, I laid there in the hospital with that necklace wrapped around my hand, holding the medallion in my palm. I held it so tight that it bruised the inside of my hand. You could see the blue mark it made for days after. There was a little nurse in there that had to pry it away from me.

I don't reckon he ever knowed about you, baby. I wrote letter after letter, but I know in my heart that he never got none of them. He wouldn't have denied you, I know it. I don't know if he died over there, or if he come back to Laurel County or if maybe he settled somewhere. As bad as this sounds, I like to think that he give his life over there, otherwise why didn't he come back to me? I have tried to reach him. I checked the state casualties every week in the paper, looked for him in all the phone books in Laurel County, wrote and wrote the army. But I never could find him, and I'm sorry. I hope that if he is still alive, someday you'll be able to meet him. Just know this—there is nothing dirty or wrong with the way you come about. You are the most pure thing that ever come from me, Clay. People say that I fall in love with every man I meet, but that's a lie. Your daddy was the only man I ever loved in my life.

Your aunt Easter is the only person in this world who knows what I have just told you. I didn't care what people thought of me, I just didn't want them knowing my business, so I never told people who your daddy was. It was my story to look back on, and I didn't want anyone else sharing it. Your aunt Easter is a good woman and not a hypocrite like most. Always be good to your Easter, for she would lay right down and die for you.

I hope to God that you never doubt how much I love you and how close you are to my heart. You are my whole life. I see your daddy in your looks, but I see myself in you. I see me in your actions already. Maybe it's a bad thing to wish on somebody, but I hope you are as filled up with living as I always was. As I write this you are three year old, so you may not be able to remember me. But I have wrote these words down for you in hopes that they will give you a sense of who I am. I can't set here and list all the things about me that make me Anneth, but I think through reading the words I have wrote to you, you can gather a lot about me. If there is anything that I wish you could keep of me, it would be my voice to play in your head—I wish I could leave you beautiful words to come to mind when it is a mother's gentle voice that you need.

I guess I ought to wind this letter up now. There is so much more I need to say, but I don't know how to get it into ink. I'm setting by the open window and I've just now heard a whippoorwill calling. I have always loved their songs. There's a piece of me you can hold on to.

Mommy—12 May 73

Clay put his face into his hands and began to cry the long, mournful weeping of true grief. He felt as if he had just sat down and talked to his mother. Easter ran her hand over his hair and down his neck. They did not speak. The rain pounding on the house sounded like blood drumming in his ears.

The phone was ringing, and even though neither of them got up to answer it, the sound seemed to break some sort of spell. Easter slowly took her hands off Clay and sat down on the chair arm beside him. He kept his head down, ashamed for her to see his tearstained face.

"I never thought I'd feel like that," he stuttered. "I can't explain it."

"There's lots of things in that box," Easter said. "Take it home and look at it when you have plenty of time. And after that, if you have any questions, I'll answer what I can."

"Seems like that letter brought up more questions than it gave answers," he said. "I never even knowed of no man called Glenn."

"He was your stepdaddy."

"And she quit him over me? Did he beat on me?"

"Naw, he never touched you as I know of. It was just his mouth. One thing I remember in particular because I was up there when it happened. Anneth had done told me she was fed up with him, but I never had seen nothing out of him until that day. That day he come home from work and Anneth had a big supper cooked for him, but he wouldn't eat a bite of it. Said he had been craving a bacon sandwich all day and that's what he wanted. You loved mayonnaise sandwiches better than anything, and you had eat up ever bit of the mayonnaise. When Anneth said they was out, he turned the kitchen table over. He throwed the empty jar against the wall. He screamed and went on and said if he ever caught you eating it again, he'd kill you.

"That evening, I went to town and bought four big jars of mayonnaise. I took them up to your-all's house and set them on the coffee table right under his nose. I told him, I said: 'That's for Clay. If I hear of you touching it, I'll come in here and slit your throat while you asleep.' He knowed I wouldn't tell a lie."

Easter stood up and went to the window. "It was things like that," she said.

Clay didn't want to hear any more now. He didn't even want to think about going through the box. His scalp crawled and his body jerked all over, like he had been up for days. Knowing how the letter had affected him, he couldn't imagine what the contents of the box might do to him.

"Just take your time with it," Easter said, and put the lid on the box. "It's just little things she always kept."

• 10 •

Winter was lonesome. The hills were black and shrunken, as if they were hugging themselves against the cold. The sky lost clouds and became one whole, slow-moving mass of casket-colored gray. The waters of the creeks and the river acted as if they had given up their will to move on and were covered by a burial quilt of brown leaves, left behind by autumn. The cemeteries became ramshackle and looked forgotten: plastic flowers cracked in the cold, and brittle branches piled atop the headstones. The air smelled like smoke and metal.

This particular winter, the season's mood had no effect on Clay. He spent long shifts in the mines, thinking about Alma. He had not even thought it possible to have so much to feel. His love affair with Alma was not instant—it did not bloom before his eyes like a flower opening in a time-lapse film. It moved slowly and steadily, subtle and quiet as the rivers of winter, and it was best that it happened this way for the both of them. They fell in love without much fanfare and before either of them had even realized it had happened.

Being with Alma felt like standing atop the mountain at Free Creek, breathing in the cool, crisp air that seemed to heal him.

Most of the time, they took long drives, listening to music and talking. They drove the curvy roads between Black Banks and Virginia or sped down the smooth parkway toward Knoxville or Lexington. Alma was still nervous about her separation and insisted that they only do things outside of Black Banks and preferably out of Crow County altogether. Clay's face began to fade from the usual roster at the Hilltop.

"When's your divorce going to be final?" Clay asked every time they went on a long drive.

"I filed three months ago and he still ain't signed the papers. He's got up to a year to sign em. I swear, I pray every night that he'll sign em. After he does, it'll only take about three more months."

They were driving slowly over a winding road toward Cumberland Gap and came over a hill to find the road crowded with cars on each shoulder. Cars were parked bumper to bumper, so close to the road that it had been made into one lane. On one side of the road sat a small church with no sign to announce its name. A piece of cardboard had been nailed to one of the porch posts. It read REVIVAL HERE TONIGHT. The parking lot was full of cars.

Alma rolled down her window as they eased by. Cold winter air shot into the cab, and along with it the loud, powerful voice of a woman singing "Wayfaring Stranger." Clay couldn't count the times he had heard Easter sing this same song, and in the same lonesome, mesmerizing way. Many times when he hadn't gone to church, he had sat in the creek across from Free

Creek Pentecostal just to hear her sing. It seemed as if every church he knew of let voices creep through their walls and spread outside.

"Let's pull in there," she said. "Do you care to?"

He backed up and pulled into the church. There was nowhere to park, so he just rolled right up to the porch, blocking cars in. Nobody would be out for a while, anyway.

Alma scooted across the seat and put her arm through his. She spread his coat out over her lap and sat as close to him as she could. Clay left the truck idling so that the heater would pump out its steady stream, but the January air slid into the car and settled on their faces. They sat very quietly and listened to the woman sing.

> I'm just a poor, wayfaring stranger
> traveling through this world of woe.
> There'll be no sickness, toil, or danger
> in that bright land to which I go.

The woman's voice carried out on the tight air so boldly and clearly that it seemed she was singing from all around them. Clay was sure that his goose bumps were from the singing and not the cold air that was streaming into the truck. Alma lay her head on Clay's shoulder and closed her eyes, listening to the music. They had never sat so close to each other, and Clay was embarrassed at the erection he felt instantly at such a small thing as her sitting beside him. He could smell her good, clean scent and feel her soft hair against his cheek.

"I wish that people would accept a fiddle in church," she said when the singing had stopped. "Can you imagine how good a voice like that and a fiddle would sound together?"

"I can't imagine what it would be like to create something

that beautiful—to be able to sing in such a way, or play the fiddle like you do. It's like your own little moment of complete creation. That must be the best kind of satisfaction. The kind you can taste."

Alma looked at him without smiling. "God awmighty, Clay. Sometimes when you talk, it's like words falling out of a book."

He didn't know what to say, so he just kissed her. He wrapped his arms around her so tightly that he could hear the bones in her back popping. He was aware of everything: the preaching that had started inside the church, the cold, dry air, the crinkling of her leather coat. He ate at her mouth, sucking her lips and running his tongue over her straight teeth. She put her hands up into his hair and then held them over his cold ears.

When they stopped kissing, he felt words pushing at the back of his teeth, fighting to get out. "You know I've done went crazy over you, don't you?"

She sat back against the seat and looked at the church. "I know it, but you shouldn't be. I'm afraid this is all a mistake."

"Why?"

"Because I know that Denzel will never let me have this," she said.

"After he gives you your divorce, they ain't a damn thing he can do about it."

"That man will never let me be happy. I know him like a book. If he ever does sign for the divorce, he'll never let me have no peace."

"That's foolish talk," Clay said.

"No, Denzel is crazy. I swear, Clay, it's untelling what he'd do if he knowed I was in this truck with you. I stay scared to death of him."

Inside the church, the preacher was screaming out about the wrath of God and pounding his fist on the podium. People yelled out "Amen, brother!" and "Hallalujer!" Clay and Alma sat listening to them for a long time without saying a word.

Finally, Clay said, "Well, what's the deal?"

"What are you talking about?" she asked.

"Do you care for me, or not?"

Alma started crying.

Clay should have seen right then what was going to happen, but then again, it wouldn't have mattered if he had. He was never going to let go of this.

CAKE HAD NEVER gone more than two weekends without having his best friend by his side at parties or at the Hilltop Club. He started to drink more and hung out in the parking lot, sharing a joint with some girl he had coaxed outside or with Frankie the doorman. He would grow angry when people jokingly said, "Clay's plumb quit you, hain't he?" but he never would say anything against Clay, although he felt abandoned and betrayed.

On Saturday night at a party, Cake was half-naked with Janine Collins, a girl who had been trying to lure him her way for months now. She was very drunk and managed to get her blouse and bra off more quickly than Cake thought possible. As she slowly unbuttoned his shirt and pulled it off him, he realized that he couldn't contain himself any longer. He wrestled Janine around on the bed, trying to get her off him, but she thought he was playing with her. She giggled, her mouth capped over his, and pressed her warm breasts against his bare chest. Finally, he pushed her off and onto the floor. She pulled the sheets off the bed to cover herself and screamed "Bastard!" over and over while he pulled on his Levi's. He left the room, slamming the door. He carried his shirt in his hand and slipped on his leather coat as he rushed down the hall. Everyone was in the living room partying and dancing. Only one or two people noticed him leaving, and they called out to him. He did not pause long enough to say good-bye.

He drove away with his foot pressing the pedal all the way to the floor, grinding gears all the way up the winding road. He put in a CCR tape and managed the steering wheel while he smoked a joint.

The pot was harsh and he could feel it burning his throat. It tasted sweet in his mouth, though, and he loved the smell of it. He wet his fingers so as to stop the fire from burning in jagged little strips around the tip and nearly ran off the road, so he put the joint in the ashtray to burn out. There was no traffic at all, and he sped around the curvy road holding on tightly to the steering wheel. His palms were sweating profusely, as they always did when he smoked pot, and he was well aware that he could easily drive off one of the curves and hurtle into the Black Banks River.

He slid into Clay's driveway and nearly sideswiped Clay's truck. He ran up the stairs two steps at a time and was surprised to find the door locked. It never had been before. He beat on the door so hard that the glass rattled in the panes.

"Cake," Clay said, sleepy-eyed, standing in the door in his underwear. "What in the world you doing?"

"I come to see what in the hell your problem is—" Cake pushed Clay aside and made his way into the living room, which was well lit by the slants of moonlight falling through the windows and the open door. Alma lay on the couch, motionless, acting as if she were asleep, although Cake was sure his knocking had woken her up. Cake stopped when he saw her bathed in silver. "What the hell?"

"C'mon, brother, let's go out on the porch. You want me to make you some coffee?"

"Shit no." Cake walked backward across the living room, studying Alma, then slipped out the door like a breeze.

Clay grabbed his Levi's off the living room floor and shook his legs down into them once he got out onto the porch.

Cake pulled a pint of Jim Beam out of his inside coat pocket and took a long gulp. He sucked in a huge breath of night air and shook the bottle in front of Clay's face. "Remember this? Or have you forgot Kentucky straight?"

"Cake, this is stupid."

"No, stupid is sleeping with a married woman."

"She's sleeping on the couch."

"Well, I don't see why."

"I can't talk about this with you and you drunk." Clay took the pack of cigarettes out of Cake's front pocket and lit one. Cake grabbed the pack roughly from his hand.

"You just piss me off, Clay. It's always been me and you, everywhere we'd go. Go everwhere together." His words came out in a drunken mumble that Clay had to string together. "Now it's just me. I never thought you'd act like this over a woman."

"Cake, I call you every day. You was just over here the other night—I cooked your big ass supper."

"I never lay eyes on you on the weekend, though—"

"You have to give me a chance to adjust to all this, then me and you can get out every once in a while—"

"No, by God. I ain't got nobody else but you, Clay. Not a damn person. We're tight, buddy, we're just like brothers, and then all at once, we just ain't no more. I got nobody else in this world. And you know that, man, you know that."

Cake's eyes were full of tears.

"I'm sorry, but you have to let me have this," Clay said after a while. He stood naked to the waist, shivering in the cold, with his hands buried under his arms.

"Shit, man, I'm drunk." Cake smoked his cigarette thoughtfully and seemed to be choosing his words before he said them, although they came out blurred and broken up, anyway. "I think you're being a asshole, Clay. Don't change for nobody. If you have to change for somebody, then you don't need em."

"I don't want to spend the rest of my life doing the same damn thing ever Saturday. There's too much to see in this life to see it drunk. Can't you understand that I want this?"

Cake sat nodding his head but not accepting it, thinking to himself, *It's not good enough*. Finally he stood and steadied himself by the porch railing, then strolled across the porch without a word.

Clay went toward him quickly and grabbed his shoulders. "You ain't leaving here drunk. You ain't able to drive all the way back to Free Creek."

"Let go of me." He shoved Clay away. They had never struck each other in their lives, and Cake still couldn't bring himself to hit Clay, although he wanted to.

"Come on in here and lay down, now. You know the law would get you before you even got through town."

"I don't care. I drove up here and I can drive back. I'm leaving," Cake said, and shoved Clay across the porch. Clay hit the wall but managed to keep himself from sliding down onto the floor.

"Go on, then, by God!" Clay yelled, and his voice boomed out over the river.

Cake started down the stairs, knowing that Clay wouldn't let him leave there drunk.

Clay stood at the top of the steps, his hands out at his sides, as if admitting defeat. "Come on, Cake. Don't leave here like this."

Cake stopped. He turned and made his way back up the

stairs. When he got to the door, he unscrewed the lid from the bourbon, took the last of it, and then threw the bottle in a high arc. It flew over the porch railing and fell silently through the trees. With a strange little smile on his face, he tucked one side of his shirt in and made his way through the door. In the living room, he stomped his booted feet on the floor and yelled, "It's five o'clock in the morning, sister!" and then laughed wildly all the way to the bed, where he went to sleep without saying another word.

Clay pulled off Cake's boots and pants and lay there with him for a few minutes, making sure he was asleep. After a while, he went back to the couch to lie down beside Alma. But he lay awake all night, watching shadows on the ceiling.

• 11 •

Clay dreaded going through his mother's box the way some people dreaded sitting with a family that had just suffered a death: he was afraid he wouldn't know what to say once he got there. He had put it in the center of his coffee table and it sat there patiently until he finally got enough nerve to open it.

He sat on the couch and stared at the box for so long that the paper flowers pasted to its lid began to spin around. He imagined that he could smell their aromas all mixed up in the air above the box. He feared being sucked into the old Bible box like a leaf being drawn into a vacuum, ripped back to a past that he could never return from. He had been chain-smoking since coming home from work and he watched the box uneasily, waiting for it to run out of patience and simply fold the lid back itself.

Inside, he found many small, trivial things that he had no way of comprehending: a dried and crumbling corsage, a quarter with a .22 bullet hole right through Washington's head, a napkin with a faded phone number written in pencil. He found an old, bone-handled Case knife that he supposed had belonged to his great-uncle who had been killed in World War II, a lid from a bottle of whiskey that he figured was from his mother's first drunken night, and a cigar that maybe someone had handed out when he was born. There was a small, carved box full of ticket stubs, and on the back of each one she had written the movie it had come from: *Bonnie and Clyde, The Sting, True Grit, The Last Picture Show.*

There was an I LIKE IKE campaign button, which he imagined she had worn proudly as she walked the clean, polished halls of her high school, and a piece of construction paper with WE SUPPORT THE TROOPS IN VIETNAM written in large, Magic Marker letters. He thought that maybe she had grown weary of the war news and had written out the Vietnam placard herself; he could see her taping it up in the front window while she thought about his daddy. There were various news clippings: the JFK assassination, the Native Americans occupying Alcatraz. He pictured her sitting on the floor, cutting out the clippings to put up for him. He figured that she had probably longed to go west and stand in protest with the Native Americans during their long siege of the island.

She had lived through so much history. He could see that, now that he was able to look back on her life. His mind rattled off events that she must have been aware of, and he pictured her reactions to every situation. He saw her standing beneath the night sky, watching for the hydrogen bombs she feared might fall at any minute, turning the solid mountains into ash that would drift away with the wind. Years later, she stood under the same sky and watched the moon, wondering if men were really walking on it. He was sure she had cried about Kent State, danced to the Doors, and gone to the drive-in to see *The Godfather.*

He dug deeper. A worn copy of *Peyton Place,* a few *Life* magazines tied together with a ribbon. A guitar pick. There was a map of Cherokee, North Carolina, and a handful of photographs showing his mother and Lolie in bathing suits, standing on the beach at Blackhawk Lake.

He studied these pictures a long time. He wondered what the air was like that day, whether their hot skin smelled of coconut tanning lotion or perhaps baby oil. He looked at his mother's eyes, then at the cigarette in her hand, the bracelet on her wrist, the careful way she had applied her lipstick. The way her arm rested on Lolie's shoulder. Had he stood in that same spot, down on the lake? Had she gotten drunk that day and closed her eyes and smelled the water-scent that only the lake possessed, the way he so often did?

He found an envelope full of fine, auburn hair wrapped in a net. A poem that looked as if it had been ripped from a *Reader's Digest*—"Nothing Gold Can Stay," by Robert Frost. A brass Zippo with 1970 engraved on the front. Autumn leaves pressed in wax paper, a red Gideons Bible, Clay's first walking shoes. Wrapped up carefully in a piece of toilet paper was a feather from a redbird, as new and shiny as it must have been the day his mother plucked it off the forest floor while roaming the great mountain. In a square white box that might have held a cool corsage, he found a collection of seashells, and he felt their cold solidity, running his fingers over the rough spots and horns at their edges, wondering where in the world his mother had gotten them. He found her senior class pin, a book of matches from Eaton's Pizza Parlor in Cumberland Gap, Tennessee. Two record albums, in their original sleeves: *Pearl,* by Janis Joplin, and Neil Young's *Harvest.*

He tried to remember her voice, singing "Me and Bobby McGee." Frustrated when his memory would not serve him, he picked up *Harvest* and turned the album over to read the names of the songs. He saw that the title of one, "Old Man," was completely circled in broken red ink. He got up with cracking knees and put the album on his turntable. The sound was grainy, but the record did not skip, and soon the melancholy guitar filled the room. In the song, a son was talking to his father, but to Clay it was as if his mother spoke through the record player.

The words, the pluck of the banjo, the swell of guitars, were all speaking to him, trying to tell him something. He stood over the record player, wondering if she had circled this song so that he might play it someday and try to interpret exactly what she meant. The song ended, and he lifted the needle and put it on its hook.

He thought now he could remember her. He could see her sitting at the kitchen table playing solitaire, or standing at the sink peeling potatoes. She put him on her hip and danced around the house when Melanie came on the radio to sing "Brand New Key." He could recall watching her ironing clothes, sprinkling water from a Dr Pepper bottle. She always kept her fingernails painted. They were a deep, dark red and always reminded him of the color a rose takes on before it dies. He was taken back to a morning when he had stood on the porch and watched her walking down the holler road, dragging her purse on the ground behind her while she cried. They were mixed-up images and scents and tastes, as hard to comprehend as a thousand photographs scattered across the floor.

He saw a velvet jewelry box lying in the box and figured it had once held her wedding band. He clicked the box open and found the Saint Christopher medallion that his father had worn. He gathered it up, and its fine, small links glided snakily over his fingers. The medallion rested square in the center of his palm. The silver chain and the medal—cold against his warm hand—sent sensations, imagined or not, shooting up into his arms. He held it close to his face, as if he might breathe in the scent of his father from the metal. SAINT CHRISTOPHER PROTECT US, it read, the words in a circle around a man packing a child on his back.

He dialed Information and asked for a listing for Bradley Stamper in Laurel County. He could hear the operator scanning her computer, then her dry, bored voice. "I'm sorry, sir, but I have no listing under that name."

"Well, just give me a listing for every Stamper you have in the county," he said, lighting a cigarette and exhaling loudly into the telephone.

"I'm only allowed to give out two listings per call, sir," she said, polite but firm. "But I only have three. Hold, please."

A computer voice rattled off three phone numbers and Clay jotted them on the inside of a book of rolling papers Cake had left on the coffee table. He clicked off the phone, lay it on his chest, and sat back on the couch. He stalled as long as he could, then finally picked up the phone again.

No answer. He tried the next number and stubbed his cigarette out while the phone rang. After twenty rings, a teenage girl said hello, hateful and quick, in a questioning tone.

"Hello, is this the Stampers'?"

"Yeah, who is this?"

"I'm trying to reach a man by the name of Bradley Stamper. Is this his house?" He heard his own nervousness and was afraid that his voice would crack, like the voice of a boy calling a girl for the first time.

"No." He could sense that she was thinking about what else to say. "Why would you want up with him?"

"He was a friend of my mother's. She passed away when

I was little, and I was just trying to find out some things about her."

"That was my uncle," she said, and paused as if she expected him to say something else.

Was, he heard her say, and didn't reply.

"He got kilt in Vietnam. They tole my family that he was a MIA, but they finally give up, I guess. My granny still won't accept it, but my daddy thinks he's dead."

Clay couldn't believe how easily these words came out of her mouth. He felt like he was watching himself from far up in the air. The house was full of winter silence, and it seemed to press in on him. He was suddenly burning up, so he walked across the room and opened one of the windows, letting in crisp air.

"Mister, you still there?" the girl asked.

"Are your people Catholic?" he asked. His mouth was so dry that chalky strands of saliva stretched from the corners of his lips like strings. He couldn't swallow.

The girl cackled out laughing. "Lord no! If my granny heard you say that, she'd die stone-hammer dead. My granddaddy was a Holiness preacher for ages."

"Well, thank you. I appreciate your help." He hung up before she said good-bye, and put his face into his hands. He felt guilty at his lack of grief, but still felt like crying. No tears would come. He held his palm up, studying the medallion, and realized that he had never even missed his father. Only now that he realized that he was a part of two whole people—their creation together—did he feel this new emptiness.

He put the Saint Christopher necklace around his neck, felt the cold of the medallion on his skin spreading out over his chest and down into his arms, and lay his head back on the seat of the couch. There was no intense sensation issuing from the medallion now—it was just cold. He wished for some feeling, prayed that his father's spirit might enter him, but nothing came. Things of the spirit never came when you asked for them. He looked up at the ceiling, one hand flat on the floor, the other running a finger over the raised figures of the medal: a man packing a child on his back.

CLAY AWOKE THE next morning on the couch, curled up with his knees under his chin. He could see his breath seeping out white on the air and jumped up quickly, as if someone were watching him. He closed all of the windows, wondering how in the hell he had slept in such cold. He looked at his hand to see if the medallion had left an imprint on his palm, but it hadn't.

He showered quickly, the hot water stinging his cold skin, and dressed while his coffee brewed. Then he was heading down the highway with the radio turned all the way up. He held a cigarette between the fingers of his driving hand and balanced the coffee cup with his other. A light snow fell like flour across his windshield. The mountains were very gray and the river did not move.

He drove through the town, which hadn't awoken yet, and up over the high, winding road to Victory. He turned down into a short holler and saw Evangeline's small rented house sitting there, pushed back into the mountain.

ALMA HADN'T GONE to bed at all the night before and was still standing in the middle of her room sliding the bow over her fiddle. A new tune had come into her mind late in the night, and she had not been able to go to bed for trying to make music out of it. Evangeline didn't care—she could have slept through a full orchestra, and besides, she hadn't gotten home until nearly five o'clock, just two hours ago.

When a song came to Alma, she couldn't do anything until she had picked the right sound out of her mind. The fiddle seemed to take control of her, but only when the music was just right, only when Alma's fingers were able to find that ancient, singular place on the strings. Now, as she played with her head tilted to the side and eyes shut, it seemed she stood above the floor, dancing about the room without moving her feet.

The song intensified, becoming wild and uncontained, and the fiddle took over. It pushed her arm up, pulled it down, made her fingers go where they needed to be.

Evangeline knocked open the door so hard that the doorknob banged back and left a mark on the wall. "Can't you hear, dammit? He's knocking so long he woke me up."

"Who?"

Evangeline breathed out hard. She couldn't even open her eyes, they were so heavy, and she leaned against the door frame as if she were about to drift back to sleep. "What about *who?*" Despite her grogginess, she managed to mock Alma in a little girl voice. "It's Prince Charles, for all I care. Go see your own damn self."

Evangeline padded down the hallway with Alma close on her heels, still holding on to her fiddle. Alma considered Evangeline's short concert T-shirt with her Looney Tunes panties showing beneath.

"I hope to God you didn't go to the door like that," she said.

"Well, I did," Evangeline said, and fell onto her bed.

Clay stood in the door looking like a cigarette ad. Tight Levi's, a corduroy jacket, straight white teeth, and that clean, wavy hair. He held a cup of coffee in one hand and a cigarette in the other.

"Let's get out of here," he said.

• • •

THEY DROVE TO LONDON and ate at a truck stop by the interstate, where coal trucks and eighteen-wheelers slid off the ramps onto I-75, speeding toward Lexington and Cincinnati, Knoxville and Atlanta. They ate breakfast and fed quarters to the jukebox. Finally, Clay got up and went to the pay phones at the front of the restaurant. Alma watched as he flipped through the phone book quickly and then came back to the table with a thin, wrinkled page of the book in his hand.

He smoothed the page on the table and pointed at a name. "Lookee here. They's only three Stampers in the London directory, and that girl said my grandpaw was a preacher. Look."

Alma leaned very close to the table and read aloud: " 'Stamper, Reverend Lee and Belle, Thirty-five Slate Ridge Road.' "

"Reverend," Clay says. "That has to be them. Them's my grandparents. Lee and Belle Stamper."

"You ought to go there, Clay," Alma said, and put her hand atop his.

"Naw, I wouldn't know how to go about something like that."

The waitress approached, holding a pot of coffee high in the air. Alma scooted her cup to the edge of the table. "If you don't want to talk to em, just drive by and see where your daddy growed up."

"You want some more coffee, honey?" the waitress asked Clay.

"One more cup," he said, and looked across at Alma to let her know he didn't want to talk about this in front of a stranger.

The waitress pulled a green ticket pad out of her apron pocket with her free hand. "You all interested in pie?" she asked.

"I'm not," Clay said.

"Ma'am, do you know where Slate Ridge is, here in London?" Alma asked, before Clay could stop her.

The waitress set the coffeepot down on the table, as if she was used to giving directions and knew that it usually took awhile to explain. "Lord, yeah. It's down the road a ways, little place called Hawk. Easy to find."

"How easy?" Clay asked.

"Just turn right out of the parking lot here and go straight on the main road. You'll pass an old coal tipple that's been shut down awhile. And two or three little jottemdown stores. Go over the bridge and you'll be in Hawk. They's a big sawmill soon as you get into Hawk—you'll smell it before you see it, the way it's been raining. Sawdust stinks worse than anything in the world when it sours." The waitress paused long enough to nod and wink to a man who had come in and tipped his hat to her. "Right there, you'll turn and go up Slate Ridge. That mountain goes way back up in there."

It was easy to find. As soon as they started up the mountain, Clay had Alma looking for mailbox numbers. The boxes bore neither addresses nor names. They saw an old man stacking firewood up against his house, and Alma leaned out the window to ask where Lee Stamper lived. The old man refused to holler out the information and took a long time about walking away from his rick of wood to lean on the truck door and ask Alma to repeat her question.

"Now, old Preacher Stamper is dead, but his wife still lives up here," he said, and spat tobacco juice into the ditch beside the road. He gave them directions and added, "Hope you all wasn't trying to find him and ask him to marry you all, cause he's sure been dead two year."

The house sat back away from the road, but it was close enough for Clay to take in every detail. He stopped right in the road, leaned on the steering wheel, and sized up the place. The house was built in the old way, with two front doors coming out onto the porch, which most likely meant that it had no hallways within and each room led into the next, making a U from one front door to the other. The porch was crowded with a dozen plastic chairs that could be stacked atop one another. There was a porch swing whose chains had been gathered up so that the arms of the swing touched the porch ceiling. A thin line of smoke made its way out of the chimney, as if a fire had just been started in the grate. The yard was wide and flat, with a huge snowball bush to one side and a row of apple trees lining the driveway. The snowball bush had a large circle of worn-away branches that suggested children had used its fragrant, flexible limbs to make a playhouse beneath the cover of summer foliage. An older-model Ford truck with a camper shell sat in the driveway. There were two stickers on either side of the bumper. One read JESUS IS SOON COMING, and the other announced NRA. Beyond the truck, he could see a car house sitting behind the house, an old metal Nehi sign nailed to its side. Two small mountains came together behind the house and sloped down toward each other like the place where a woman's hip meets the side of her belly.

"That's it," Clay said. "That's where my daddy growed up."

"Clay, won't you go to the door? You ain't got a thing to lose. If you don't, you'll wonder about it from now on."

Clay said nothing and acted as if he had not even heard her. He kept his eyes on the house. He knew his own grandmother was sitting inside, but there was no use in going in there and introducing himself. He saw no reason to start a relationship that had no beginning.

"I just can't do it," he said. "One of these days I might, but not now."

"It's what you ought to do," she said. "You bound to have wanted to, or else you wouldn't have come got me so early this morning and come to Laurel County. I'll go right in there with you."

Clay shifted the truck back into drive and pulled away. "Not now," he said. He spoke carefully, afraid she might hear the tremor in his voice. "I just wanted to see where my daddy growed up."

They drove home without speaking. Alma sat close to him, one hand on his leg, listening to the hum of the tires on the blacktop. All the way home, he tried to picture what his father had looked like. He never had seen a picture of him and was certain that he never would.

• 12 •

God was loose in the church house, and the Holy Ghost ran rampant among the people, sizzling through the air and hitting the women until they were forced to shake with wild abandon, succumbing to the spirit, throwing their heads back and speaking in unknown tongues, dancing out into the pews and rushing round and round the church, swaying like waterless swimmers in front of the altar, screaming loudly and taking off to run up and down the aisle.

The men stood with their arms raised heavenward, their eyes tightly shut, their mouths moving with silent prayers. The pastor paced back and forth on the altar, throwing his arms straight up while he shouted, "Have your way, Lord! Have your way!" The guitarist ripped his strap from around his torso, threw his guitar down, and began moving about the altar. He had never received the Holy Ghost before, and when he began to call out in tongues, the whole congregation felt the breath of God upon them. They danced and hollered, shouted and swayed.

Only Easter stood still. Her hands clenched the pew in front of her as she stood with her head bent low. Surely the Lord was among them, she knew that, but she could not feel him this Sunday night. It was like being sober and walking into a honky-tonk at midnight: everyone else so happy, so filled with life, while you felt nothing in particular. She couldn't understand why she was being left out, and she kept her eyes shut tightly, praying that the spirit would come to her.

Guilt rested upon her soul as heavily as the spirit weighed on everyone else around her. Why was she condemned to feel such pain for something that was really not her fault, something that would have happened regardless of what she had said? She kept going back to that day while the rest of the congregation churned about her.

It was New Year's Day, and it had been snowing ever since the night before. The cold was bitter, more severe and freezing than Easter could remember its having been in a long while. She had awakened with a feeling of dread and burden but had no clear sight as to what was troubling her. She tried to shake the uneasy feeling and go about her chores.

El was stuck on the interstate somewhere between Black Banks and Cincinnati, so she was left to fend for herself during the storm. She had to get coal to feed the Stokermatic. She put on a heavy mackinaw and a pair of El's work boots and trudged out in the knee-deep snow with coal bucket in hand. The snow had stopped that morning around daybreak. Easter had heard all of her life that sometimes it got too cold to snow. She felt the cold grind into her bones and set into her teeth.

A large drift had shaped itself right in front of the lean-to. She got a shovel out of the pump house and cleared a way into the coal. The snow was so thick that it seemed as heavy as clotted dirt. She bent over to gather the first pieces of coal and nearly blacked out. She was not one to give up easily, but her head swam around so fast that she feared passing out and falling into the drift. She carried the empty bucket back into the house. When she got inside, the phone was ringing, and her fingers were so numb that she dropped the receiver on the table before she was able to regain some feeling and bring the phone up to her ear.

"Easter?" Anneth said from the other end of the line. "We've got the rest of my stuff from Glenn's and we're fixing to head home. I was afraid you'd call up here while we was on our way and be worried to death."

"You better just stay there at Lolie's until this snow melts," Easter said breathlessly. "Hain't no way you'll make it over Buffalo Mountain in this."

"Naw, I'm coming home, now. Clay don't like staying in a strange place, and he's begging to come home. Besides, we done went all the way over to Glenn's and got my stuff, and we didn't have no trouble. We'll be taking it slow, though, so I'll see you in a little while. Love ye."

"Anneth!" Easter said into the dial tone. She slammed the phone down and went to the stove to warm her hands. She said a silent prayer: *Lord, watch over my people.*

It was always something with Anneth. Never mind a winter storm or closed-down roads or whatever. She had quit Glenn after the New Year's Eve party where they had fought in front of everyone. Anneth had called early this morning.

"I've quit him this time. I'll never go back to him."

"Where you at right now, then?" Easter had asked.

"Over at Jewel's."

"At his sister's house! You ought not be there, if you're wanting rid of him."

Anneth had talked very clearly, as if she had everything figured out at last. "She knows how Glenn is. She takes up for me over him. Besides, she lives right over next to Israel and Lolie. Israel said he'd help me load my stuff up and bring me to your house."

Easter had swallowed her coffee hard. "In this big snowstorm?"

"I need to do this today, Easter. It's my New Year's resolution—get plumb and final broke away from Glenn Couch—and that's what I'm going to do, blizzard or no blizzard," Anneth had said. "If I don't get my stuff right now, I'll never get shed of him."

"You can get that stuff later, Anneth. Just stay still," Easter had said.

"No, I'm going, now. Lolie'll keep Clay while I run over there. He's still asleep. He stayed there last night while we went partying," Anneth had said. "We'll be all right. Glenn's still laying drunk up his brother's house, and I know that big coward—he won't be going back home until this snow lets up."

"What if he is home, though? He'll go absolutely wild if he sees you there, come to get all of your stuff."

"You worry too much, Easter," Anneth had said.

That had been hours ago.

Easter said another prayer and ventured back outside. The day was so gray and overcast that it looked like early dusk. The sky churned and seemed to moan overhead, like some sick living thing. She raked coal into the bucket and took it inside to dump in the pail that stood by the stove, then went outside again to fill the extra bucket. As soon as she stepped outside, she heard a vehicle making its way up the holler.

The vehicle, a rusty green four-by-four that she recognized as Glenn's work truck, pulled into Easter's driveway. As she sat the coal bucket on the back stoop, she saw him come around the side of the house with his hands shoved deep in his pockets. He was an extremely tall man—tall in the way she remembered men being in her childhood, when men seemed bigger and more stout—and he always wore a derby hat, just as men had when she was little. She figured this was what had attracted Anneth to him in the first place, this singular sense of style, this big presence he had. When he entered a room, he filled it up and everyone looked his way.

His black eyes homed in on her from under the rim of his hat. His pupils were abnormally large, so that he seemed to look at you harder than other people did. Easter felt as if Glenn was reading her face.

"Say there, Easter. How are you?" he asked, as if he had just come to visit. He had barely spoken to her since the day she had taken the jars of mayonnaise to his house and told him not to touch them.

"Froze to death," Easter said.

"Well, I won't keep you out here long, and I hain't got time to come in. I was just looking for Anneth. I got home while ago and seen she had took all her stuff off. I was hoping that I could talk to her before she done that. You know, patch things up."

"She ain't here, Glenn. She's on her way home from Lolie's. I told her that she was a fool, getting out in this, cause Israel's bringing her, and I know he don't have no four-wheel drive," Easter said. She wanted to let him know that Anneth was leaving him, and she figured this would do the trick. She wanted to see defeat on his face, but it did not appear.

"Well, they'll never make it over Buffalo without one. I'll just head back that way and see if I meet em. They'll prob'ly need to be pulled out of a ditch line."

A strong gust of wind blew down the holler and pushed the

snowdrift off the roof of the back stoop. The snow scattered between Easter and Glenn like tiny bits of broken glass.

"We'll see you later. You get warmed up now," he called out through the silver wind.

Easter stood in the freezing cold until he had driven out of sight. The wind died down, but the awful chill did not.

When it became dark, she still hadn't heard from Anneth. She called Gabe and made him come over to worry with her. She paced the floor and stopped only long enough to glance out the window for approaching headlights. Gabe sat at the table and drank his coffee in long, hot gulps and bounced Dreama on his knee.

"If anybody knows how to take care of theirself, it's Anneth," he told Easter. She wished she hadn't called him.

And then she saw the lights of a car making its slow way up the road. She ran out onto the porch in her stocking feet, thinking it was them. But when the car pulled in, she saw that it was the sheriff. She leaned on the icy porch rails as he walked up the yard. "Have they wrecked? Are they all right?" she asked.

"They never wrecked, Easter," the sheriff said. He started to take off his hat but did not. "But it's bad, I'll tell you. Ain't El at home?"

"No, no," she said. "He's on the road. I want to know what it is. I want to know right now."

"Clay's all right," he said, and paused for a long moment. He didn't know how else to say this. "Anneth was shot, Easter, and she's gone."

Easter didn't pass out, but they all scrambled to her, yelling, "She's fainted!" She never lost consciousness. She simply lost the will to stand, to keep her eyes open. Her whole body went limp and she began to slump to the ground like a rag doll before the sheriff caught her under the arms and carried her into the house.

They laid her on the couch, and even though she was aware of being awake, she heard nothing. She saw only the backs of her eyelids, felt only her chest rising and falling with each breath. After a little while, she slipped into a kind of sleep.

Later, she heard the low cries of Clay and awoke. The living room was full of people. Gabe, with Dreama on his hip, was speaking quietly into the telephone. She could hear people milling about in the kitchen. She smelled coffee and bacon grease and lemon Joy. When she raised herself up on her elbow, she saw Paul moving down the hall, packing Clay in his arms. Sophie was sitting on the love seat with her arms wrapped around Lolie. Lolie was leaned over, her face in her hands. She shook her head back and forth, as if in strong denial. She rocked herself, and Sophie had to move with her to keep her arms in place. "Shh," Sophie whistled in Lolie's ear, as if she were a child.

None of them noticed Easter stirring until she cried out, "Clay?" Someone had placed a quilt over her, and she threw it aside and swung her feet out onto the floor. "Where they taking him?"

"Hush now," Gabe said, suddenly beside her. "He's asleep."

"I heard him cry," she said. She pushed Gabe aside and went to the first bedroom. Paul was stepping back from the bed, where he had just placed Clay. She stood in the door. When she spoke, her voice seemed somehow dulled. "Is he all right?"

"He just woke up for a minute," Paul whispered, "and went right back to sleep."

Clay was sound asleep, covers pulled up to his ears. She couldn't bear to go in there to him. She held on to the door frame with both hands, knowing she ought to go to him, but she couldn't make herself do it. She wasn't ready for that. She hadn't been there when he had awakened, hadn't been there to bring him home. She could not face him right now.

Paul led her back into the living room. Then she saw Lolie's face, shining with wetness. Her eyes were red and swollen. There were little cuts all over her cheeks and forehead, small enough to be razor knicks. Her hands trembled and she held them together in an attempt to still them.

"Was it Glenn?" Easter asked.

Lolie nodded slowly. "He killed my Israel, too. And Jewel."

Paul made Easter sit. She was barely aware of him beside her until she felt his hand on the back of her neck, directing her where to go.

"We was stopped on the side of the road. Israel couldn't drive no more," Lolie said. "The road was getting too bad. And Glenn pulled in behind us. Me and Jewel was so tickled. We'd been setting there so long. But Anneth knowed. I could see it on her face before he ever got to the door."

Sophie smoothed Lolie's hair back off her forehead. "You don't have to talk about this right now," she said.

"Tell me," Easter said.

Lolie ran both of her hands down her face. She held them there a moment, but her fingers jerked so badly that she had to fold her hands together, knuckles beneath her nose. "Only thing Glenn said was, 'You leaving me?' Anneth was hollering for Israel to go, to drive, but before she could even think to lock the door, he jerked her out of the car. Clay fell right out, his little face down in the snow."

Easter made a curled sound in the back of her throat.

"And he pulled Anneth up by the arm," Lolie said. "She fought him, though, Easter. She busted his mouth. Kicked him in the shins, but it never phased him. Blood was running right down his chin, but he never flinched. All I could think was *Get to Clay, you got to get the baby.* He was trying to get up, but the road was too slick. Jewel and Israel was both on Glenn, trying to get him off of Anneth, but Glenn slapped Jewel's face. Knocked her plumb down, he hit her so hard. Jewel had been beating him over the head with her purse, and when she fell, she reached in that purse and pulled out her little gun. She always packed it."

Easter pictured all of it as Lolie spoke: Anneth struggling in Glenn's arms, the way every little movement must have been intensified in the crunching of snow.

"Glenn was fighting Israel with one hand and holding on to Anneth with the other. He never made one sound. Jewel pulled that little pistol up and said, 'Let her go, now, Glenn.' She said, 'You my brother, but I'll shoot you if I have to.' "

Easter was aware of nothing but Lolie's words and the images of it all that played in her head. It all made so much sense to her. Why hadn't she known such a thing would happen? She listened to Lolie and saw Glenn kicking Israel away. She saw Jewel fire all nine rounds of the pistol. First three, shot up into the sky. Then the rest of the bullets right at Glenn. All of them missing except one, which seemed to do nothing more than tear a small hole in the shoulder of his coat. Glenn acting as if he didn't even feel it, as if he didn't even know that he had been shot. Anneth hollering, "Get Clay! Get Clay!" and Lolie covering Clay up with herself, her long coat spread out on the snow around them.

"When I looked up again, Glenn had his pistol out," Lolie said. "He shot twice at Israel and hit him both times. One of the bullets went right through his arm and hit Jewel in the chest. They both fell down, and I knowed right then. It was so loud. It echoed off them hills. I screamed then. I couldn't move, couldn't leave Clay. I just hunched down over him, put all my weight on him, and I heard the other shot."

Easter listened. She listened and she pictured Anneth lying on the snow. Completely and suddenly still. Israel and Jewel lying just steps away from her. Not a sound on the cold air as Lolie turned to look back, as she took inventory of what had happened. Then Easter came back to Lolie's voice.

"Oh God, I can't tell it," Lolie cried. "I can't tell how it was." She began to rock again. Sophie ran her hand over Lolie's back. Lolie's eyes stared out as if she didn't know where she was, but it seemed she couldn't stop talking. "Glenn was running back to his truck, and I slid around on the ice and finally got Clay up on my hip and I run down the road. I could hear that truck shift into drive. It was so hard to run in that snow, and I had to keep Clay's head pushed down against me. I didn't want him to see."

She stopped for a long time and cried. She lurched forward with grief, but couldn't hush.

"I thought he was after us. I could hear the truck coming. It was like I was running in wet cement, its engine so loud. Clay kept saying my name, over and over. I looked back and there was Glenn, in his truck, right at my heels, seemed like. I just jumped over the guardrail and let myself fall down the mountain. We rolled. Ice and snow in our eyes. I just held on to Clay, held to him tight as I could while we rolled down that mountain through brush and briers."

Easter could see them tumbling, Clay's fingers gripping Lolie's arms. A flash of his eyes, snow drifting away from saplings that their bodies rolled past. She thought she could hear it, the crack of tree limbs, the truck engine rumbling up on the highway.

"We finally hit a big tree, and it knocked the breath out of me," Lolie said. "I don't know how long we laid there."

EASTER FELT LIKE crying out, loud enough to stop the whole church service. God was here, in this very church house, and she wanted to ask him—face-to-face—how she could live with this burden. The Bible said that the Lord would not put more on us than we could bear, but this was too much to bear, this was asking too much. *I am not strong enough*, she wanted to cry out. *It is too much*. She had been given this gift, this curse, this knowledge of what the future held, but still she had not seen what was going to become of her own sister. She had ignored the feeling, had not tried to make the shape of dread more clear, had accepted that it would have something to do with the ice and the snow. Even worse, she had led Glenn right to them.

"It's too much!" she said aloud, but only those closest to her turned, for the rest of the church was filled with the Holy Ghost and paid her no mind.

She ran out of the church house. As she crossed the parking lot, she could hear the people hollering and praying inside the church. She could hear their feet pounding the floor, the preacher shouting, "Have your way, Lord!"

Snow bit at her face as she walked back down the holler toward her house. By the time she got home, she was trembling with cold. She got into her car and didn't give it time to heat up before she backed out of the drive and went across the bridge to the highway. She drove to Clay's house by the river.

She pulled in and put the car in park. Only now did heat begin to pour out of the vents in a solid stream. The windows of Clay's house were lit yellow and his truck sat in the driveway. She could hear the dull thud of music.

The night after they had buried Anneth, she had sent Clay off to bed with two of his cousins while she and the rest of the family discussed what had to be done in the aftermath of Anneth's death. When they had left, she had sneaked into the bedroom and scooped Clay up into her arms. She had wanted him to sleep with her.

When she lay him on her bed, she realized that he hadn't even been asleep. He had looked at her as if he didn't know where he was. She had gotten into the bed with him, her good dress and stockings still on.

"Can't you sleep, honey?" she had asked.

"No."

"Will it help if I sing to you, then?"

"It might." His voice had been so small, so quiet.

She began to sing an old church song to him. He had not protested and had watched her, his eyes open wide, full of questions. When she'd finished, he had said, "She always sung songs from the radio to me. Do you know any of them?"

"No, all I know is church songs, baby."

"Well," he had said with finality.

Easter couldn't go to the door and spill her old fears to him. He had lived through so much disappointment, and she wasn't about to add another. It was bad enough that he had to live with the knowledge that his mother had been murdered. She backed out of the driveway and drove home.

• 13 •

When Alma and Clay walked into the Hilltop Club, she felt like she ought to be wearing a scarlet letter on her blouse. As soon as the cigarette smoke and perfume and loud music washed over them, she felt very ashamed. It was bad enough, she reasoned, that she was here, in this place her parents had always regarded with such fear. To make it worse, she was not even divorced yet, and on the arm of Clay. The guilt she carried along with her was so real, so solid, that she could actually feel it biting into her ribs.

She had been raised better than this. She was not like Evangeline, either. Evangeline didn't care about anything as long as she was having a big time. Even though Alma danced and played a rollicking, skirt-twirling fiddle and kicked back shots of Jim Beam until daylight, she was still saddled with this awful shame that she could not get rid of. Her mother had once told her that she possessed "a conscious heart." She knew that this was true, but she wished that she could be like Evangeline. It would be nice not to give a damn about anything. People like that certainly lived longer, free of grieving themselves to death.

"What's wrong?" Clay asked as they made their way through the swimming crowd. He held her hand tightly and nodded to everyone they passed.

"Nothing," she lied, and noticed that all eyes were upon her. She knew it was because she was with Clay Sizemore. She and Clay had been here together twice already, but she still couldn't get used to the fact that everyone watched them. Women saw her with Clay and envied her. Men looked her up and down and realized that Clay had seen something in her that they had missed when she had gotten up there and played that fiddle. She found herself pulling the top of her blouse together; she felt downright naked in her outfit, which Evangeline had picked out for her.

Clay went to a round table near the dance floor and turned the RESERVED sign facedown, then held two fingers up to the waitress. He put his arm around Alma's shoulders and breathed hot into her ear, "You're lying. What's on your mind?"

"Nothing, I told you." Dozens of scents swirled around them, and she breathed them all in deeply, thinking she might be able to soak enough sin into her body to free her mind. "I hope you're in a dancing mood. I want to dance all night."

Roe came to the table with two bottles of Miller Lite and two shots of bourbon balanced on her cork-lined tray.

"S'that what you wanted, baby?" Roe asked Clay as she slid two napkins onto the table and placed the drinks on them.

"That's right," he said.

"How are you doing, Alma?" Roe set her tray down long enough to give Alma a shoulder-crushing hug. She gave Clay a peck on the cheek that left a set of pouty, bright pink lips on his face. "I already told you Clay's my special customer. If you jealous, you might as well get over it, cause I have to love on him, he's so pretty. Anything you'uns want, just holler."

Without even thinking beforehand, Alma scanned the crowd with an intent look on her face. She had done this every time they had come before, as she was always sure that Denzel would be among the drunks. Clay threw back the shot of Jim Beam and chased it with a gulp of beer, then breathed out as if his mouth were on fire. He had told her that he planned on getting wild tonight.

"You gonna get drunk with me?" he asked.

"I might do it, but I can't chase liquor with beer," she said, and scooted her icy bottle toward him. "Sorry, but I need a Pepsi. Then I can outdrink you."

Cake, Geneva, and Goody came in, their boot heels announcing them like a trio of galloping horses, and hollered to Clay and Alma from the door. They scuffled about the table, trying to find places to sit, and Geneva screamed out across the crowd for Roe to bring her and Goody a fifth of Wild Turkey.

"Alma, this is my cousin, Geneva, and her man, Goody." Geneva smiled politely and lit an incredibly long cigarette. Goody reached out across the table and shook Alma's hand. "They're both crazier than hell."

"You damn straight," Geneva said, exhaling a square column of blue smoke. "I'm Clay's favorite cousin."

"He's got more cousins than anybody I ever seen," Alma replied.

"Old mountain family, honey. We kin to everybody in Crow County one way or another, legitimate or not. Clay said you was from way up on Victory. I figured he'd have to go to the edges of the county to find somebody he wasn't kin to."

Roe brought the fifth, and Goody ordered another round for Clay and Alma, and a Pepsi. "Let's party!" Cake hollered out, and people at several tables behind them squalled out in agreement. Saturday night had begun.

ALMA PROVED TO BE a good drunk. Her personality was not so much changed as it was heightened. She made friends with Geneva and Goody quickly and tried to talk to Cake as much as possible. He warmed to her, admiring her ability to sling back shots of whiskey. He wrapped his arm about her neck to sing along to songs he liked.

"Let's go dance," Cake said loudly to Alma.

"Lord, no," Alma said, wiping her mouth with the back of her hand.

They all egged her on.

"I'm too drunk, and Cake's too good a dancer," she said. "I don't know if I can keep up with him or not."

"You'll keep up fine," Clay said.

"Go on," Geneva said, and poked Alma in the ribs. "Dance with him."

"I ain't much of a dancer no way," Alma said, leaning over the table so they could all hear her. "When I was growing up, my daddy wouldn't let us dance. Me and Evangeline would sneak and practice dancing in front of the mirror with the radio turned down low."

"Shit, now," Geneva said, "I've seen you dance."

Alma laughed loudly without knowing why. She caught herself laughing and felt absolutely free.

"Come on," Cake said, and pulled her up out of her seat.

She bent down and kissed Clay on the lips and took off for the dance floor.

Evangeline was in top form tonight, moving seamlessly from one song to another, bringing down the house with her growls on a Lynyrd Skynyrd song, killing them all with her famous cover of Loretta Lynn's "You're Looking at Country," which got her wild applause and moved people to stand up on their chairs, clapping and hollering. By the time Cake and Alma reached the dance floor, Evangeline was launching into "Sunspot Baby."

Cake was a wild dancer, never staying in one place for long. At first Alma followed his moves, but then she took off on her own, circling him, shaking her hips. She closed her eyes and listened to her sister singing, to the band playing. She and Cake danced so well together that it seemed they had practiced their moves. He grabbed hold of her and twirled her on the chorus, laughing wildly in her ear, and she snapped her fingers and stomped her feet. She thought of nothing but the music.

Evangeline was dancing all over the stage, too. She had sung for the last hour without taking a break, and if she was tired, it didn't show in her voice. The band members were all sober and had played their fingers nearly to the bone by the time they took action on their own, calling for a break. While Evangeline took a breath, Lige, the lead guitarist, stepped forward and announced that they were going to take fifteen minutes.

Cake walked closely behind Alma as they left the dance floor. "See, you're a good dancer, just like Geneva said."

"That was fun," she said. "I'm having a good time. Ain't been drunk many times in my life."

"I see now why Clay's so crazy over you," Cake said.

When they got to the table, Geneva, Goody, and Clay clapped and laughed. "Best two on the floor!" Geneva yelled.

Alma bent down to whisper in Clay's ear. "I'm going to go talk to Evangeline while she's on break."

Alma burst into the room behind the stage, where Evangeline was sitting in a metal folding chair, killing a whole beer in one long swallow.

"How's it going?" Evangeline asked, taking the bottle from her lips.

"Good. Real good. I'm having a ball."

"Hellfire, girl." Evangeline looked into the mirror and applied a fresh coat of lipstick. "You're in love with him. It's wrote all over your face. God awmighty, a blind man could sense the hots from you all."

Alma smiled and lay her head on Evangeline's shoulder for a second.

"Plus you're drunk as Cootie Brown," Evangeline said nonchalantly. "You'll be climbing into bed with him tonight."

"Shut up," Alma told her, and took the lipstick away to use herself. "I feel like playing some fiddle. Got anything you need me to play on?"

Evangeline stood up quickly and dusted off the lap of her dress. She eyed her sister. She put her hands on her hips, looking at Alma like she didn't know what to say.

"What is it?" Alma asked.

"Alma, Denzel's here."

"What?" She felt herself grow completely sober.

"I seen him come in while I was doing the last song. He come straight in and started playing pool. He can't see your-all's table or the dance floor from up there."

"Oh, God. Oh, shit."

"Don't freak out, now. He might not say a word."

"I thought you told Frankie not to let him in. He'll definitely say something if he sees me—he'll show his ass good and proper."

"Frankie wasn't at the door when he come in, and besides, they'd had a hell of a time if they'd tole him he couldn't come in. He's just been up here two or three times and hain't never caused no trouble."

"I wouldn't here when he come them times, though. I knowed we shouldn't have come here." Alma walked toward the door. "I'll see you in the morning. We're leaving."

"No," Evangeline said firmly. She grabbed Alma by the arms. "Honey, you can't run away from him all your life. If you're gonna live in this town, you're gonna see him. Just have a good time, don't worry about it. He can't do much—I done tole Frankie to keep his eye on him."

ALMA WALKED BACK through the crowd. She kept her eyes focused on Clay, who was laughing and slapping the table because of something Cake had just told him.

"Alma, you all right?" Geneva asked as soon as Alma reached the table. Geneva put her hand to Alma's cheek. "You pale as a ghost."

"I ain't been drunk since I was a teenager. I guess I pushed it."

"Did you throw up?" Geneva prodded. "Need me to walk outside with you?"

"Naw, I'm all right."

Clay was drunk. He wrapped his thick arm around Alma again and kissed her on the jaw. She put her hand on his face and drew his lips to hers, suddenly not caring if Denzel saw them or not. *I am in love with him,* she announced to herself. She knew she should make up some excuse to leave, but she couldn't bring herself to do it. She didn't want to run from Denzel the rest of her life. She kissed Clay for a long time, and she felt tears well up in her eyes.

"Clay," she said, but when he turned around and looked at her with his glossy, red eyes, she knew if she told him Denzel was there, he would go wild.

• • •

After several songs that she claimed she didn't want to dance to, Alma finally got up the nerve to walk to the bathroom with Geneva. They had to walk right by the pool tables, and she breathed a loud sigh of relief when she saw that Denzel was no longer there. If he wasn't playing pool, he must have gone home. There was no way he would be dancing.

"I know my head has to look like a rat's nest," Geneva said as they slid through the crowd, but Alma paid her no attention. There was a line to the bathroom, as always, and Geneva talked ninety miles an hour while Alma scanned the crowd. She didn't see him anywhere.

As soon as they came out of the bathroom, Alma saw Evangeline step into the white glow of the spotlight and look out over the crowd silently while the band warmed up for a song. Alma heard the notes Lige strummed on the guitar and the slow, steady beat of the drum, and she knew what Evangeline was about to say.

"You all know that my little sister is the best damn fiddle player in Crow County, now don't you?" Evangeline announced, and the crowd burst into clapping and wolf whistles. Everyone turned to Clay's table to look for Alma, then looked around the room until they saw her and Geneva standing at the bathroom door. "Come on up here, baby."

The crowd continued to clap while Alma shook her head no.

"They all want to hear you play for em," Evangeline said. "Come on, now."

It seemed as if she would never make it to the stage. She felt every eye on her. Evangeline handed her the fiddle that she had sent Frankie out to the car to retrieve. She capped her hand over the microphone and whispered, "He's gone. Play your heart out."

The band's low strumming began to grow louder. "We gonna

do a killer for you, now," Evangeline said. "This is 'Bile Em Cabbage Down.' I know you all like to clog every once in a while, so get the hell up."

Alma began sawing away on her fiddle. It was a fast, exhausting piece that called for a banjo to back her up, but Lige and the band were keeping up. People rushed the dance floor. It was one of those songs that seemed to play on its own—the kind of song that let Alma know why people had once considered the fiddle the devil's instrument. It was wild and loud and set everyone to dancing or squalling or stomping their feet.

Clay loved this song. He had said it sounded like the sound track to his life, and she loved that. So she gave the fiddle all of her strength, finally giving herself up to the song or the devil or whatever it was that filled her body with sensation and took control of her. She kept her eyes on the neck of the fiddle, moved her head back and forth to the sweet, spinning sound, and shuffled her feet to the beat. She could see Evangeline dancing, holding up her skirt and clogging so hard that the people in the crowd could hear her heels stomping along with them.

Clay and Cake clogged with their arms limp at their sides, but Geneva and Goody stood watching Alma, clapping and keeping time. When they came to the bridge, Alma let the fine guitar-picking of Lige take over for a moment. She tapped her bow against the strings and patted her foot. She grinned down at Clay, who was dancing near the stage. And then she saw Denzel making his way across the dance floor. He moved careful and stiff, like a man stepping across rows in a garden. His eyes were fixed on her face. He did not blink.

Evangeline looked up from her stomping feet just in time to see the smile sliding off Alma's face. Lige waited for the fiddle to kick back in as the bridge ended, then started playing faster so the people might not notice that Alma had not put her bow back to the strings.

Denzel walked slowly to the stage, no sign of emotion on his face. He did not look angry, and he certainly did not look happy to see her. His eyes were slightly squinted, as if he were trying to be certain that it was her. Alma scanned the crowd for Clay, and when she laid eyes upon him, Denzel followed her gaze. He looked back and forth from her to Clay and then to her again.

"I've watched you tonight," he hollered, but she couldn't really hear him. Somehow she knew what he was saying, as if she were able to read lips.

He walked around to the little set of steps that led up to the stage. *He intends to come right up here, then,* she thought. She dropped the fiddle with a dull thud and moved back slowly. The microphone issued an awful shriek as she knocked the stand over. The whole crowd stopped. The band's music faded for a moment, then picked back up.

Clay pushed his way through the people and got to Denzel about the time he stepped up onto the stage. The music stopped and Lige ripped the guitar's shoulder strap off himself. The drums' cymbals sent out a sweet, shivery splash as the drummer got up. Alma kept backing up, unaware of where she was going.

Clay caught Denzel by the shoulder and turned him around. When Denzel pulled his arm back, Clay hit him square in the mouth. Denzel's broad back crashed against the side of the stage, but he came back with his fists ready. He hit one side of Clay's face and then the other, landing each punch squarely.

Clay went at Denzel with fists flying. He struck Denzel's face and then punched him in the stomach. Denzel fell to the floor again and Clay straddled his chest to punch either side of his face. Denzel bucked Clay off him and stood quickly, moving around in a half-circle, then pushed Clay down with both hands and leaned over him. Alma could see his elbows rising up into the air behind him as he hit Clay in the face.

Alma scrambled down off the stage and pulled at Clay, screaming and sinking her fingernails into Denzel's face. She felt his skin peel back underneath her nails. She wrapped her arms around Clay's head and she pulled him up onto her lap as Denzel's fists pounded against her hands. "Don't hit him!" she screamed, over and over, her voice a high, scratchy thing that she had never heard before.

Cake broke through to pull her away. He hooked his arms through Alma's from behind while she continued to scream. Clay managed to get up and went at Denzel as if reinvigorated. As he pounded Denzel's face, everyone in the honky-tonk began to fight. The crowd surged forward and people fell onto one another. Glass shattered. Tables were turned over; chairs were thrown. A lot of the women were fighting, too, but some of them stood up in their chairs to get a better view. They hollered and laughed. Geneva ripped a girl's blouse half off. Goody attacked one of the pool players. The bouncers tried in vain to pull people apart.

A man pulled Clay off Denzel, who was lying in between table legs, with blood running out of the side of his mouth. The man held Clay back as Denzel got up, his big hands spread across Clay's chest as he said, "He's had enough now. Drop it."

Denzel didn't look at Clay again but stepped over an upturned table to go toward Alma, who was still being held by Cake. Cake let go of her, thinking that Denzel intended to fight him, but when he did, Denzel slapped Alma across the face.

Evangeline ran at Denzel and hit his face with open hands. She yelled close enough for her spit to land on his lips. Tears ran down her face in a black mess of mascara. The bouncers grabbed Denzel, hustling him across the dance floor.

The pool player released Clay with a little push, right into the grip of Frankie, who took his arm and began walking him out of the club. Alma was suddenly at his side.

People were still fighting as Frankie led them out. Cake, Geneva, and Goody followed, but Evangeline had to be packed out. A bouncer wrapped one big arm around her waist while she kicked and hollered.

Frankie sent them outside. He stood in the open doorway, out of breath. "God awmighty, Clay," he said. "Don't you know better than to mess with that feller? That sumbitch is crazier than hell, and on coke. Get the hell out of here."

GENEVA DROVE THEM all back to Clay's house. Alma insisted that Clay put his head in her lap, though Geneva assured her that he was fine, she had seen him in far worse fights than that.

"He ain't hurt!" Geneva squalled out. "Damn, that was a rush. I ain't been in a fight in five year. Uh, Goody, you bleeding!" Geneva let out a peeling laugh and beat on the steering wheel.

Clay sat up dizzily and blew his nose onto a wad of toilet paper that somebody had handed him. "Did I do all right?" he asked.

"All right? Hell's bells, buddy, you whopped his ass, looked like to me," Goody said. "I don't see how he kept getting up."

"Cause he was so coked up he didn't feel nary punch, that's why," Geneva said loudly. She lit a cigarette and clicked off the radio. A light rain began to fall and the wipers grated across the windshield. "That bastard was higher than hell on coke. Couldn't you tell that?"

"Who in the hell was that anyway?" Cake asked. "We didn't even know him."

"I never seen him before," Goody said.

"That was Alma's ex-husband," Clay said.

Alma looked at Clay. "How did you know?" she asked, but Clay didn't answer.

"Well, he won't mess with you all no more," Geneva said, driving carefully around the curves of the wet road. "I guarantee his nose is broke, plus a lot more."

Alma ran her sweaty hand over Clay's and leaned over him to breathe out, "I'm sorry, Clay. I shouldn't have never went there."

"They ain't nothing to be sorry about," Clay said.

• 14 •

"Lord God, Buddy," Gabe said, sitting upright in his seat at the kitchen table. "You are beat plumb to death."

"He looks worse than I do," Clay said as he sat down at the table.

Dreama came down the hallway, ready to start breakfast.

"Oh my God, Clay. You need stitches," she said, and touched his face softly. She looked as if she was about to cry. "If Easter sees your face tore up like that, she'll die, absolutely die."

"Don't touch that cut, Dreama, it'll mark the baby!" Gabe boomed, and Dreama pulled her hand away quickly.

"Was it over that girl you seeing?" Gabe asked.

"Naw. I tole you, I don't know what it was over. He just come up to me and—"

"Buddy, don't lie to me," Gabe said, standing and hitching up his jeans. He walked to the counter and poured himself and Clay a cup of coffee. "You know I know everbody up at that Hilltop. They tole me that was Alma's husband."

"He signed the divorce papers today. It'll be final in three months."

"It don't matter, son. They ain't divorced yet, and you ought not be out with her."

"Shit, Daddy, what are you so moral all of a sudden for?" Dreama asked, wild-eyed.

"What?"

"Like you ain't had married women." Dreama laughed loudly.

"They was separated when I met her. It ain't like I took her away from him," Clay said, eyeing his uncle for a response.

"Still, you can't blame the feller. If he went in there and seen you two together, he didn't have no choice but to fight you. When you going to realize how people work, Clay? How the world works?"

"All I know is, I'm marrying her soon as that divorce is final," Clay said.

If anybody knew how the world worked, it was Gabe. Clay remembered the first time Gabe had taken him hunting. He remembered the sound of falling leaves, cooing like women whispering among the trees. Leaves had drifted down in fiery quilts, patchworks of gold and red and orange.

"You know this path, now don't you?" Gabe had asked.

"Why yeah," Clay answered. "I travel it ever day."

"Well, you go on down yonder, and I'm going up on this ridge. Now walk easy, buddy, and kill you one." Gabe straightened Clay's camouflage jacket, which was much too big for him. "Walk like I tole you."

Gabe slid away and Clay walked carefully down the path, trying to bear the feet of his ancestors. Gabe had always told him how their Cherokee blood allowed for them to walk silent as a spirit over the mountain paths. Clay moved down the mountain without making a sound. He fancied he could walk right up on the most timid bird without its knowing he was close.

He had walked silently on the path until he came upon a walnut tree, its limbs weary with their load. The ground below had been decorated by the nuts, and each time the slight morning breeze moved, a few more bounced onto the forest floor, like heavy rocks plopping into deep water. He quickly went about gathering them, shoving as many as he could carry into his hunting sack. When it was full, he felt the sack, the way he had patted Gabe's so many times before, and judged them to feel the same. Gabe's hunting sack was always pressed tight with squirrels, and when Clay smoothed his hand over it, it felt like a dozen little babies in a woman's belly. When he and Gabe met back up, Gabe shook his head.

"Walnuts?" he said, and his tone made it clear that he would never understand his nephew. A boy was supposed to be crazy over hunting, should mark off the days until the season opened, want to lay out of school just to go on a hunt. It was the mountain way. Gabe walked on down the trail, hitching up his pants and muttering to himself.

Clay took his hands away from his face and tried to clear his nostrils of the sharp, green scent of walnuts from so long ago. He heard Gabe laugh in a forced manner.

"Talking about marrying a woman that hain't even divorced yet," Gabe said. "I swear, buddy, you a sight."

EVANGELINE HAD BEEN playing solitaire. Now she took a card off the top of the deck and formed a perfectly straight line of cocaine on top of her wobbly nightstand. She rolled up a dollar bill and leaned over, snorted the coke up in one long nose-gulp. She breathed in deeply, threw her head back, and shook it madly, then took her index finger and dotted up the tiny particles she had left behind and put them on her tongue. She closed her eyes, pinched her nostrils tightly, snapped off the radio, listened to see if the water was still running, and said aloud, "What in the *hell* is she doing?"

Alma had been in the shower for more than ten minutes. She turned round and round beneath the showerhead, her eyes clenched tightly shut, feeling nothing but the water, hearing nothing but the steady pounding on her cold body.

Evangeline lurched down the hall. Soon she would feel the cocaine and it would wake her up, sizzling up to hit her right in the forehead. She felt awful right now, and she badly needed the rush this instant. She had to be at the club for warm-ups in thirty minutes, and the boys would be pissing and moaning if she was late. Evangeline banged and kicked at the bathroom door, mad as hell. "Alma Leigh! What in the hell are you doing? I have to get cleaned up!"

The water beat its monotone song against the tub.

"Alma? Are you all right?" Evangeline's voice was suddenly tinged with worry. Ever since the lawyer had called and said that Denzel had signed the divorce papers, Alma had been acting crazy. She hadn't responded at all the way Evangeline had expected. If it had been Evangeline, she would have jumped up and down, screaming, "I finally got rid of the son of a bitch!" but Alma had just hung up the phone, called Clay to tell him, and gone to the bathroom. She had been there ever since.

Evangeline kicked the door so hard that the wood cracked around the doorknob, and her toe instantly began to swell up. "Alma, what in God's name are you doing in there?"

"Leave me alone," came Alma's voice, full of water.

"Shit-fire," Evangeline muttered, and gave up.

Alma hugged her arms about herself and felt the lukewarm water beat on her face and spread its sensation all the way through her body, from the top of her head to her fingertips and down into her legs. She leaned against the tile, her hair tangled in the corners of her mouth, her eyes still clamped shut, and slid down the wall. She sat in the tub with her knees together in front of her face and gave herself to the water. It felt so good, so cleansing, that it reminded her of baptism. She could remember that sensation clearly, even though she had been very young when her father convinced her that she had been saved and that she had to go beneath the water to enter Heaven. She remembered how cold the November river had been, and the preacher's huge hand in the small of her back. "In the name of the Father and the Son and the Holy Ghost," his rising voice announced, and then she was under the water so long that she thought he might never bring her back up. That water had felt so clean, and she had been convinced that it had been water blessed by the Lord. When she came back up to the late autumn air, she had felt so pure; she had felt sterilized from sin, bathed only in the goodness of the world. The people on the bank began singing "Down in the River to Pray," and the presence of God had washed up onto the shores. She felt as good now, as full of spirit.

She was free.

"*Free.*" She said the word aloud, the water filling her mouth. She ran the word over and over in her mouth, swishing it around like mouthwash, feeling its slick texture on her tongue. It was the first time that it had come to her that she was loose from Denzel, that she could actually be rid of him. She was going to get away from him; this must be the same satisfaction, the same rush, she thought, that someone felt when they got away with the perfect crime.

It was no small thing, after all. At one point in her life, she had thought it completely impossible to ever get away from Denzel. She could remember sitting down on her own front porch as Denzel left in one of his fits, watching his truck bounce down the road as she thought to herself, *There is no getting out of it now.* At that time, the notion of freedom had been a dream, or even less than that: the thought had been purely ridiculous to even dream about. Sitting in water that was beginning to get cold, she wondered what had given her the strength, the gumption to actually walk out that last time, to leave and just think, *To hell with it all.*

She reckoned now that Denzel had been the one to give her that strength. All the times he beat her, cussed her, and talked to her with a snake's venom in the back of his throat—that was what had made her strong. She hadn't minded the beatings all that much, to be honest. After the first two or three, they had become a relief in a strange sort of way. After he beat her, she had had the satisfaction of not crying, and that had built up such rage in her that he must have seen it brewing right in her eyes. It had not been the beatings that had hurt her the most; it had been his constant mouth, his spirit-killing mouth. When she bought a new dress, he'd say, "No dress in the world could hide your big ass." She had not played the fiddle while he was at home for fear of his breaking it into pieces. He said her fiddle playing sounded like "two cats hung up together." When she mentioned going back to college, he told her, "Stupid, ignorant people ought not waste the government's money." When she was unable to hide her disgust at his doing a line of cocaine, he'd push her face into the powder and make her lick it up. He raked his hand across the supper table, saying that her cooking wasn't fit to feed a hog as he stomped around in the broken dishes and steaming clumps of food. The words he spewed out were like a poison that deadened every good thing about herself.

Denzel had thought these cruel words, these put-downs and cusses, would break her. He had been wrong. "What does not kill us makes us stronger," her mother used to say. It was one of her endless streams of clichés, and she had been right, so right. *Maybe I ought to thank the son of a bitch,* Alma thought.

But it was Clay who had brought her back to life. If he had pulled her drowned body from the lake and pushed air back into her lungs, it would have been no more or less, because he had saved her. He had reawakened her to something she had known so well once before, although she couldn't really say how she had learned it. Her parents had always been so intent on having their souls saved that they forgot to appreciate anything around them, forgot to live. Now she had life and the freedom to live it.

"Are you dead?" Evangeline screamed from the other side of the bathroom door. She began knocking frantically, genuinely worried.

Alma turned off the water and leaned against the cold, hard tiles of the shower wall. "No," she whispered. "I'm alive."

PART TWO

FLYING BIRD

• 15 •

Darry stood in the yard with tiny feathers of snow falling around him. He had knocked for ten minutes, nearly beating down the front door, but still refused to give up. Leaving, he turned around in the yard once more, staring at the windows, knowing they were watching him. He yelled to the trailer again: "Dreama! I know you're in there. Answer the door!" Slowly, she opened the door and stepped out onto the high porch.

"What is it, Darry? There hain't nothing you can say that's going to change a thing."

"Dreama, please come home." He spoke quickly, knowing she wouldn't give him long. "I love you, baby. I've loved you all of my life, as long as I can remember."

"Shit, Darry. You make me sick." She stroked her big belly. The baby had been kicking and squirming inside her all morning, as if it knew its daddy was on his way. "If you love me so much, why'd you go out on me? That don't make no sense."

"I can't change the past, Dreama. I've quit that girl. I don't know what was wrong with me."

"My God, Darry, we'd only been married three months before you started going out on me. You expect me to forgive that?"

"That ain't what I'm saying. Dreama—" She saw the tears welling up in his eyes but knew he wasn't going to cry. He had cried the last time he had talked to her on the telephone, and even that hadn't melted the ice that had formed around her heart.

"Get on out of here. You're pathetic," she said.

"Won't you come for a ride with me, Dreama? Let's talk about this."

"No." Her voice grew loud.

"If we could just talk awhile, alone, and go riding around—"

"Don't come up here no more, Darry. I'll call you when this child is born, and you can come to the hospital to see it, but I don't want you about me no more till it comes. I hain't having you back, not now, not ever." She stood with her hands on her hips, her face a slice of stone. He put a knuckle into the corner of his eyes but didn't let the tears come, and she was glad. She got no pleasure from seeing him cry; it only made her more angry.

She puffed up her voice again, hoping everyone in the whole holler would hear her. "This is your child I'm a-carrying, so we're connected for the rest of our lives, but that's all. That's as far as it goes. I'll file for divorce after the baby's born. I don't want it coming into this world and us not married."

She went into the house and closed the door quietly.

Inside, Gabe was loading his pistol so quickly that some of the bullets fell from his hand and bounced across the carpet. Clay watched out the window as Darry climbed back into his truck.

Gabe looked from the pistol chamber to the door and back again. Dreama waddled toward him and capped her hand around the cold metal of the barrel.

"Put that damn gun up, Daddy. You hain't gonna use it no way."

"I'm bout tired of you talking to me thataway, Dreama Marie," Gabe said, standing up and hitching his pants up awkwardly. "Ever since you come back here you ain't had no respect for me."

"I'm a changed woman," Dreama said in a wildly dramatic voice, shooting Clay a big-eyed look. "Liberated!"

Clay laughed into his hands.

"You talk plumb foolishness," Gabe said.

"I'd talk about foolishness," she said, stirring the cabbage she was frying in a cast-iron skillet. "Foolishness to me is getting a gun out to pull on the father of your unborn grandchild. That don't make a lick of sense. And I've lived twenty years with you and I couldn't count the times I've seen you run and load that little pistol, but there hain't been nary time you've used it. Not that I'd want you to, but just the same—"

"That's where you wrong, Dreama," Gabe said, standing so close to her that her belly almost touched his. "When somebody fools with my baby girl, or any of my people, I'd kill them before even thinking about it."

Clay felt blood rush to his face. He nearly blurted out, *Well, why didn't you kill the man who shot my mother?* and then he thought to himself that for all he knew, Gabe had done so. Clay had never even considered what had happened to the murderer before, and realizing this, he couldn't believe his lack of curiosity on this matter. He had been so haunted with his mother's death that he had never even asked about her killer. But whenever he had brought up Anneth's death to Gabe, his uncle had always looked off with blank eyes, as if he could not bear to speak of it.

"I know that, Daddy." Dreama ran her hand down her father's cheek.

"I would. I'd kill anybody over any of you all." Gabe unloaded the pistol slowly, rolling the bullets around in his palm as if he appreciated their light solidity.

Clay watched him with mixed feelings and then wondered why he felt this way. Gabe had taken him in, raised him, given him clothes and food and support in almost every situation. Clay had been told plenty of times that Easter had been all set for him to move in with her when Anneth was killed, but Gabe had begged her to let Clay stay with him. He had looked her in the eye without wiping his tears away and said, "Please, let him stay with me. You can raise him, Easter, but I want him to live with me." And Easter had not been able to refuse him.

Clay did not understand the tension that had come between him and Gabe, like black smoke that overtook everything. He didn't know how to speak to his uncle, the only father he had ever known, and that was not right. He could not understand what had carved this great divide. He watched Gabe and felt a pang of homesickness in his gut. Gabe put his pistol back in the kitchen drawer, hitched up his pants again, sank into his recliner, and flipped on the television. Clay looked at the long lines in Gabe's face, his strong, stubby hands, and his thinning hair.

"What happened to the man that kilt my mother?" Clay asked suddenly. His words hung in the air like breath on a winter morning.

Gabe turned his head quickly and looked at Clay's eyes. His face grew pale. "What's that supposed to mean? You throwing it up to me that I never kilt him?"

"No." Clay lit a cigarette. "What you said made me think of that. I'd like to know what happened to him."

Dreama ran a fork through the frying cabbage, looking back and forth from Clay to Gabe, who sat on opposite sides of the room. The whole dead space of the living room floor lay between them.

"I did go after him," Gabe said finally. His eyes burned into Clay. "Soon as they come and tole us. I took my thirty-eight and I had ever intention of blowing his brains out. I went up and borrowed Harold's truck. I don't know why I didn't wreck. I was flying over Buffalo Mountain and that was the awfullest snow I ever seen. I had to go right by where it happened. The law was still there, they was hooking a wrecker to Israel's car to pull it off that mountain. Down to the foot of the mountain, I seen more law. All their cars on the side of the road, and men going down over the side of the mountain. One of the law was standing out in the road, and he stopped me. He knowed what my intentions was."

Gabe paused for a long moment, and the house was filled with nothing but the sizzle of grease from the frying cabbage. The hinges of the oven door creaked as Dreama checked the browning corn bread, pretending she wasn't listening.

"Glenn had wrecked. His car was over the side of the road. Drove right through the guardrail and come to rest in the deep part of the creek. He was bout a hundred foot down the creek, like he'd been running away from his truck. Facedown in the water. I wanted to kill him. Would've gived anything to, but I was beat to it. Law said it looked like he'd wrecked and tried to run off, but he fell through the ice on the creek. Drowned."

"So he fell and drowned?" Clay asked.

"That's what they said. He was dead, and that satisfied me. I just wished I'd been the one to do it."

Dreama's movements in the kitchen bit into the silence. Gabe and Clay were both looking at the floor. She cut up the corn bread, sliced a juicy, ripe tomato into thick wedges, took up the cabbage, and made them all plates.

"Eat, now," she said.

CLAY LET HIMSELF out the back door of Gabe's house and walked toward Easter's. There was a full moon tonight, but the mountain behind Gabe's was so high that it blocked out any sign of it. The top of the mountain was lit with a silver glow, and the clouds above the moon were streaks of white, liquid light. He considered the mountain and felt like climbing it. He hadn't been up there at night in ages. He heard it calling to him, telling him that if he would go up those old paths, he might see something that would answer one of his many questions, but he turned away and went on into Easter's yard.

He could see Easter's shadow on the kitchen window as she washed dishes. Even through the steamed glass, he could hear her singing.

> Sometimes I feel discouraged,
> and think my life's in vain.
> Oh, but then the Holy Ghost
> revives my soul again.
> There is a balm in Gilead
> to make the wounded whole.
> There is a balm in Gilead to head my soul.

He did not watch her silhouette there, in the yellow window, but closed his eyes and savored her fine, clear voice, floating out onto the night. He missed all of this, and he knew what everything was leading to: he wanted to come home, back to Free Creek. He walked on into Easter's, wondering why he had ever left in the first place.

EASTER SAT DOWN at the table with Clay, who was slowly eating an apple and running his tongue over each piece, thinking how everything always tasted better at her house.

"Where you and Alma going tonight?" she asked, smiling. She was crazy over Alma, now that she had met her. Alma had greatly pleased Easter by cleaning her plate and having the good sense to ask for more, when Clay had brought her up to eat the week before. Alma had refused to leave until she had helped wash the dishes and wipe down the kitchen.

"Nothing much. We'll probably just cook supper and set around the house."

Easter read his eyes, and asked, "What's on your mind?"

"Gabe told me about him going after the man who killed Mommy. Said he drowned. It don't make no sense."

"Why don't it?"

"Well, it just seems awful convenient for him to just fall and accidentally drown, after killing three people. Are you sure the law beat Gabe to that man?"

"Gabe never killed him, Clay."

"Well, it just sounds too perfect that he died like that, just down the mountain from them."

Easter nodded. "Well, to tell you the truth, sometimes I think it could've been any one of us that done it."

Clay looked at her, feeling exhausted. Sometimes he wished he didn't know a thing about what had happened to his mother. He often wished they had just lied to him about everything, told him she had died a natural, peaceful death and left it at that. There were too many twists and turns to this story, too many oddly shaped pieces to fit into this quilt. "What in the world do you mean?" he asked.

"We all wished it so hard. I know it's a sin, Clay, but when they tole me Anneth was dead and who done it, I set there and prayed and prayed that he would die, too. I've repented over that many a day, but I can't help the way I felt. I can't lie about how full of vengeance I was." She put both elbows on the table and moved closer to him, then folded her hands one atop the other and settled back into her chair. "We all wanted so bad for him to be dead, that he just was. Something took care of it for us."

Her words were final, and that was enough for Clay, anyway. He pictured the death wishes of everybody that had loved his mother—Easter, Gabe, Marguerite, Paul, Sophie—all of those vengeful prayers rising up into the air, becoming one solid and real entity. He imagined that they became a mass of red, crying birds, flying over the mountains, casting a shadow on the land beneath them. They were redbirds, and their bright bodies were stark and beautiful against the gray sky, the white earth. They sliced through the winter air as they zeroed in on Glenn. The murderer was so frightened by the oncoming flock that he lost control of his vehicle and plummeted off the side of the road. He tried to run, until he fell into the creek, where the birds rested heavily upon him—the thousand of them. They sat on him, flapping their broad, shiny blood wings, their eyes perfectly round and opaque. Finally, all of his breath was in the creek, and ice started to collect back around the corpse. Then the birds took off, one by one, like drops of blood being sucked up into the clouds, up to become a part of the gray, rolling sky of January.

"It don't make no sense, to pray for something like that," Easter said, breaking apart his thoughts. "The Lord don't answer them kind of prayers. But how else can you explain it? I was glad he was dead, though. I won't lie about that, neither. I've grieved over the way I wanted to avenge my sister, but never over him dying. I was glad, and I'll prob'ly have to pay for that one day. You can't get into Heaven with hate in your heart."

Clay picked up the apple again and bit into it. Juice ran down the corners of his mouth. He didn't want to hear any more. He had always wanted to know about his mother's life, about the things she had been, not about her death, but it seemed he could not learn about one without knowing the other.

"Easter, you always told me if I wanted that little piece of land off to the side of the house, that it was mine."

She nodded. "This land was left to me, Gabe, and your mommy, so it's part yours."

"I been thinking that I'd like to come back to Free Creek. I've worked six year in them mines without spending much, and I've got bout enough money saved up to build a little house. I'd rather do that than move a trailer in."

"Lord, Clay, it'd tickle me to death if you'd build on that land. I'd give anything if you'd take it."

"I want to," he said. "That's where I want my children to be raised. Right here on this creek, where I was."

Easter smiled, and Clay could see that she was trying to hide how pleased she was.

"It'll be for the best. A family ought to live together. Seeds won't grow if they tossed to the wind."

Clay slapped the table hard, and it issued a short, high shriek. "I will then," he smiled. "Just a little square house, with big windows so I can see the creek."

"I can picture it," Easter said.

• 16 •

THEIR LOVEMAKING WAS tangled and moist, like summer vines—a wild mess of arms and legs, warm skin against cool, Clay's silver Saint Christopher necklace mingling with Alma's gold chain and small, plain cross. The room was thick with milky gray shadows, and the window was a silver square in the wall.

The sleet was loud and constant, but Alma heard it as if from a great distance. She watched the beads of ice beat against the window, feeling both melancholy and exhilarated. Winter seeped into the house. The room was so cold that the chill ate through to her bones, but her skin was warm with the heat of their lovemaking. Beads of sweat stood on her shoulders. He had thrown the covers into a heap on the floor beside the bed, but their bodies were naked to nothing more than shadows; only the lights of an occasional car moving down the winding road lit their bodies silver and speckled them with the bits of sleet on the window.

She moved her hands down the backs of his arms, which seemed to be the only parts of his body that were cool. Her hands went from the smooth darkness of his back to the chaps in his hands, thin gashes lined with grit. She breathed in that smell of earth, and the aroma of coal, dirt, rock, and roots caused her to shudder from head to toe, her head arched and her teeth firm upon her bottom lip in pleasure. There was no sound except that constant lull of sleet.

He ran his hands down her legs and put his stubbly jaw against her belly. She could feel him inhaling her. Alma listened to every little thing: the small, soft wrinkle of the sheets, the quills of the feathers in the pillow as her head sank deeper and deeper within, the click of a gasp caught halfway in her throat. She caught the scent of ice overtaking the room, and the sweet, damp flavor in the bowl of his neck. Neither of them spoke, and it seemed to her that he wanted to holler out but did not.

Afterward, they lay very close and didn't say a word for a long time. His breath played against the nape of her neck, and she ran her hand up and down his arm, trying to translate everything she felt. She memorized the texture of his arm and kissed his shoulder. She ran her hands over his face, feeling it the way the blind might do to identify someone, and her fingers lingered on his lips, pushing against them as though they were the strings of her fiddle.

She didn't know how to feel. She thought this might lead them somewhere that they need not go. It was too soon, she reasoned. Every doubt ran through her head until she just shook them away and concentrated on the matter at hand. She had wanted to do this, and now she had. She didn't know if it was the right thing to do or not, but she had wanted to do it. And she was glad that she had.

"I've got to have a cigarette," Clay said, in a tone that made it clear he knew this was a cliché. She watched him walk naked out of the room, lit only by the gray, twisting shadows. She pulled the covers up over her face, so that only her eyes were showing, and felt like laughing without knowing why. She had never been made love to before in her life, and she didn't know what would be the acceptable thing to do. She felt like getting up and doing cartwheels through the house, although she knew that he would have thought she was crazy, and besides, her legs were still much too weak for that. Maybe she ought to come right out and tell him that she had never known anything like this. Honesty usually followed making love in the movies, and the movies were about her only source of information on sex. Denzel had certainly never taught her a thing about it.

Alma followed the orange glow of Clay's cigarette as he came back into the room. He got into bed and lay on his back, pulling her to turn over and lie on his chest. He smoked with one hand and twirled her hair around his fingers with the other.

"You want me to put a CD on?" he asked.

"Naw, I'd rather listen to the sleet," she answered. "Sounds like it's dying down."

He didn't answer, and she knew that he was listening to the beating ice. They lay there like that for a long time, not saying anything. After a while, the sleet grew more and more quiet, as if they could hear it making its way to the other side of the world. When another car passed, maneuvering carefully over the slick road, their bodies glowed like fox fire in its headlights.

"You ever seen the ocean?" he asked.

"Are you crazy? My daddy thinks going to a ball game is so worldly it's a sin; he'd fell dead before he'd let any of us go to the beach."

"I ain't neither, but I want to someday. Me and you ought to just take off for two or three days and go," Clay said. "I'd give anything to stand on the beach and just look out across that water. I can't imagine what it'd be like."

"I've had a recurring dream for as long as I can remember," she said in a breathless voice. "I've dreamt of standing by the ocean and just sawing away on my fiddle, with the water sliding up under my feet and the hot air making my strings soft and loose. In my dream, I play so hard and wild that eventually my body raises plumb off the ground to drift way out over that water."

"That's some intense music making," Clay said, laughing softly.

"I swear, I've felt like that before. Not just in my dream. Sometimes, when I get a song just right, it's like I become a part of the music."

"I've seen that on your face."

Before long, the sleet came back, pounding against the house like a flurry of gravel, and they were sung to sleep by its steady rampage. Alma's sleep was plagued by dreams of muddy water. It seemed like one dream that lasted all night, consisting of nothing except her standing on a narrow bridge, looking down into a wide, shallow creek filled with water the color of rich soil. When she woke up, her neck ached, as if she had really stood looking over the side of the bridge. Her skin felt gritty and tight, as if she had actually swum in the filth, and she went into the bathroom, careful not to wake Clay. She stood at the mirror, splashing cold water onto her face and looking at her reflection. She had heard all of her life that dreams of muddy water meant only one thing: death.

DREAMA'S SON WAS born at five o'clock in the morning, screaming with a set of lungs that he had surely inherited from his melodramatic mother.

"Call Darry," she had said when she had dilated far enough and the doctor said it was time. "Tell him to hurry."

Easter dialed the number over and over, and when she rushed back into the birthing room with a pale face and slack shoulders, she had not even had to tell Dreama he wasn't home. Dreama told her to look up Evelyn McIntosh in the phone book, and that was where he would be.

When the woman answered, Easter felt blood rush to her face. Times like these, she wished she didn't go to church; her faith was the only thing that kept her from cussing Evelyn McIntosh all to pieces. "This is Dreama's aunt," she spat out. "I know Darry's there. Tell him his child is being born and to come on if he wants to be here." After she hung up, she wished she'd been more hateful. She wished she had said, "You old whore," or something to that effect. She fumbled in her purse for another quarter and dialed Clay's number.

CLAY, ALMA, AND CAKE were still up partying. Alma and Clay had gone to the Hilltop for the first time since the fight. Clay hadn't gotten drunk, but Cake had not stopped drinking all night long.

Clay stood at the stove, cooking Cake a fried baloney sandwich to sober him up before they went to bed, while Cake sat close to Alma on the couch telling her the long, complicated story of how he had found himself alone in a bedroom with Janine Collins, one of the Hilltop's most notorious women. Alma pealed wildly with laughter and stomped one foot on the floor. He jumped from the couch and imitated Janine's walk, swinging his hips with jutting force and putting each foot so far in front of the other that he nearly fell down.

"Talk about walking like you got a cob up your rump," Cake said. "She does."

Alma lay her head back against the cushion and laughed with her eyes closed. She wasn't completely drunk, but she was feeling good. Cake was still jealous of her, but he was trying to like her, and from the looks of it, she already loved him. He'd had plenty of Jim Beam and pot, and he told the story with the grace and comedy of a talkative drunk. He moved all over the room, showing her how the girl had chased him and finally pinned him to the bed. Cake paused long enough to fill his shot glass with another hit of whiskey and down it in one slug. He breathed out with pleasure and smacked his lips. "Mmm-mmm good, just like Campbell's soup," he said.

"Dammit, don't drink no more, Cake!" Clay hollered, pointing with his fork. "You're already wasted, and I ain't setting up all night with you. I'm done sober."

"Yeah you will, little boy," Cake said in a slurred voice. "You'll take care of baby brother."

The phone rang and Clay threw the fork into the sizzling skillet and turned down the stereo. He yelled for the two of them to stop laughing as he got the phone.

"Clay, Dreama's having the baby," Easter said matter-of-factly. "She's asked for you."

"Be right there," he said, and hung up quickly. He spun around and his eyes fell on Cake and Alma, who were laughing into their hands. Alma beat the couch with one hand and held her stomach with the other. Cake sat with a very straight back and giggled a low, annoying *hunh-hunh-hunh*. "Shit," Clay thought aloud.

"What's wrong?" Cake asked loudly, hopping onto the couch cushion and standing up.

"Dreama's had her baby, and you two are both drunk."

Clay had never seen Cake sober up so fast. When he and Alma and Clay piled into the truck and headed down the wet, shiny highway toward the hospital, Cake tried to keep from crying. He leaned against the door and put thumb and forefinger across the bridge of his nose, holding back his tears. "Aw, man," he kept repeating, not realizing that his words were audible.

"What is it, Cake?" Alma asked. Clay was flying around the curves, his eyes fixed to the blacktop, and paid neither of them any mind. "You sound like you're crying."

"No. I just can't believe Dreama's had a youngun." He wiped his nose on the back of his hand and sucked all of his unfallen tears back deep inside himself. He wasn't about to cry in front of Alma, and he actually didn't know why he felt like it. "She's so little."

"Are you all right?" Alma stretched her arm out on the seat behind Cake and cupped the ball of his shoulder in her hand.

"He's just on a crying drunk," Clay said solidly, but he knew that Cake loved Dreama. He did not take his eyes from the road, and said, "You need to straighten up, brother. Can't go in there drunk."

"I'M GOING TO call him Tristan, after that movie," Dreama announced.

"What movie?" Easter asked, considering the name.

"*Legends of the Fall,* her favorite movie of all time," Clay answered.

"Besides *Gone with the Wind,*" Dreama chimed in. "You know, Easter. I showed you that picture of Brad Pitt. That was his name in that movie."

"Dreama, you know I wanted to call my first boy that," Clay said.

"Tough titty. I beat you to it." She looked from Clay to Gabe, laughing. Gabe stood close to Dreama's bed, his hands shoved deep into his pockets, staring at the baby. Dreama nodded toward Gabe and laughed. "Daddy, you look like you're in shock. Look how much it looks like Daddy, right through its eyes."

Gabe beamed and remained silent. Only Cake looked more uncomfortable, standing there beside Dreama's bed, as if he wanted to lie down right beside her and go to sleep. He hadn't said a word since they had gotten to the hospital.

"Here, hold him, Clay. You the closest thing to a daddy he'll ever have, my pinion," Dreama said, and wrapped the blanket tightly about the baby. She handed the baby to Clay and fixed her own bedcovers around her. She looked down as she spoke, smoothing out the blanket into a neat, straight fold that disappeared on either side under her arms. "If Darry wanted to be part of this baby's life, he'd done been here. Any other woman wouldn'tve even called him, but I wanted to be able to say I done right by him."

"That's all anybody can do," Easter said.

Clay held the baby nervously. Its small body heated up the crook of his arm. He could feel the baby filling up with air, then exhaling it. He could feel life, right there in the palms of his hands. Clay fished the baby's hand out of the blanket and watched as it wrapped its long, narrow fingers about his own. Tristan's grip was tight. Clay couldn't help leaning over and kissing his wrinkled forehead. He had Dreama's high brow and a fine down of black hair.

Clay handed the baby to Gabe, who was standing closest to him. Now they were all looking at Tristan, and only Easter looked at Clay, puzzled by the strange wash of bewilderment on his face. Clay walked quickly out of the room and onto the balcony to smoke a cigarette. Easter found herself ready to go after him, as she always had, but realized that now it was Alma's place to do so. Easter folded her arms and bemoaned the fact that she was losing her boy.

"What is it, Clay?" Alma said from behind him. She had been around men enough to know that they didn't want you to look at them when they had been crying. Men were allowed to weep only in church. She put her hands above his waist, careful not to get too close. "Tell me."

Clay turned quickly so she could not catch sight of his face, and engulfed her with his arms. Her face buried in his chest, she breathed in his good coal smell, feeling his frame quiver. He seemed to have fallen into her arms, and all of his weight was on her.

"Another fatherless child," he said finally. His breath sizzled onto her neck and sent shivers down her back. "It kills me."

"What does?"

"That Darry don't care no more than that bout that baby. My daddy never even knowed I existed. Never even had a chance."

"Darry'll regret it soon enough. People like that can only be happy so long. Eventually, he'll be miserable, and then it'll be too late."

"No. I used to think thataway. People like that just go on, looking out for theirselves. They don't have to pay for their mistakes."

She didn't answer him. He pulled away from her and leaned on the railing. He looked out over the town, where daylight had spread itself out white and flat without their even noticing. Smoke wound out of the buildings below, black against the winter sky. A thin snow dusted the ground, but the air was still.

"God, you must think me and Cake are a couple of crybabies," he said.

"No, it looks to me like you both care about Dreama. That's why I've went so crazy over you, Clay. You care about people. Seems like you care about everything, and I ain't never met nobody like that."

He didn't take his eyes from the town and stayed leaning over the railing, looking at the squat buildings, considering the tarnished sky. Silver breath pumped out of his mouth as he turned to her and said, "Marry me, then."

She folded her arms one atop the other and held her elbows in each hand, hugging herself.

"Is that what you really want? I'm not for certain you're ready to settle down."

"I already have, Alma. I ain't going to stand here and tell you that I'll plumb quit partying and drinking, cause that's right in my blood, and I can't change that, but I'll always be right there with you, and I want you with me, too. I know you love me— I don't doubt that for a minute. I want you with me all the time. That's the best way I know to say it."

"All right, then," she said, and she reached out her hand. He pulled her inside his big arms and held her as close to him as he could, feeling her solid and real against him.

• 17 •

Marguerite sat on her high front porch, thinking about Anneth. Upon her lap lay an open book, and she stared down at its full pages with the intent and concentration of a concerned reader, but the pages might as well have been blank. She had been thinking of Anneth all day, and her memories were all happy ones, so they were that much more troubling. Most people went through their lives trying to forget the dark corners of their past, but Marguerite was cursed to live with those good images that sometimes swam before her eyes. She had had a miserable life and she had built her friendship with Anneth up into the greatest thing that had ever happened to her. Ever since Anneth had died, she had been trying to purge herself of the time she had spent with her.

The first time Anneth had taken her up on the mountain, they had stopped halfway up and lain on huge, flat rocks that jutted out of the mountainside like dinner plates. It was near dusk, but the rocks had sucked in the summer day's heat, and the stone was warm and dry beneath them. Anneth lay flat on her back and held one arm up in the air, studying her hand.

"My granny could read coffee grounds," she said. "When I was thirteen, she read in my grounds that I'd die before I ever seen thirty."

"She told that to a child?" Marguerite asked.

"Why yeah," Anneth answered, as if it was nothing unusual. "She said that every day of my life I'd be happy and sad, both in the same day. That's true. I can't recall a day that I ain't been happy as a lark, then all at once, just felt blue as I could be."

"Seems to me you're happy all of the time," Marguerite replied, looking up at the sky.

Anneth ignored her, caught up in her own thoughts. "Granny said I'd sure die young, but I'd live more than most people ever do. Sometimes I wonder if I've been trying to live up to what she seen in them grounds. Trying to make that come true all my life."

Marguerite didn't know what to say, and it seemed that Anneth didn't expect or need a reply, because they both fell silent and lay upon the heated rocks, letting the wind rush over them. The birds had stopped singing, and finally the wind stopped, too, and Marguerite lay there entranced by the stillness.

Marguerite did not hear the boot heels on the steps or on the old planks of the porch, but when Clay said her name, she slid back out of the past.

She saw only his silhouette, big and straight against the evening sky. "Clay. Lord, I haven't seen you in ages."

"I know it."

"I miss seeing you. Remember when you were little, you practically lived here."

Clay had known Marguerite all of his life, but he had never

known what to expect from her and had certainly never known how to talk to her.

"That's what happens, though, when children grow up. I never see Cake, either. Sometimes I can't believe that he still lives here, because he's never home."

"Where's he at?" Clay asked, nervously.

She either had not heard Clay or didn't want to cut the conversation so short, because she didn't answer. Instead, she closed the book silently and looked up at him. Clay was struck by her beauty. It was true, he thought, what the people said: she really did seem to be growing younger. Instead of looking like a fifty-year-old woman, she could easily have passed for a blooming woman in her early thirties. Her skin was tight and fair, her hair shiny and full of body—the curls about the sides of her face bobbed every time she moved her head. Her lips were perfectly drawn, full and bloodred without lipstick, against her straight, white teeth. Her wrists were small and smooth, as were the tops of her hands, free of veins or wrinkles.

"Do you still have those records I gave you, when you were a teenager?" she asked.

"Lord yeah. I listen to them all the time. I was just listening to that one by Paganini the other night. Easter found a box full of some of Mommy's things, and I was going through it and listening to that record. I found a record album in that box, too."

"What was it?"

"*Harvest,* by Neil Young. It must've been one of her favorites."

"It might have been, but I don't know. She bought so many records that I couldn't keep up with them all. She listened to every kind of music there was. She used to tell me that the only musicians I liked were dead ones." Marguerite opened the book again and smoothed out the page with the flat of her palm, as if the paper gave her skin a sense of satisfaction. She fell silent, and Clay began to wonder if she had started reading again.

"Do you remember her?" she asked, but did not look up.

"Sometimes. I try to remember her voice, but I can't."

"Her laugh was something to hold on to," Marguerite said, and squinted up at him as if sunlight were in her eyes. "In the evenings, you could hear it all up and down this road."

Clay shuffled his feet and looked around the porch.

"She took you for walks every day. Even in the winter. She'd bundle you up and carry you on her hip, up that mountain. She'd point things out to you. Make you run your hands over the bark of trees. She'd sit for a long time, just listening to birdcalls."

"She was here a lot, when I was little? I thought we lived with Glenn, on the other side of Buffalo."

Marguerite laughed quietly. "She left him every other week. She'd come here and stay a night or two, then go right back. She couldn't decide which she loved best—Glenn or Free Creek. And even when they were together and getting along fine, she came up here all the time. She'd leave him playing poker with his brother, or out drinking, and come stay all night with Easter. You was here more than you was over at Glenn's."

"What did you think about Glenn?" Clay asked.

"I despised him," she said, and closed the book. "I can't even talk about how bad I hated him."

"Where'd you say Cake was at?" Clay asked, shoving his hands down into his pockets.

"In the house. Just go on back," she said, looking past him.

Cake was in his room, looking through a pile of CDs. His stereo emitted a faint guitar and mumbling, as Marguerite would not allow him to turn his music up loud enough for her to hear.

"Let's ride up the holler," Clay said.

They jumped on the four-wheeler Clay had borrowed from Gabe and raced down the road, across the old bridge, and up into the head of the holler, toward the old mine. The winter air was like metal against their faces, but neither of them cared. Clay drove, hunched over the steering handles like a racer, pressing his thumb as hard as he could against the accelerator. The lights of the houses faded behind them, and the darkness seemed barely penetrated by the dim headlight on the front of the four-wheeler. The creek widened as they traveled farther up into the holler and was soon so wide that they could hear its roar even over the rough purr of the engine. The mountain was even blacker than the darkness, thick with pines and crooked trees. Clay goosed the gas, sending them speeding over a smooth, round hill that made their stomachs sink.

They came to the steep ridge where Anneth was buried. When the headlight cast its yellow gaze across the gravestones, they shone like the surface of water in sunlight. Clay cut the gas and sat silently. It was more quiet here, as the creek was on the far side of the graveyard, but still the water covered every other sound.

"Been a long time since you come up here," Cake said.

"I'd come more often if I knowed how to act."

"You want to walk up there?"

Clay swung his leg over the seat and jumped off the four-wheeler. He had no flashlight and would have to do with the gleam from the single headlight. He pulled his coat tightly about himself and walked slowly to his mother's grave.

Easter and Gabe had made sure that she got a headstone as soon as it could be chipped and delivered. A single rose had been cut into the stone, and below the rose, it read:

ANNETH SIZEMORE
Born 1940 Died 1974
Beloved Mother and Sister

A birth certificate had so many more words, he thought. The rose was all wrong, too. Even though Easter and Gabe had had nothing but the best intentions, if he had been big enough to make such decisions, he would have called for a bouquet of wildflowers to be carved into the gravestone: tiger lilies, daisies, jack-in-the-pulpits, Queen Anne's lace.

He crouched down and put his finger inside the lines of the rose. He touched the letters of her name, the years she had lived. The stone was so cold, so icy, that he feared it might blister his fingers. It felt just the way her skin had felt when she lay in the cedar casket. He could call up that image any time he wanted to: a lavender church dress, a wide purple belt with a plastic buckle, long eyelashes. Her hands had looked so alive that it had looked like blood was flowing right through the round veins. She had never seemed so still before. Even her sleep had been plagued by motion. He had wanted to breathe her scent in, but the smell of cedar had overtaken everything.

"You all right?" Cake asked, and put his hand on Clay's arm.

"Easter must have just cleaned her grave off," Clay said. The headstone was free of branches and leaves, and yellow mums had recently been planted on the grave.

"She walks up here once a week to see to it," Cake said. "I see her heading up the holler ever Friday. Mommy brought them mums, though. She made me go to town and buy them the other day. Said the more it frosted, the prettier they got."

"It was wrong of me, to never come tend to her grave," Clay said, and stood.

"What are you doing up here tonight? Where's Alma?" Cake asked.

"Staying all night up her people's house."

"I didn't think they was speaking."

"That's why she went up there, I reckon," Clay said. "I guess she was tired of being cold with em. I ain't stayed with Easter in a while, so I'm going to stay there tonight. You ought to come up and set around with us."

"Might do it. UK plays tonight, at ten."

"Well, we'll watch it," Clay told him. He shoved his hands deep down into his pockets and kicked a square of coal across the dirt. "Can't smoke in Easter's house, though. That's the only thing."

"We'll sneak outside, like we used to." Cake fished around in the inside pocket of his denim jacket and pulled out a half-pint of Jim Beam. "Lookee here."

"That'll warm us up," Clay said, and watched Cake throw down a long shot. "Better not drink much, though, if we going back to Easter's."

"Like a half-pint would get both of us drunk," Cake laughed, and handed the bottle over to Clay.

The bourbon was strong and hot. Clay felt like it was flowing into every part of his body. "Cake, I didn't get you to ride up here with me to see Mommy's grave. They's something I wanted to tell you."

Cake took a drink from the bottle.

"I asked Alma to marry me. We're getting married, soon as it gets warm weather."

"Well, I'm glad," Cake said, and Clay knew he was lying.

"You don't sound glad. I've knowed you my whole life, and I know when you're glad."

"It's just that so much will change. Everthing will change."

"That's what life's all about, buddy. Change. This is a change I want."

"I sure hope so," Cake said. "I hope you want it, cause that's what you gonna get. No doubt about it."

"Well, I've thought long and hard about it, and it's what I want. I need to start my life." Clay got back on the four-wheeler and spoke with his back to Cake. "Don't you ever get sick of working all week long, then getting stoned and drunk on the weekends? That ain't no kind of life."

"Well, you tell me what else I got to do. That's all I got. What else is they in this life for a man to do, if he don't go to church?"

Clay started the four-wheeler up and let it idle softly. "I guess you know I want you to be my best man."

"I can do that, I reckon," Cake answered.

"I wish you'd be happy for me, though. I know that ain't something I can ask you to do, but I wish you would be."

"It's just that I'll miss you. It won't be the same. Never again."

Clay took the last drink out of the bottle and handed it back to Cake. Cake started to throw it against the cliffs on the other side of the road, but instead he shoved it into his inner pocket and wrapped his arms around Clay's waist again. Clay tore out of the dirt patch and headed back over the hill, racing toward the houses. They flew down the holler, as if they were floating on the darkness. Clay's eyes watered in the cold air as he raced down the road, but Cake lay his face against Clay's back.

• 18 •

THE MORNING HE WAS to be married, Clay went for a walk up into the mountain. The air was thick with the new smells of spring, and the woods were so filled with sighs and whispers that Clay thought to himself that this must have been the way it sounded before people ever came to these hills. He stopped for a moment, listening to the birds singing above him, the ones that called from far across the holler. The wind spread itself through leaves the color of green water.

Many days before, he had noticed the hills growing red with buds, but only now did he realize that winter was over. It seemed to Clay that seasons crept up slowly, hardly changing their progress from day to day, and then one morning they were suddenly and finally here. Spring had come overnight, sneaking in, the blooms working throughout the darkness to be ready when sunlight hit the mountainsides. He considered the sounds of the mountain, listened for something more, and felt the desire to go on, as if someone were pushing him from behind. The first trees to show their new colors—sarvis, redbud, and dogwood—were in bloom, and their petals pushed at his face as he made his way up the old trail.

He stopped to study one of the dogwood flowers, tracing his finger over the crimson stains on each petal. Jesus' blood, that's what he had heard all of his life. The flower was shaped like the cross, with a bushy middle that people said looked like the crown of thorns, the stains on each petal the blood of Christ. He touched the stains and felt wetness on his fingertips, sweet dew from the early morning.

He remembered that his mother's letter had said she'd often taken him to a field of wildflowers atop this mountain. He had traveled this mountain every day of his life while he was growing up, but he had never known of such a place. He was sure that he had been over every square inch of this land and began to wonder if the field was a figment of his mother's imagination. She'd written: "I came to the clearing on the mountain's top, where the yellow and purple flowers bend their heads. This is your favorite place, Clay. I pack you there on my hip all the time and lean over so you can put your face to the flowers."

Maybe only a child could find it, he reasoned. Maybe he had been the one that had led his mother there. Perhaps he had not been meant to go back there yet; maybe it was too soon. But he wanted to find it—maybe that was where her spirit stayed now. When he was a child, he had often imagined that the morning mist was his mother's ghost, easing down the mountain to seep out over the valley and watch him. When he got older, he was dismayed by how the white fog always burned away by midmorning. A field of wildflowers would be a better place to think of her living.

Sarvis and dogwood sliding over his face, he found himself

climbing the mountain quickly, crushing the bluebells accidentally beneath his feet, as he did every spring when they popped up in the middle of the path. He saw scraps of sky above him and was vaguely aware of the call of sparrows and the thud of a woodpecker somewhere across the ridge. When he reached the summit, he walked from one end to the other, searching for a sacred field that might have existed all of these years without his knowing. He went off the path, making his way through tangled groves of mountain laurel and into brier thickets that pulled blood out of his hands with quick bites. He climbed over felled, moss-covered trees as big as ancient columns and over rocks that were still cold from the long winter. He walked down into a deep cove where springs bubbled out of the mountainside and ferns grew thick and low beneath the pines.

At each turn he was sure that he saw a clearing where sunlight fell in a wide block on the ground, where the trees stepped back to make way for a field full of Cherokee roses, Queen Anne's lace, jonquils, jack-in-the pulpits, black-eyed Susans, purple daisies. He wondered if it was a place all of his ancestors had gone to, and if it was where his grandmother had picked out the names for her children. Anneth and Easter had both been named for wildflowers: Queen Anne's lace and Easter lilies. He imagined that every person in his family had journeyed to that tightly stretched field, so high atop the mountain that only flowers could grow there.

But there was nothing. He had known this mountain all of his life, and there was no such field. There was no bald spot on its summit, only jagged spears of rocks that stood in the ground like gravestones, surrounded by thousands of trees that moved as if they were underwater.

He lay down on a flat rock and peered up at the sky. He felt sunlight upon his face, and he could feel it all through his body, beginning at his head and spreading down his chest and arms, into his legs and feet. He felt as the rocks and cliffs must feel, after a long, gray season of soaking up nothing but chill, when they suddenly find the sun. He felt like pulling off all of his clothes and lying there, but he was too relaxed to move. The field of flowers *had* to be close by—what else could have given him this sense of intoxication, if not the soup of a whole field of wildflowers?

He wanted more than anything to drift off into sleep and awake with a blue-black night sky filled with stars above him. Below, they would be looking for him, and it would be good to wake up and hear them hollering his name, down there. For once everybody else would be looking for something, and he would be content. He wanted to stay right here, up above reality, where no one could touch him, no one except God.

CLAY REALIZED THAT he had to go back down to be married. When he came off the mountain, he found that it was still morning, although he felt as if he had been on the mountain for hours.

Although Pastor Morgan did not believe in marrying someone who had been wed before, he agreed to marry Clay to Alma because he had known the boy all of his life. He stood on the porch with Easter's husband, El, who had taken his first day off in years to attend the wedding. When the pastor saw Clay, he smiled the way he did when he shook hands with everyone after church, and he folded the boy up in his long arms.

"Still climbing that old mountain, Clay?" the pastor asked.

"Yeah. I guess I always will."

"I haven't been up there in years."

Clay breathed deeply and laughed. "I'm nervous."

"Well, a big breakfast'll cure that," El said, putting his arm about Clay's shoulders. "Easter and Lolie been cooking all morning."

Inside, the table was crowded with bowls and platters bearing biscuits, fried apples, potatoes, tenderloin in a pool of redeye gravy, fried baloney, and eggs. Lolie was scraping brown gravy out of a skillet into a bowl while Easter poured coffee and directed everyone to their seats. This was the first time that Clay could ever remember the two of them cooking together. Uncle Paul sat at the table beside Aunt Sophie, who looked mad because Easter wanted her to rest and wouldn't let her help with the cooking.

El and Pastor Morgan sat down while Clay went into the bedroom to make sure that Cake and Jimmy Darrell, Alma's brother, were up. Everyone had stayed at either Easter's or Gabe's the night before, and it was good for them all to be together here like this on the morning of the wedding. Evangeline refused to stay all night at anyone's house, no matter the event, but would arrive later to sing. She had decided to head out for Nashville, along with her band, in hopes of finding a recording contract. She had put off their journey just so she could be at the wedding and would leave for Music City as soon as the vows had been spoken.

Dreama had insisted that Alma spend the night with her at Gabe's, the two of them sleeping in the same bed like sisters. Clay and Cake had slept together at Easter's, on a pallet on the floor beside the bed where Jimmy Darrell lay snoring like an old woman and hollering out in his sleep.

Gabe had made his way across the yard, and Clay was glad to see him. He hardly ever took meals with the whole family, and it was especially strange to see him seated at the table next to Pastor, although they talked like old friends. They had grown up together, and Pastor was one of the few men Gabe respected. All of the men were at the table, while Easter and Lolie fluttered about them like birds around corn in the hottest part of the day.

"You all go on and eat now, then we'll set down and eat," Easter said. Clay couldn't remember ever sitting down to eat at the same time as Easter during a big meal, not even at holidays. The women always ate last, when the men had finished and made room for them at the table.

"No, I want us all to eat together," Clay said. "They's enough chairs. Call Dreama and Alma, and we'll all eat together."

"Why, it'll be cold by the time them gals get over here," Lolie said. "You all go ahead and eat. The women will eat later."

"Call and tell them to hurry. I want us to eat together, now. That's what I want for my wedding day."

Dreama and Alma came in laughing, and when Alma looked up, her eyes did not meet Clay's at once. Her face looked so clean and clear that it seemed to Clay she had found some blessed water to wash with. A noticeable silence fell across the room as everyone looked at her; then, just as quickly, Easter ordered them to sit.

"Lord, bless this food we are about to receive, and thank you for providing us with it," Pastor said, without announcing that he was about to say the blessing. "And Lord, bless this day when these two young people commit their lives to each other, and help them to overcome the obstacles a couple face in life. Help them to receive your love and accept them into your life. We all know that you are the only way and the light, forever. Amen."

"Amen," echoed Easter and Uncle Paul. Then a great hum arose from the table as they all started passing bowls and plates and eating as though they were starved to death.

They did not have a big conversation while they ate. They ate quickly and only spoke to comment on the food or ask a quick question that would get a quick reply. They said things like,

"Lolie, this gravy's so good I have to pat my foot to eat it," or "That jelly you eating, I picked them blackberries myself." But when they finished, they pushed their chairs back a little from the table and talked for a long time, nursing coffee and mixing molasses and butter together in their plate to smooth over the extra biscuits.

Clay felt like he should jump right up and start getting ready for the wedding, but he didn't want to leave the table right away. He pushed back his plate and asked Uncle Paul to tell them all about the way he and Sophie had first come together. Clay had heard the story many times, but he never tired of it.

Uncle Paul loved to tell stories, but no one would ever have guessed by the way he went about starting. At first his tone was low and soft, with long pauses between sentences.

"Well, way back, I was the worst drunk ever was. I'm not ashamed to say it, cause the truth's the truth. I worked for a long time at a lumber camp in Laurel County, over on Blackwater, and one night me and some boys drove over to Manchester to play poker. We'd been drunk on moonshine two days. Now, a drunk don't need to get in a card game, but that's what I done, and I lost everthing I had. Even bet away my little truck that we'd drove over there in. By the time the game folded up, I was drunker than a monkey's uncle, and my buddies had run off and left me. The man that won everthing was a good feller, and I reckon he felt sorry for me. He talked me into letting him give me a ride in my own truck, and he took me to the train station to send me back home. Put me right on a car and paid my way, but when he asked me where I was living and I said 'Blackwater,' he must've thought I said 'Black Banks,' cause that's where he sent me. When I got off the train there, I was still so drunk I barely could walk.

"Now Sophie worked in the theater there at town, and when

she got off work she always went to that little restaurant to get her a piece of pie and a pop. It was right there at the train depot, and when she was leaving, she seen me laying out on one of the benches outside. I was so drunk I don't remember none of this, but it's got told back to me, you see. She found me and seen I was drunk and didn't have a dime, so she pulled me up off that bench and took me over to her sister's car. Her sister always come and picked her up from work. She took me to her sister's house, where she was living at the time. I don't know how that little girl ever walked me in there, cause I know I was dead weight against her.

"Anyway, she brung me in, flopped me on the bed. She tole her sister's man that I was an old drunk and didn't have nowhere to go and that it was untelling what would happen to me if she'd just left me there. So Sophie and her sister went to doctoring me up. Put me in a cold bathtub and put some of her sister's man's clothes on me, cause I was so drunk I'd ruined my clothes and everthing else. That cold water sure enough sobered me up, cause I can more or less remember everthing after that. I remember thinking these was the strongest two little women ever was, cause they lifted me up and throwed me on the bed like I was a rag doll. Sophie set up with me all night. I was in real bad shape, I reckon.

"All the next day, Sophie fed me tater soup. Put so much pepper in it that it cleaned me out good and proper, felt like I was breathing fire. She'd set right on the edge of the bed and feed me until I was able to myself, and I recall the first time she put that mush to my mouth, I was so hungry that I bout swallowed spoon and all. She'd wipe my chin and sing songs. She'd sing that song that says 'I sing because I'm happy' and 'The Great Speckled Bird.' I'd hear her in the kitchen singing, too, and then I'd know she was in there fixing me something to eat."

Everybody laughed quietly, but he didn't look up.

"Well, eventually I got feeling better and got up out the bed. I told her I had to repay her somehow, but she wouldn't let me. She said her sister would drive me back home, plumb back over on Blackwater, but I wouldn't let her and told her I'd rather walk back to Black Banks and find me a ride somehow. They knowed better than to argue with that, cause they knowed it would insult me, you see, and they both stood at the door and told me good-bye. Soon as they closed the door I went to chopping firewood and piling up their coal for em. I couldn't stand the thoughts of being beholden to somebody. After a while, I lit out and got back to Laurel County, and didn't touch nothing to drink. I'd work in that lumber camp and think about Sophie singing 'I sing because I'm happy.' That's all that was on my mind. When I got me a little money saved up, I went back to that little house and we started courting."

Uncle Paul stopped for a long moment, looking at the table. His big hands were still in his lap.

"She'd sung to me, you see. She'd fed me when I was hungry, and I didn't have no choice but to come back for her."

THEY WERE MARRIED in Easter's side yard, just across the grass from the skeleton of the house that Clay was building for them. The lumber looked damp and bright yellow in the fine spring day. Folding chairs had been borrowed from the funeral home and set up in neat squares; bunches of dogwood and sarvis were tied with wide ribbon to the aisle chairs. Dreama and Alma had cut the flowers early that morning from the trees along the creek.

Before the wedding, Alma had sent Evangeline and Dreama out onto the porch every few minutes to look for her parents' Cadillac making its way up the holler; she had called them a week ago and asked her father to come and give her away. Her father did not come, but when Dreama spotted an unknown Blazer heading up the road, she was sure that it had to be some of Alma's people. Alma ran out into the yard, her train flying behind her like the wide tail of a kite, and fell into her mother's arms when she stepped down out of the truck. Her oldest brother, Elihu, got out of the driver's side.

"These two are enough," Alma told Clay. "If Daddy don't want to be here, I ain't letting it bother me."

Elihu walked up the aisle with her and said, "Her mother and I," when the preacher asked who gave Alma in marriage. Evangeline and Dreama were matrons of honor and Jimmy Darrell served second to Cake as best man.

Clay had invited only the members of the immediate family—Geneva and Goody, a few more cousins, Gabe and Lolie, Easter and El, Uncle Paul and Aunt Sophie—and, to everyone's shock, Marguerite, who had walked down the holler and quietly found a seat in the back row, by herself. She sat with her back very straight, her head held high. She had dressed well for the occasion and looked like a woman who went out all the time. Tears fell from her eyes, but she wept silently, wiping them away so quickly that no one even saw her put a tissue to her face.

Alma marched in to Alison Krauss singing "Baby, Now That I've Found You" from Dreama's portable stereo, which was perched on a small wooden table and hidden by dogwood flowers. Since the wedding was held outside, the traditional unity candle could not be lit, so when they came to that part of the ceremony, Evangeline stepped out and sang "Let It Be Me" while her guitarist, Lige, strummed softly behind her.

When Pastor pronounced them man and wife, Clay bent Alma back dramatically and kissed her for a long time, one of the first times that Clay Sizemore did not have a thousand thoughts rushing through his mind. He heard nothing, saw nothing, but felt her lips, smelled her good, clean scent.

He felt that his mother was watching from the shadow of the giant cedar across the creek.

• 19 •

ALMA WALKED THROUGH the shell of their house, running her hands over lumber that felt ripe with juice. She breathed in the scent and thought that standing in a half-built house must be the closest thing to being inside a tree, smelling it. The scent was so strong that she could even taste it.

It was getting dark and the sound of Clay's hammer was loud in the dusk.

The house was completely framed now and the roof had just been finished, so she was picturing what it would look like when it was done. She made a list of furniture she would have to buy and where certain pictures would hang and the way it would feel to stand at her sink and look out the little window over it, where she could see the backyard. She stood in that spot and imagined her hands in soapy water, the smell of a just-eaten supper lingering in the kitchen air.

Suddenly Clay's hands were upon her. He held her from

behind and kissed the back of her head. "Won't be much longer," he said.

She turned around and put her face in the warmth of his neck. He was sweaty and bare chested.

"We'll put the windows in tomorrow," he said. He had enlisted everyone he knew to help with the house. Clay didn't know a thing about carpentry, but he was learning as he went.

For a long moment they stood there at the place where their sink would be, and she was very aware of his breathing. Night closed in quickly, and before long there was no light except the bare bulb of the droplight in its cage. Clay had run an extension cord over from Easter's house, and the bulb burned in what would become the living room, where he had been hammering on the windowsills to get them square.

She put her lips to his arms, but instead of kissing them, she just let her lips linger on his skin. When she opened her eyes again, she saw that lightning bugs had floated in. They hung in the air, glowing brightly, then darkening. There were more than a dozen, and they were all so close that she could reach out and touch them.

"Look," she said quietly, as if the bugs might be scared away. "Lightning bugs always make me think of when I was little."

He pulled away from her and caught one of the bugs in his hand. He held his palm up to her face, and the lightning bug glowed, casting a greenish yellow hue on her cheeks. The bug steadied itself, then spread its wings and took to the air.

"I remember when I was real little, my mother woke me up in the middle of the night to look at the lightning bugs," he said.

"I thought they only came out at dusk," she said.

"That's why she got me up. It must've been three in the morning. She had been sitting up all night, drinking right by herself. I could smell the whiskey on her breath."

"How old was you?"

"I couldn't have been more than three. People don't believe that I can remember that far back, but I can. She got killed when I was four, but every once in a while a little memory comes to me out of nowhere. I remember that night just like it was yesterday. Everything about it. The way the creek sounded, the little slice of moon hanging on the sky. Them lightning bugs, so many that it didn't seem possible."

Alma took a step forward and put her hands on his face without knowing what she intended to do. She put a thumb against his lips, but he kept talking.

"I never seen so many in my life. Just floating everywhere, so thick it didn't seem real. And you could smell them. You know how a lightning bug has a real distinct smell? That covered our clothes. She carried me and every few seconds she would say, 'Look,' just the way you did a minute ago. And before she carried me back in the house, she said, 'Remember this, Clay.' And finally I did."

Alma kissed him. Free Creek was quiet and hot tonight. No one was stirring outside.

WHEN THE HOUSE was finished, they did not have a dance to usher joy over the threshold, as people did in the old days, but moved in before the electric company had turned on the power. They spent their first night there in the blue black of springtime darkness on a mattress in the middle of the living room floor. They raised all of the windows and listened to these sounds: a chorus of crickets and katydids, a damp April breeze stirring in the burning bushes that Clay had planted on either side of their front steps, the chirp of the chimes Alma had hung from the porch eaves, and the rush of the creek.

After they broke the house in properly, they lay back on the mattress with the breeze coming in sweet and cool against their sweaty bodies. They fell asleep tangled about each other and awoke when the uncovered windows welcomed in the sunlight coming over the mountain.

Clay pulled on his Levi's and went outside. Alma didn't get up. She turned Clay's pillow over to the cool side and put it between her knees.

He stepped off the porch and out into the yard, where the grass was wet but already warming with the new day. He looked up and down the holler but saw no one. The only sign of life was a blue stream of smoke from the big house at the mouth of the holler, where Aunt Sophie was standing on her own porch savoring her forbidden cigarette.

He sat down on the grass and looked at his own house. He had spent his whole life listening to stories from the past, and now he had his own, and it was slowly building, chapter by chapter. It was just like a book that he could pick up and hold in his hands. He could feel its weight, could put his face against cool pages and breathe in the scent of words. That's the way it felt, looking at his home the first morning after it had been lived in.

"Feels good, don't it?" Easter said, walking into the yard. She carried two cups of coffee and offered one to him.

"You must have read my mind," Clay said. The coffee was strong and black, so hot that he could feel it sliding all the way down his throat.

Easter sat right down on the grass beside him. She made a lot of noise getting settled—popping bones and a barely audible grunt—but finally they sat there and looked at the house, drinking their coffee.

"I remember when they built my house. I was real little—probably bout eight year old—but I remember it plain as day,"

Easter said, leaning back on one hand. "Soon as they got the door hung, they cooked the awfullest big meal you ever seen and all the men set in to drinking. I never will forget how happy my granny was to have a solid house. We was always poor, and I still don't know how they managed to raise such a good house. But that house meant the world to Granny. She turned to me and said, 'When I'm dead, this'll be your and Anneth's. This is where you meant to be.' "

"I stayed homesick the whole time I was gone from it."

"That's the way we all are. I never knowed of none of our people that could stay away from here long. I swear, I half believe that's why Anneth had such a hard time staying married. None of her men would live up in here, and she couldn't stand living off. Even if it was just a few miles off, she couldn't tolerate it. Bout ever six months, I'd be in the kitchen and turn around to see her standing in the door with a suitcase in her hand."

Clay laughed. "Marguerite said the same thing."

"It's a good thing, being able to find your place in the world," Easter said.

Clay drained his coffee and lay back on the grass. He laced his fingers together and put them behind his head. "I never will leave here," Clay said.

"I sure hope you don't," Easter said. She looked into the bottom of her cup and dashed the cluster of grounds out onto the yard. "I dreamt last night of you leaving, though. In my dream, I thought you had two horses standing by your porch. I was at my bedroom window, watching you pack everthing out of the house and pile it up on the yard. Alma would come out and tie stuff up on one of the horses' backs."

Clay didn't say a word. Easter was not one to share her dreams.

"After she had everthing on there that horse could carry, you and her climbed up on the other horse and took off. Never used the road, though. You splashed right through the creek and took off up that mountain. That horse never faltered, went up them steep cliffs like it wasn't nothing. Up, up. The trees parted for you."

"Was that all of it?"

"That's all I can remember," she said. "I woke up sick from it, though. I'm going to tell you just like my granny did—this is where you meant to be. Remember that."

THAT WHOLE SUMMER was marked by thunderstorms and heavy rains that lasted no more than twenty minutes but left the world a changed place; the earth steamed and hissed, leaving the air to smell like cooked greens. When the storms were not pounding down on the mountains, the sun was, so that the water dried up as soon as the showers ceased.

Sometimes Clay would go out onto the porch and watch the pelting rain, which fell so fast and straight that it seemed to be coming up out of the ground. When lightning turned the holler silver, he always jumped with a start, and he savored that good spook-house sensation of his nerves curling up all at once for a brief half-second. He watched the tops of the trees bending in the short gusts of wind, lime-colored leaves being beat off limbs. The thunder echoed down the little valleys like cannon fire. He had always assumed that thunder was the mighty voice of God, and he could not help the chill bumps that ran up the backs of his arms with every shaking of the earth.

When the lightning flashed, he imagined he could see all of the dead people he had ever known of, standing in line down the road. They stood about six feet apart in different poses: his mother bent over with her hands on her knees, like the picture of her on the railroad tracks; his father, faceless and standing very erect, as if at attention before a ruthless general; his great-grandmother, whom he had only heard tales of, standing with her arms hanging limply at her sides; his mother's murderer, Glenn, stooped and broken with the weight of a dozen redbirds perched on his shoulders and atop his head. The white light ran down the holler and he could see them plain as day, always looking at him. When he was young, the past had haunted him here on this creek. Now, he was comforted by it. Maybe he was conjuring these ghosts up himself, but more than once he had felt they really were there, and had felt like calling for Alma to come out and look at them.

He took off his shirt and stood on the top porch step so the rain could beat against his chest. He felt as if the stinging rain beat messages into his skin.

Alma came to stand in the open door and chided him over the booming thunder. "You better get in this house fore you get struck by lightning."

When he didn't reply, she stepped out onto the porch and stood behind him, one side of her cool face to his hot back, her arms encircling his waist, with a few of her fingers curled around his belt loops. She didn't say another word, and considered the storm with him. The warm mists of rain blew under the porch eaves and wet Clay's belly.

Clay knew how erotic the storms were to Alma. The whole summer, she had grown so aroused by the thunderstorms that they ended up landing on the floor or the couch or the bed. She had always been scared of storms but could not help the jolts that raced up and down her thighs when the rains came.

He turned around and wrapped her up inside his arms, kissing her. He walked her backward into the house and fell on top of her on the couch.

"Wait." She laughed, crawling out from under him. "I got beans on the stove."

She went into the kitchen, and he followed her. She stirred the pinto beans and opened the oven to check on the corn bread.

As soon as the oven door shut, he turned her around and they sank to the kitchen floor. Her summer clothes slid off easily. He loved how quickly he could peel off the thin cotton dress, simply unfastening the top and letting it fall away, like the skin of an onion. He put his mouth on her neck, which was salty with sweat.

"Clay, I'm afraid lightning will come in this kitchen," she said, her chin arched back. "It'll strike the stove and kill us both."

He imagined them charred and black on the linoleum. Someone would come in and find them, sculpted out of ash. He could feel pleasure and fear pulsating down her body and knew that they had become one feeling intertwined. He kept kissing her, kept moving, and finally she relaxed against the floor.

Lightning crashed and thunder shook the house. Rain beat against the windows in sheets, as though someone were dashing buckets of water onto the glass. They rolled all over the floor, the legs of kitchen chairs all around them. Clay finally smelled the burning corn bread as he fell into an exhausted heap. Alma caught its scent and jumped up.

He laughed at her as she ran around the kitchen, naked. She found a dry rag and pulled the skillet out of the stove. She let it fall into the sink and crawled back down on the floor.

"Now I have to make some more bread," she said, laying her head on his chest. His sweaty back was stuck to the linoleum.

"I believe that was worth having to stir up more bread," he said. "I'll do it."

After supper, they sat out on the porch and watched the cool of the day settle down over the mountains. The sun had set, but night hadn't moved in yet, and it wouldn't for a while. It was one of those summer evenings when time stretched out long and peaceful, as if all the clocks had been slowed. The evening light was purple and still. The only things that moved were hidden along the creek—crickets and katydids preparing to make their night sounds.

Alma finished the supper dishes and swept the kitchen. She carried her broom on out to the porch, where Clay was still sitting. He watched her as she swept, and the sound of broom straw against the porch floor reminded him of childhood. Easter was always scooting dirt out of the house with wide strides of her broom.

Alma put the broom on its hook by the door. A little breeze lifted her hair and caused the leaves to sound.

"A big salad would be good after while, wouldn't it?" she asked.

"Surely to God you ain't hungry after that big meal," Clay said.

"Naw, but I will be after while. I love a cold salad on a summer night." She stepped down into the yard, letting her hand trail on the railing. "You stay here and rest."

Clay got up and followed her around the house. Their garden stretched long and narrow, snug against the rough mountain, extending from their backyard into Easter's. The plants were full and dark green. The corn had not come in well yet, but the tomatoes hung ripe on the vine, and the green onions were already growing so tall they needed to be pulled.

Alma went to the little wooden square at the edge of the garden and began to snap off the last of the leaf lettuce. She worked carefully and her face reminded Clay of the way his uncle Paul looked when he was quilting. She was concentrating as if each lettuce leaf had to be broken just right. He pulled off two tomatoes and mashed the imprint of his thumb into the side of one. It was soft and still hot from the day's sun. He jerked up a half-dozen onions and clicked off three long, warm cucumbers.

"I wish the carrots was ready," she said.

"Them won't be in till the last of summer."

"I know that," she said, and sat down on the dirt to gently work the radishes out. "I was brought up tending garden, buddy."

Clay squatted down beside her and watched as she broke off the stems and shook dirt from the radishes. He could smell her and the soil and the juice in the tomatoes.

"I forgot to tell you—Evangeline called me today while you was at work. From Nashville. They still ain't got in to see nobody important, but she said they was making contacts. She's giving herself one more year, and if the band ain't got a contract, she said she was coming home."

"I didn't figure she'd give up that quick," Clay said. "You don't get a record contract overnight."

"Well, she ain't one to give up, but she's impatient. She claims she's off coke, too. Said it was hard to get when you didn't know who to get it from."

"I'd say it ain't too hard to get down there," Clay said. "But I'd say they are running low on money to get it with."

Alma lay the radishes atop the mess of lettuce she had on her lap and put her hands behind her to lean on, letting him know she wanted to stay right here. He put the onions with his tomatoes and cucumbers and sat down on the dirt.

"Clay, they's something I've got to tell you," she said. He could tell by her tone that she had been swirling her words around in her mouth to get them just right. "I seen Denzel today, when I went to the grocery store."

"He didn't say nothing, did he?" Clay could feel blood collecting in his face. "He better not be fooling with you."

"He never said a word." She looked at the mountain and then back to him. "But he looked at me like he was dying to spit. I ain't never seen such a look of hate on somebody's face."

"You've just hurt his pride, marrying so quick. To hell with him," Clay said.

"I'm just so afraid that he'll try to cause us trouble. I can't believe he'd let me have this."

"He don't have no control over you no more, Alma. There's nothing he can do."

"I lived miserable for so long that it's hard for me to accept the life we have."

Clay knew exactly what she meant. He had spent his whole life mistrusting anything good that came along. Until he had met Alma.

"He can't touch you now," Clay said, and picked up the vegetables. He stood and reached out his hand to help her up. "Come on, let's go in."

20

ALMA WAS IN the backyard, pacing back and forth like a lunatic, trying to scratch a new song out of her head. She held the fiddle lightly in her hands even though her anxiety had grown so fierce that she felt like throwing the fine instrument to the ground and stomping on it. She had woken up with the song swirling around in her mind and couldn't make it sizzle down her arm and out onto the stiff strings of her fiddle. She sawed away, closed her eyes, and walked all over the yard, aware of nothing but the fiddle. She hummed the song to herself, but she couldn't get it right. The bow screeched across the strings.

The October evening was beginning to get cool, but a line of sweat stood on her brow. She straightened her back and tried again. She stroked the taut strings like a woman touching her child's hair. She would stay out here until tomorrow morning if she had to, until blood ran down her arms and dripped from her elbows. She reckoned if she didn't get it out of her system, she would blow up.

When she caught the tune in her mouth and let it buzz on her lips, its melancholy melody reminded her of a life story being told. A history. She got the chorus down and played it over and over, making it perfect, like a man running a lathe over a thick piece of rosewood.

The chorus sounded like a throaty lullaby, and within its notes she caught the name of the song. She played the chorus through again and sang to herself: "And that is the history of us."

"She finally got it," Cake said.

Cake, Clay, Dreama, and Easter were in the front yard, breaking up late beans. Their chairs sat in a circle, and they had all been bent over their laps, popping the beans out of rhythm, listening to Alma.

"She's far from having the whole thing, though," Clay said. "She's liable to be up all night."

"Well, if that's the case, I hope to God she goes in the house," Dreama said. The baby, Tristan, sat at her feet on a small, square quilt, playing with jar lids and rings. "I never would go to sleep with her sawing on that thing all night."

"I could," Clay said. They all looked up at him. "That would sing me right to sleep."

"You've got it bad, son," Cake said, laughing. "I never seen a man so crazy over a woman."

"That's how a man ought to be over his woman," Easter said.

"Clay, let's see who can break em the fastest," Cake said, nodding down to the pile of beans spread across a newspaper on his lap.

"No sir," Easter said firmly. "I want them strung right. You all get in a race and they'll be so haggled up, nobody won't be able to eat em. You might as well not be in no hurry—we've got to put em up yet."

"You canning these?" Cake asked. "I figured we was going to eat them tonight."

"I'll cook us a mess tomorrow," Easter answered. "But to-night, me and Dreama needs to can most of these. They have to be put up tonight. They'll keep longer if they're put up in the old of the moon."

"I never knowed of beans to still be on the vine in October," Cake said.

"It don't happen often," Easter said. "But it's been such a warm fall. I'm thankful for it."

The voice of the fiddle and the loud pops of the green beans began to form a kind of music. The song rose and fell, the strings seeming to emit the troubled moans of a woman. Clay listened and pictured a woman walking the mountains, dying of grief.

"Lord God, that's the saddest old song I ever heard," Dreama said.

"It's a lament," Easter said. "A song of grief."

Dreama leaned down and buttoned up Tristan's sweater. "What do you think will become of all of us, Easter?" she asked.

"Lord, I can't see the future of people I love," Easter said, never looking up from the beans strewed across her lap. "I can't see the future, period."

"Everbody knows you see things, Easter," Dreama said. "I don't know why you deny it."

"I wish I was like that," Cake said. He had stopped breaking beans and sat there with his hands in his lap, looking at Easter with a broad smile etched across his face. "I'd give anything to be able to do that."

"No, you wouldn't." Easter's voice was hard, but she still

didn't look up from her work. The beans tumbled across her fingers, a blur in her able hands. She broke them perfectly, each one snapping out four singular pops. The pieces fell into the dishpan like green knuckles.

"Let's hurry and get this last mess broke so me and Dreama can start the canning," Easter said. "It's starting to get too cool for the baby to be out here, anyway."

"I'll set up with you all," Cake said. Cake had been staying at Easter's a lot. Dreama had started going to church with Easter and had recently been baptized. When she moved in with Easter to get away from Gabe's parties and crowds, Cake started showing up on Easter's porch in the evening.

"Good, you can occupy Tristan while we put up the beans," Dreama said.

"I ain't got nothing else to do," Cake said.

Clay tapped his foot along to the beat of Alma's fiddle, whose soprano had intensified into a fast breakdown. He finished the beans that lay in his lap, put the strings and ends aside, and got up to clog around the yard, squalling out.

"That's the kind of music I like," Dreama said loudly. She threw her newspaper on the ground and got up to dance with Clay.

"Come on, Easter," Dreama called, but Easter just capped both hands over her mouth and laughed.

The song twisted and spun on crisp air. It echoed up the holler and went into homes, slithered around porch posts, beat against the faces of old cliffs.

"Dance with us," Dreama begged. "Ain't no sin in music that pretty."

Easter got up and began to dance around the yard with Clay and Dreama, looking embarrassed and happy. "Lord have mercy, if any church people drive by, they'll throw me out of the meeting Sunday," she said.

Cake sat in his chair and clapped in time to the music. He looked like he was in love with all three of them.

TRISTAN COULDN'T GO to sleep with all the excitement in the house, and it was nearly midnight before he finally fell over while Cake played with him. Cake pulled the baby up into his arms and packed him into the kitchen, where Dreama was putting the caps on mason jars full of beans.

"He's finally out of it," Cake whispered.

"Just lay him down back yonder on my bed," Dreama said.

Cake walked slowly down the hall, holding Tristan tight against his chest. He lay him in Dreama's fragrant bed and pulled the covers up beneath his neck, then put two pillows on the edge of the bed and leaned down to kiss Tristan's cheek. He ran his hand down the side of the baby's face and walked carefully from the room.

"He's dead-asleep," Cake said. "I played with him so hard that he'll sleep till ten o'clock tomorrow."

"Well, good, cause it'd sure be nice to sleep late for once," Dreama said. She put a lid on the last jar of beans and tightened it. "How long till them are done, Easter?"

Easter was wiping down the counter while the pressure cooker jiggled and steamed. She wore a cardigan even though the house was hot from the canning. The kitchen smelled so strongly of cooked beans that Cake's mouth watered.

"Be a few more minutes," Easter said. "Go on to bed, if you want to, honey. I can do this last batch."

"Go out here with me, Dreama," Cake said, holding open the door. "I'll set and smoke one before I go to the house."

The night air was growing cooler. The heat from the kitchen poured out of the door behind them as they sat down on the floor of the back stoop. Cake lit a cigarette and listened to the silence of an autumn evening. He wondered where the crickets and katydids went in the fall. Across Easter's backyard, he could see the light in Clay and Alma's bedroom just being turned off.

"Give me a draw off that cigarette," Dreama said, smiling.

"You better not let Easter see you, and you going to church now," he said before handing it over.

She took the cigarette from him and sucked on it awkwardly. He could see that she didn't know how to inhale, but she didn't choke. "I'm trying to live for the Lord, not for them people down there at the church," she said. She handed it back. "Here. I just like to take a puff off one ever once in a while. I smoke about one whole cigarette a year, just to be doing it."

He looked across the yard, feeling animal eyes upon them. He could hear an owl screeching, far up the mountain.

"Pretty night, ain't it?"

"It sure is. I love this time of year," Dreama said, looking up to the sky. "Seems like they's more stars in the fall."

Cake could smell the beans on her clothes and in her hair. She sat with one palm up and the other hand massaging her wrist. Her fingers were red and indented from tightening jar lids.

"I swear, Tristan is crazy over you," she said. "It's a sight his own daddy don't never fool with him. I'm glad you're around to play with him so much."

"You still care for Darry?" Cake asked.

"Lord no! At one time, I would've laid right down and died for that man, too. Now I wouldn't spit on him if he was on fire. Love dies so easy when somebody hurts you that bad."

Cake nodded without really thinking why he was doing so. He took one last, satisfying draw on his cigarette. He jumped when she touched him on the shoulder as she was getting up.

"I'm going to have to go and lay down, Cake. I'm so tired, I can't make it no longer."

"Well, good night."

She opened the door and stood with one leg in the house and one on the porch. "Thanks for playing with the baby. I don't know what we'd do without you."

"It's all right," he said.

"Well, good night," she said, and slipped into the house.

Cake didn't feel like getting up and walking home. He wanted to sit right there on Easter's back porch and smell the damp, colored leaves up on the mountain. He lit another cigarette and looked up at the crowded sky. He thought about what Dreama had asked Easter earlier: "What do you think will become of all of us?" He took a deep breath of the scent of beans that floated out onto the night, and listened to the pressure cooker clucking and Easter moving around inside. He thought about Dreama snuggling up against the baby when she climbed into bed, and Clay and Alma just drifting off to sleep across the yard.

He whispered to the mountain: "I wish this is what would become of ever one of us. I wish we could stay just like this."

• 21 •

MARGUERITE WAS AWARE of a silence so thick and heavy that it made its presence known, hovering like a metal mist. It seeped about the squat houses, the black trees, the objects bound to the earth. She had never known such silence as Free Creek possessed at night. It was intensified by the snow that covered everything that night. The slicing February wind was gone now, and the air stood still and frozen, like curtains of ice that she was able to pass through. The tree limbs were bent low, nervous above the icy ground. The cliffs were too cold to hold snow against their faces, and gray stands of rock stuck out from the whiteness.

Marguerite had never grown accustomed to the quiet of a holler at night, and as she walked down Free Creek toward Easter's house, she found the hush maddening. She felt like screaming out for someone to come to her, but she didn't dare to pull the scarf away from her mouth. She could hear the blood pumping inside her body—the only sound besides the crunch of her feet in the high snow, which was so loud that it sounded as if she were walking over bones that cracked beneath her. She turned to look back at her house on the mountainside for a moment and felt strange looking back at its dark silhouette against the snow: suddenly she felt an overpowering feeling of homesickness, but she wasn't thinking about the house. The snow made her miss the past.

She turned back and focused on the yellow glow of the coal-oil lamps that burned in Easter's windows. She felt that she would never make it that short distance down the holler, with the snow up to her knees and the scarf wet about her mouth and nose, the air freezing the skin around her eyes. But she could smell the fine, clean aroma of winter, and it soothed her throat, like taking a deep breath of liniment. She had lived in Kentucky for more than a quarter of a century now, but she still couldn't get over the snow. The smooth, undisturbed ground, like a shimmering beach of white sand, the ice clotting the trees and encircling the power lines. Winter was the worst time in the mountains; she could remember three or four miserable winters when she was snowbound in the house with Harold. But at the same time, it was the best season, too. She loved the way a draft in the house sometimes gave her a forgotten, erotic shudder, and the way the children's laughter echoed down the holler as they rode sleds off the mountain.

The sky opened up, just as quickly as it had closed before, and the snow came down like a million damp feathers. First it fell straight down, then to the side in a frenzied rush that looked as if it needed music to accompany it. It began to snow so hard that she could barely even make out Easter's windows. The big, square flakes blew behind her scarf, stung her lips, and stuck to her eyelashes. She felt as if she were fighting against a flood, each leg heavier and heavier as it pushed at the snow.

When she reached the porch, she ripped the scarf from her head and let the cold sink into her skin. She knocked twice before letting herself in. Heat surrounded her.

"Marguerite!" Easter cried happily, jumping up to help her in. "Come in, come in. Anything wrong?"

Marguerite kept her eyes cast down as she took off her coat, then her boots. "No. Just lonesome's all. Harold's been asleep all evening, and I was tired of listening to his snoring."

She had known everyone would be here, and patting down her hair, she surveyed the whole room, where everyone sat smiling at her.

Dreama was rocking her baby to sleep and quietly singing "Barbara Allen" into his face. Alma and Clay were hugging each other beneath an old quilt. Gabe and El sat on the couch, laughing at a private joke. Cake jumped up from the Mennonite chair in the corner to take his mother's arm and direct her toward a seat. She smiled and pulled away. She hated it when Cake treated her like an invalid.

The room was lit by three coal-oil lamps made of old, heavy glass. A kerosene heater sat in the center of the room, pushing out warm heat and its acrid, biting scent. The power had been out since early that morning, and when such things happened, it seemed everybody always gathered at Easter's.

"Here, Marguerite. This'll warm you up," Easter said, pushing a cup of steaming coffee into her hands. "Good thing we got a gas stove. I couldn't make it through a snowstorm without coffee," she said to the whole room, settling back into her place on the couch between Gabe and El. "We heard on the radio that the governor was sending the National Guard down here to take doctors and the sick to the hospital and start digging us out."

"You ought not to have walked down here by yourself, Mommy," Cake said.

"You must not have been too worried about me, or you would have come to my house instead of Easter's," she answered, and sipped her coffee.

Everyone fell silent after that, and Marguerite wondered if they had all been talking and cutting up before she came in. Finally, Easter spoke up to break the silence.

"Well, I'm glad you did come up. It's good for everbody to be together on a night like this. We ought to make some peanut butter candy, since we all here."

Outside, the wind howled, and they all leaned forward to listen to it. They had been listening to the wind all evening, and every once in a while they heard the crack of another limb snapping from the weight of the snow and ice.

"I hope that big oak don't fall in on our house," Clay said.

"Well, there ain't nothing you can do but set here and let it," Gabe said.

Marguerite drank the last of her coffee and sat up very straight, putting her hands on her knees before her. She cleared her throat with her hand balled to her mouth and began to speak.

"I'll never forget the first time I saw snow. Real snow, I mean, here in Kentucky. I had only lived here about six months, and I was still not quite sure *how* to live here, and one evening, it began to snow. I stood at the window a long time and watched it fall. I expected it to come down a few minutes and then clear up, but it just kept falling and falling. The only snow I had ever seen was inside those little snow globes you shake up, and I couldn't get over it. I stood there for more than an hour, never moving a muscle. I had never seen anything so perfect and simple before. That's what I think of when I see snow—perfection."

They all listened. They had never heard her speak at such length.

She looked into the air in front of her, as if she could see the picture before her.

"It was far past time for Harold to get home from work, and I suddenly realized that the snow had rushed in so fast and thick that he would never make it over the mountain and back from the mines. It came to me to put on a record to watch the snow by. I thought about one of my favorite pieces, 'La Campanella,' and I put the needle to the record, then went straight and raised the window. The cold air rushed in and filled up the room. The music was a perfect match to the way the snow fell. They kept time with each other, like they were meant to be played together. I turned up the volume as loud as I could, and I'm sure that everyone heard it, although they probably had no idea where it was coming from."

She breathed out with a short shudder.

"And then, no sooner than the violins began to saw, I caught sight of a woman coming out into the road. She wore a bright red topcoat that struck her just below the knee, and a black beret that she had pulled down just over her eyes. She made her way out into the middle of the road, bouncing and twirling just like a little ballerina. She thrust her arms into the air, spinning round and round, then skipped back up the road, twirling around with her head thrown back to catch the snowflakes on her closed eyes. She was a sight! That red blur against the snow, dancing like she was celebrating life."

She looked directly at Clay, smiling broadly. "That was the first time I saw snow and Anneth."

"I remember that red coat, " Easter piped in.

A loud gust of wind and the bonelike crack of a limb took everyone's attention. It was as if the tree had broken right there in the living room. Everyone jumped up like they expected a limb to pierce through the ceiling.

"Oh my Lord!" Easter hollered out.

"I better go over there and check on the house," Clay said.

"They ain't no use in it, Clay," Easter said. "Don't get out there in that storm."

"I need to go make sure the heater's all right," Clay said. "I can't get no peace for worrying over it."

Cake followed him out.

CLAY AND CAKE lit cigarettes as soon as they got inside Clay's house. They could barely taste them for the sharp air that they had breathed outside.

"God, I was bout to have a nicotine fit," Cake said. "I was ashamed to smoke in front of Easter, though."

"Me too. That's mostly why I wanted to come over here." He leaned down to check the heater, then walked to the back door to look at the trees closest to his house. They were bent low with ice and snow, but they looked too frozen to break.

In the living room, Cake was standing at the picture window with one side of the curtain lifted. He was staring out at the road.

"Clay, they's somebody setting out in the road, staring at your house."

"Who is it?"

"I don't know. He's just setting there on a four-wheeler, looking dead at the front porch."

"Probably some of them boys out fooling around," Clay said. He pushed Cake aside and looked out the window. A man sat on a four-wheeler in the middle of the road as if he was taking a break from a long ride. He had a wool cap pulled low over his eyes and was outfitted in coveralls that made his body look bigger, but Clay recognized him. He could tell who it was, even through the blowing snow.

"That's Denzel," he said. "He's set home in this big snowstorm and got drunk. I guarantee he's rode that four-wheeler all the way up here."

"Ain't no other way he could've got here," Cake said.

"Well, I'd like to know what that son of a bitch thinks he's doing." Clay went to the bookshelf in the living room and took down his .22. He shoved the pistol down into the back of his Levi's and ripped open the front door.

"Aye!" he hollered, standing on the porch. His call was lost on the wind. "What're you doing here?"

Denzel swung one leg over the four-wheeler seat and jumped down. He strolled into the yard and walked halfway to the porch. For a brief moment, as Denzel walked toward him, Clay found himself blinded by the white that covered everything. But over the wind Clay could hear Denzel's boots in the snow as he shifted from one foot to the other.

"Where's Alma?" Denzel called. "Send her out here."

"She ain't here, Denzel. You might as well just go back to the house," Clay said. He looked for a pistol in Denzel's hands but could not see one. There was no doubt he had one on him, though. "Just go on and they won't be no trouble."

"She's my wife and I want to see her," Denzel muttered. The snow swirled and danced about him. Snowflakes caught in his eyelashes.

"She ain't your wife no more." Clay could hear his voice echoing off the frozen cliffs lining the creek.

"Sure she is," Denzel said, almost smiling. "Bring her out here."

Denzel walked into the yard without taking his eyes off Clay's face. He walked right up onto the first porch step, so that he appeared a head shorter than Clay. "Alma!" he hollered. "Get on out here, now, I said!"

He was so close that Clay could smell him, and their breath trailed out of their mouths to collect silver between them.

"Denzel, I don't want no trouble with you. You ain't got no business here."

"Alma is my business. I want her to come out here to me."

"I want you the hell out of here," Clay yelled. He thought of pulling the gun out of his pant waist and putting it in Denzel's face, just to scare him off. But he thought of what Gabe had always told him: *If you pull a gun on a man, you better be ready to use it.*

Denzel didn't flinch. He stood still and studied Clay's face, looking into his eyes the way Easter did when she was trying to read him.

"Go on, now," Clay said, and quickly ran his hand over the pistol's handle, as if to reassure himself it was still there.

Denzel cut his eyes away and reached into his coat. He felt around as if patting his pocket for a pack of lost cigarettes, then pulled out his gun. He brought his arm up, and Clay could see the silver of the barrel, Denzel's finger on the trigger. The sound of the hammer being thrown back made a grinding click.

Clay heard the sound of his own pistol bounce off the mountains before he saw the blast of light. The sound echoed down the holler, booming louder and louder with each reverberation. His ears rang with the explosion.

Denzel staggered down off the steps and out into the yard. He pulled his hand away from the wound in his chest and slung blood out across the snow. His unfired pistol fell out of his hand and disappeared in the snow. He slumped down onto one knee and looked up at Clay. "Goddamn you. Goddamn you, you've shot me."

Clay dropped the pistol onto the porch floor. It bounced down and fell heavily onto the first step. Denzel eased down onto the ground, and his body twitched. His arm jerked, and then he was still. Snow blew down the neck of Clay's shirt.

Clay screamed. He let go of all the screams that had been latched away inside him ever since he was a child, ever since he was a little boy lying facedown in the snow with his dead mother's scarf wrapped around his hands.

• 22 •

When the law came for Clay, Easter fought them with all the combined strength of herself and her dead sister. One of the troopers tried to get hold of her, but she tore at his face with her fingernails, ripped his hat from his head, kicked him in the shins. The trooper tried to ignore her at first, as he was used to mothers acting in such a manner. But she struck out at him with such ferocity that he had to fight back.

The other trooper shook Clay awake. Clay looked around as if he didn't know where he was, then up into the eyes of the officer. The trooper helped him up and Clay leaned against him as they walked to the car, Clay's feet dragging in the snow. Easter broke away and ran after them, screaming an unintelligible barrage of entreaties. When the trooper caught up to her, he shoved her away to make his way around to the car door. She stumbled back, then reached down to pull up handfuls of snow that she threw at him in great, wet sprays.

Dreama screamed, her voice full of tears: "Easter, please quit!"

All at once Marguerite breathed into Easter's ear. "It's all right. Let them go now," she whispered. "They're just going to talk to him."

Through a haze of tears, Easter saw the blue lights of the police four-by-four moving away, the red taillights. She brought a clenched fist up to her face, fingers toward her, and saw the blood caked underneath her nails. A ghost had come into Easter, a strong ghost, full of life. She had felt Anneth slipping into her, just stepping into her as easily as a woman steps into a beautiful gown. She had felt Anneth directing her hands, opening her throat. She had felt all of the life she had never possessed before—all the raw strength she had always longed for—course through her blood vessels and make the frame of her body a crowded place. *This is what it feels like to be truly alive,* she had thought. *This is what's it's like to be strong.* When the state Bronco pulled away, Anneth slipped back out of Easter's skin and became air again.

Marguerite lifted Easter up out of the snow and lay her across her arms. She stood straight-backed and carried her as gently as a mother packing her growing child off to bed. Easter was aware of being packed away, aware of figures moving in the yard, but she had no comprehension of them. She didn't see Dreama walking slowly behind them. She did not notice Cake standing in the middle of the road, watching the taillights move farther and farther away. She did not know that Gabe was having to sink his thumbs into Alma's arms to keep her from running after the police car.

Marguerite maneuvered through the deep snow, stepping high to keep her balance. She made it up onto the porch, slid one hand beneath the bend of Easter's knee to twist the doorknob, and carried Easter into the bedroom. Marguerite lay her on the bed and kneeled down in the floor, running a hand over Easter's forehead. Easter could feel Marguerite's warm, coffee breath playing out across her forehead.

"I'll set up with you all night," Marguerite cooed. "I'll take care of you."

Easter didn't know if she was dreaming or simply remembering, but an image came to her so plain and clear that she felt she might have stepped back in time.

She was sitting on the ground in her garden. A garden of October, made up of nothing more than crisp fodder, yellow pumpkins, and rows of leafy mustard. She was snapping off the mustard and shoving it into a brown paper bag.

Clay was standing at the edge of the garden, holding a bulging hunting sack. He was ten years old, and Gabe had outfitted him in clothes twice too big.

"Kill anything?" she asked, and looked back at her mustard.

"Naw." He came closer and set his hunting sack down between rows. The top of the bag slumped over and a few walnuts spilled out and rolled toward her fingers.

"What's this?" she asked.

"Walnuts," Clay said. "I wasn't doing no hunting, so I figured I might as well gather them."

She smiled and watched the mustard as she broke it. He began to help her, and the sound of breaking stalks chattered between them.

"You ought to concentrate more on something like this," she said. "You a good hand in the garden to be so young. If you don't want to hunt, just tell Gabe. Ain't no shame in it." She put another handful of mustard in the paper bag and shook it so the dirt would gather at the bottom. "It's a lot better way, if you ask me. Raising up food beats killing it any day."

Clay said nothing, but he nodded in agreement. The mist moved down low over the garden, slipping off the mountain. High up on the ridge, another shot rang out, but neither of them acknowledged it.

"You never wasted the morning," she said. "That's the awfullest big bunch of walnuts ever was. This evening we'll hull them."

"It was a pretty morning, too," Clay said.

"It sure was. I been up prob'ly before you."

"No, I mean from up there," he said, nodding toward the mountain. "It's different."

She stopped momentarily and looked at him. "I know," she said.

Now Marguerite was talking to her again, her voice just like a sweet little song. So easy, so soft. "Try to rest," she said.

Marguerite got up and took a quilt off the foot of the bed, then spread it out over Easter. She tucked the edges in around Easter's body. Beyond the room, the house was busy with talking and crying: Alma wailing uncontrollably, Dreama singing in a cracked voice to the baby, Cake asking questions that Gabe did not answer.

• 23 •

Alma was crying into the telephone, holding it close against her face, as if it were a hand upon her wet cheek. She looked into the living room, where Clay sat with his face in his hands. She sank back into the kitchen, unable to watch him.

"I think he's losing his mind," she whispered. "I don't know if I can stand this much longer."

"Maybe you all ought to get away for a while. Get out of that town—get out of Kentucky, period. I'd hit the interstate and drive as far away as I could," Evangeline said. She was on a pay phone in Nashville, on a loud street in front of the apartment she shared with every one of her bandmates. They still hadn't been able to get their demo listened to. "You all could come see me. I'm so lonesome for home I'm bout to die."

"No, that's when he's the worst, when we're round a big bunch of people. Some days he's all right, but usually he comes straight home from work and sets down in that chair and just stays there the rest of the evening."

"Well, God awmighty, it ain't like he murdered Denzel. He didn't have no choice but to kill him. Even the police told him that."

"I know it. I think it bothers him on account of his mother dying the same way."

"Can't Easter do nothing with him?"

"No. You know if I can't talk no sense to him, then nobody can. I swear, I don't know what to do." Alma wiped her face with the back of her hand and tried to get ahold of herself. It was funny how you could be so hurt and go without crying, then talk to somebody you love and just lose it. Talking to Evangeline in bad times had always made her break down. "I feel like everything's done."

"I tole you what to do. Talk him into getting out of there. You know they'll let him off from the mine. Time and distance is the only thing that can heal a wound. I know. I've been running from things all my life."

"You can't run away from your problems, Evangeline," Alma said hatefully. All she could think of was the way Evangeline had always gotten away from her troubles: by being so doped up that she didn't even know where she was.

"Sure you can," Evangeline said with confidence. "Out of sight and out of mind. That little saying is true."

"Well, it ain't that easy for most people," Alma replied, but she couldn't help thinking about what Evangeline had said. She wouldn't mind getting the hell out of here herself. She was tired of walking through town and seeing people looking at her as if she had somehow manipulated Clay into killing Denzel.

She was not happy that Denzel was dead, but she was not sad

about it, either. In a way, she felt almost responsible for it: she had certainly wished him dead enough times while she was married to him. The only thing she ever felt was an occasional pang of guilt because she was finally free of Denzel. You couldn't get much more free of someone. Still, the shame did not last long, and now she knew how people without souls must have felt—empty. It was a real, physical feeling, and it made her feel like she carried a stone in her belly.

"Alma? Honey, are you all right?" Evangeline asked, as if she had read Alma's mind. "You're the one I'm worried about."

"I'm fine, Vangie. It's just Clay. If you seen him, you'd know why it hurts me so bad. He's grieving himself to death."

"I'll call you back in a day or two and check on you," Evangeline said, soft and out of character. "Things'll be all right. Love ye, now."

"Love you, too. Bye." Alma hung up before Evangeline could drag out the conversation any longer. She ran cold water onto a dishrag and held it to her eyes, then walked to the doorway and looked out at Clay. He had turned on the news, but she knew that he was not watching it. It seemed he was looking through the television, through the walls of the house, through the mountain across the creek, and seeing nothing. Dusk had fallen outside, and the living room was lit by gray winter shadows and the square, blue light of the television.

She dreaded going to him. Only two days ago, Easter had come to him—pale and red-eyed—and asked him if he would let her pray with him. He had looked at her with ice in his eyes, a stare so cold that he might as well have screamed out to her that he felt as if God had left him and there was no need to call him back. But she had prayed anyway, and her voice had shaken the whole house. She asked the Lord to help him through this torment, to save him before he slipped away. She prayed for a long time, with tears falling down her face. Alma had stood watching, not doubting for one minute that God had dropped everything to listen to her.

Finally, Easter had taken Clay's hands in hers and said, "Sometimes you just have to accept that some things in this life are unbearable, and go on."

But he had not replied, and Easter had left without another word.

Alma sank down on the floor in front of Clay. She wrapped her arms about his leg and lay her head on his knee, but he did not move. He had not bathed or even changed out of his dirty clothes since coming home from the mines, and she felt the gritty black against her face. She could smell the earth, the coal, and the cold from outside on his pant leg. He looked straight ahead, and she forbade herself to cry. They sat there like that for a long time.

"Clay," Alma finally said, "let's get out of here. Let's just pack up and leave for a week or two and try not to think about all this. You have to take me out of here."

He looked her in the eye, but his face did not change. His eyes looked like coins.

"We have to get through this somehow," she said quietly.

He put the rough, broken skin of his hands to her face and ran a thumb under her eye, then pulled her up onto the chair with him. He encircled her with his arms, holding her tightly about the waist so that her head had to come to rest upon his shoulder. She thought that he had done this so that she would not see him cry, but when he spoke, his voice was neither tear-stained nor broken.

"That's the one thing I never wanted to do," he said. "Kill somebody. The one thing I thought I'd never have to do."

"Well, you need to go on. That's the past."

She wondered if he was seeing everything all over again—his mother lying on the bloodstained snow, Denzel's eyes just before the gun sounded. He had not told her as much, but she knew these two incidents were now like a picture that has two negatives developed on it, one atop the other.

She felt his tight body relax beneath her.

"Let's go, then," he said. "Let's leave this place for a while."

• 24 •

When they left Crow County on Highway 25, there was no sign that announced what county they were about to enter; instead there were three crosses on a grassy slope that ran off the mountain lining one side of the road. The cross in the center was bigger than the two that flanked it and was painted a blinding white. The white was so solid and shiny that Alma thought someone must have climbed up there every six months and applied a new coat of whitewash. The smaller two were as yellow as highway stripes.

This was the last thing Alma saw when they left Free Creek behind them. She looked at the three crosses silently, then closed her eyes as tightly as she could. She thought she might be able to burn this image into her mind, marking the three crosses on her eyelids. She had been trying to memorize the landscape that she had never been away from, but this was the image she chose to take to the ocean with her: a soft, rolling bank—smooth and pronounced as a woman's hip—sliding down from the jagged mountain, and three crosses.

She lay her head back on the seat and tried to imagine how many times she had passed those crosses on her family's trips to sing the gospel throughout the mountains. On those thousand drives, she had always looked at them and thought of them as marking the boundary between home and the other places, and when her family had come back by cover of midnight, she had waited until she saw the middle one—so white it glowed in the blackest of nights.

She thought that if Evangeline had been wrong, if you could not leave your troubles behind, these crosses would be imprinted on her eyelids for strength. She prayed silently, hoping that her father's belief that God did not hear sinners' prayers was wrong, and scooted over closer to Clay.

They rode in silence all the way out of the state. They got to Cumberland Gap and headed through the long tunnel that would carry them into Tennessee before they entered Virginia. The hum of their tires filled the truck. Other drivers laid on their horns, as people always do in tunnels, but Clay did not join in. His face was so straight and firm that it looked as if it had been sculpted out of coal. When they came out of the tunnel, they were in Tennessee. Alma didn't need a border sign, for she felt the line cross through her, felt home recede farther and farther behind.

"Well, there it goes," she said.

"What?" Clay asked solidly.

"Home. Before too long we'll be standing on the beach. I can't imagine it. Can you?"

"No," he answered, with no inflection in his voice, and lit a cigarette without taking his eyes off the road.

Alma felt smothered in the close quiet of the truck and she

cracked her window. It was late March, and still cold. The air streamed through the window with the sound of a never-ending *shh*. She dug around in her purse and finally found a tape of driving songs she had made before they left home. When she slid it into the player, Bob Dylan started singing "Mozambique," accompanied by a sad fiddle. A perfect song, Alma reasoned, a place where magic and love were easy to come by. She took Clay's hot hand into hers and fell asleep, dreaming of crosses.

Clay drove across five states without noticing anything they passed. He played the tape that Alma had made, but couldn't have told her one song that was on it. All he could think about was the movie that had played out in his mind the night he shot Denzel. When he had realized that Denzel was dead, he had seen everything so plainly that he might have been looking down upon it from a high vantage point. He had remembered what happened that day after his mother was shot, and he had been remembering it ever since.

He had cried uncontrollably, and his wails slid out over the snow and echoed across the valley to the mountains. The sound spread through the woods, over the creek, slapped against frozen cliffs. It floated through the air and over the dead bodies on the side of the road.

He had been silent the whole time he and Lolie were rolling down the mountainside, and had lain there a long time without making a sound after Lolie's breath had been knocked out of her by the big tree. Most of her weight was on him, and he had suddenly had the great fear of smothering to death beneath her bulk. Although he was having trouble breathing, he cried out. He didn't know what else to do. Little flashes came to his eyes: the car fishtailing over the icy road, his mother's gloved hands folded over his, the woman's face turning into that of an old woman, sparks flying out of the end of a pistol, blood on the snow.

He could hear a car motor now, moving away from them. He could see up the steep ridge, and through the black, straight trees he could make out the side of the road, where they had jumped over the guardrail. He couldn't see the vehicle, and the sound of its motor was growing more and more faint. He cried out again, reckoning that they might hear him and rescue them.

A redbird, its blaze even more brilliant against the snowy backdrop, lit on a tree branch above Clay's head. The redbird considered him, looking concerned, and then darted off.

Lolie sat straight up and pulled Clay up onto her lap. She held one arm tight about his chest and put the other arm around his head so as to protect his ears from the cold. She began to rock back and forth, as if she was trying to get him to sleep.

Clay felt the bruising on his back and the pains that radiated out from it each time Lolie rocked him in her arms, but the pain was warm. Snow stuck to their clothes like bits of wet paper.

"Shh, shh," she whispered. "Hush now, baby. It's all right. Lolie's here."

"I want to go home, Lolie."

To one side of them, there was nothing but woods. On the other side, there was the straight-up incline back to the road, where Glenn's truck had driven away.

"Come on, baby," she said, and when she stood, she cried out in pain. A crew of redbirds flapped noisily out of the tree overhead. "You keep your arms around Lolie's neck, now, and put your face down on my shoulder. Don't pull your face away, now. Keep it down. All right?"

"Well," he said, his voice full of tears.

Lolie began to climb up the mountain, leaning forward. With each step she took up the incline, Clay was certain that she was going to fall backward and they'd roll down. He held on to her with all of his strength and never took his face away from her shoulder. His mother's scarf had come unwound and it trailed in the snow next to them.

They reached the shoulder of the road, and Clay could feel Lolie's heart pumping against his chest. His body rose up and down on the great heaves of breath she took. She stood for a moment, leaning against the guardrail, and then stepped over and stood on the side of the road. There were no sounds.

He knew she was going back to see if any of them were alive, but he reckoned they weren't. He had heard the gunshots, the screams, but had kept his face in the snow. He knew what the gunshots meant. He knew all of them had been shot except for him and Lolie, but now she was going back. He started to rise up from her bosom, but she capped her hand over the back of his head and shoved his face back to her pounding heart.

"Keep your little face down, now, Clay. Whatever you do, don't raise up, baby."

She walked toward the car, and when she got there, she stopped for a moment and there was nothing but the sound of cold. All at once, he could hear her. She was not crying but sounded as if she were choking, like there was a scream stuck in her throat. And he could smell the blood, although he could not put a name to the scent. It smelled like metal.

Clay tried to pull away from her, and before she could push his head back down again, he saw blood streaked across the snow in long, crooked fingers. Then his face was against her breast again and she was running. Her feet slapped against the frozen road. He knew she was running back down the mountain, back to where the houses sat close to the road. He could smell the coal smoke pumping out of their chimneys. Lolie began to run faster and faster.

• 25 •

THEY STOOD ON the beach, looking out at the blackness. The darkness over the ocean was so thick that it looked made of syrup. There was no moon, and even the stars were dimmed by the bright lights of the tall hotels lining the shore. It was beautiful and frightening at the same time. Clay thought about that darkness stretching for miles and miles over cold, deep water. He wondered if that was what death was like, so tight and thick that it smothered you just to look into it.

"It's scary, ain't it?" he asked.

"It's scary to me knowing we're standing at the end of America," she said. "This is where it ends, besides some islands out there."

The wind came at them in a constant, unceasing breeze. Back home, a wind came down into the valley and then moved on, leaving trees shivering and chimes singing; here the wind seemed never to stop. It didn't give anything time to grow still before it attacked again. The water was different here, too. Back in Crow County, water was always moving, always racing to get away. It spilled over rocks in white frenzies, frantic to keep going. Here, the water went nowhere. It seemed caught in a sad purgatory. It washed out to sea, then came right back in again, never getting anywhere.

"It's not how I had it pictured," Alma said. "I thought they'd be a moon."

"Don't you like it?" Clay asked.

"It's beautiful. I ain't never seen nothing like it, but I thought it'd be different, somehow." She began walking down the beach.

They had arrived in town at midnight. They had parked on the street and run right down to the beach, standing in silence for a long time without touching each other. Now Alma put her hand out behind her, and Clay took hold of it. He felt like pulling her to him, but he couldn't. He wanted to stand there on the beach and hold her, looking over her shoulder with hopes that a moon might pop out of nowhere, but he couldn't bring himself to do it. He felt awkward and ashamed without knowing why. She had convinced him to take off his shoes with her, and as they walked, the surf ran beneath them, sucking against their feet as it went out again. The water was still cold. He had not expected this at all. He had figured it would be so hot that they could have run right out in the water when they arrived.

There were a few other people on the beach. A group of teenagers sat on a deck near the sand, smoking cigarettes and laughing. An old couple walked down the beach, holding hands, watching the ground before them. Everyone they passed talked low and none of the people looked up to speak as they went by. Some people carried small flashlights and buckets. They stopped to glide their hand across the sand to search for seashells. Clay watched them and felt sorry for them. It seemed they were all people looking for something that they would never be able to find.

They came to a place on the beach where sand had worn down to large rocks that looked like the hard, speckled backs of whales half-buried on the beach. Alma sat down and pulled him beside her. She put her hands between his knees and lay her head on his shoulder.

"It *is* beautiful. I never seen nothing so powerful," she said. "I won't know how to describe it to everbody when we get back home."

He didn't speak, and for a long time they sat listening as the water pounded the shore and the wind beat against them.

"Clay, I can't lose you now," Alma said. Her voice was a whisper over the roar of the surf.

"I never meant to kill him, Alma. You know that, don't you?"

"Why yeah. He didn't leave you any other choice. He had a pistol, Clay. He would have used it."

"Sometimes I feel like I ain't no better than the man that killed my mother. Taking a life is all the same, whether you mean to or not. You've still done something that only God is meant to do."

"That's foolish talk, Clay. Some things just can't be helped."

"Well, you don't know what it feels like, to have to carry something like that with you."

She put her hand on his leg and ran it up and down his thigh. "I know, but if it wasn't for me, none of this would have happened."

"If it wasn't for you, then I would still be alone. I'd still be miserable inside."

She dug her feet deep into the sand. "Well, we have to just go on."

"That's all a person can do, I guess," Clay said. That's what he had been trying to do his whole life.

THEY RENTED WHAT the manager called a suite at the Misty Bay Motel, a stack of stucco boxes painted turquoise and vermilion, which seemed to be the two requisite colors in the town.

The suite was a small room that held two beds, a card table, and a scarred dresser with a built-in desk and yellow sheets of stationery in the drawer. A television sat on the dresser so it could be seen from the two beds. There was another room in the back, crowded with a couch and a dinette set that stood beneath a large, paneless window. A small refrigerator was built into a counter, along with a half-stove and a coffeemaker.

The motel sat two streets back from the beach, but they could catch a glimpse of the ocean between two tall hotels standing shoulder to shoulder on the shore. The water looked like a smudge of dark paint against the white sky. Their room was on the top floor, the fourth, but they couldn't see much of the town through the palm tree leaves near the balcony railing. From their picture window they could look down on the surprisingly clean pool, where people lounged around reading paperbacks and drinking cocktails. Beyond the pool sat rows and rows of cars, all with different license plates.

"It ain't too bad," Clay said.

Alma sniffed the air and ran a finger over the dresser. "It's clean. That's all that matters to me."

Alma pulled open the nightstand to make sure a Gideons Bible rested inside.

"Thank the Lord," she said. "There's a Bible in here. I wasn't about to sleep in a strange room without one."

"How many days did you pay for?" she asked.

"I paid for a week," he said. "If we stay longer, I figured we could go renew."

Alma sat down on the bed while Clay went out to carry the rest of their things in. She lay back and stared at the ceiling, wondering what it had seen in its years. Here was a place where countless people had had sex, where women had sat and rubbed suntan oil on their pasty thighs. People had gotten drunk in here, or had little spats or sat laughing at each other's jokes. Lots of plans had probably been hatched here. For all she knew, somebody might have died in this little motel room. She wondered if anybody had ever come here as they had, running away, thinking a different geography would change their insides.

She got up and slid a tape into the stereo Clay had packed. Bill Monroe and the Blue Grass Boys started playing "Cheyenne." Mandolins, banjos, and fiddles swirled in the air. She was tempted to get out her own fiddle and play along with them, as she had so many times before, but couldn't bring her fingers to unlatch the case.

"What's wrong, baby?" Clay asked, and ran his hand down the length of her body. She had not felt his touch in a long time. His hands felt big and familiar, and his voice was almost the same as before. It seemed he had already begun to heal, though she knew that that was not possible.

"I'm wore out."

"Lord God, you slept more than halfway here."

"I know it, but I'm still tired. Just lay down here and we'll get up early in the morning and go to the beach. I want to lay here beside you and not worry about a thing."

The promise of rest was a thing he had come to know better than to expect, but he lay down with her. For the first time in a long while, he slept through the night. He dreamed of blackness and nothing else. When he woke up in the morning, Denzel's face wasn't the first thing that came to his mind.

26

CLAY FLOATED ON the ocean, a part of the water. He lay flat on his back, his arms stretched straight out on either side, his feet one atop the other. His eyes were open against a white sky. If they had had enough sense, gulls flying overhead would have thought him crucified. He watched the birds but couldn't hear their chatter because his ears were under the water. He heard only the dull roar of the ocean and felt as if he were listening to the machinery that moved the earth, toiling far beneath him. It was a constant churning sound that he had to focus on to keep hearing.

He had always thought that working back in a coal mine was about as close as a person could get to being a piece of the world, but being in the ocean felt even closer. He closed his eyes and entertained the thought of floating like this all the way to Ireland or Spain. As a child, he had watched white leaves glide down onto the waters of Free Creek and be washed away. He had wondered if they were carried on to the Cumberland and then to the Tennessee, and finally into the Mississippi River. He had thought of the towns that the leaves would pass, and the smells that would come to them before they were finally pushed out into the Gulf of Mexico on a rushing wave, lost forever. Now he knew that little leaves like that would not have made it very far. They would have been caught in tree limbs that littered the creek, or sloshed up onto shore and stuck against a mossy cliff. Even if they had reached the ocean, they would have been washed right back up onshore by the determined surf, where they would have crumbled in the hot sun and flown away on the wind in a hundred different pieces.

He lay back with every muscle in his body relaxed and tried not to think.

ON THE BEACH, Alma lay on a beach towel, reading *To Kill a Mockingbird* for the tenth time. She never was able to read much at a time, since she got headaches easily, so after every fifteen pages she put the book facedown on the towel and looked out at the ocean, her eyes scanning the waves for a sign of Clay. The day had turned out to be unusually hot, and people had crowded onto the beach. The water was still too cold for most people to dive in, and there were not many people in the ocean. She could see him out there, floating, as he had been for the past twenty minutes. She couldn't figure how anybody could float that long. It wore her out just to watch him. He had the strange ability to completely relax on the water, though. Beyond him she saw a large boat drift by on the horizon. Its solidity seemed smudged in the haze that burned along the line where sky met water. She couldn't get over the flatness of the ocean and the land that met it. The flatness made her nervous and short of breath. She couldn't stand having everything all laid out before her.

Wide-open spaces forced her to take in every little thing at one time.

She lay back on the gritty towel and felt her skin burning. Radios were playing all up and down the beach. She could hear a blend of everything from rap to George Strait. Next time she came to the beach, she would definitely bring her own radio so she wouldn't have to hear that wild mess. She eyed the bronze, blond girls lying on a blanket just down the sand from her and wondered what they would think if she played some of her tapes of Jean Ritchie or Bill Monroe.

Alma had been thinking all day of the beach back home. Over on Blackhawk Lake, there was a long strip of sand that had been hauled in. The sand was dark yellow, but when you stepped in it, you left perfectly shaped white footprints. Along the shore, the lake was still unless a boat went by and stirred up some waves. Pines and sandbar willows pressed close to the water's edge. Buckeyes—round and black as marbles—floated just below the surface of the water, along with light green leaves that had blown out of summer trees. People pulled pontoons up on one end of the beach and set up tables on the sand. They had grills attached to the front of their boats, where they cooked barbecue ribs, whole heads of cabbage, and baked potatoes. People sometimes danced on the beach and everybody got to know one another. Boys climbed up onto the cliffs to jump off, and the women lay out in the sun on air mattresses, making a circle on the water as they held on to each other. Clay and Cake would hold their beer bottles up and sing "Looking for Love" together or swim over to flip the women off their air mattresses. Once, she and Clay had swum right up under one of the pontoons and made out like a couple in high school.

Alma opened her eyes to the big South Carolina sun when Clay fell onto the towel beside her. He ran his hand down her oiled leg and shook his head, sending cold drops of water onto her back.

"What're you doing?"

"I was thinking about the sandbar back home," Alma answered.

"Yeah, this beats that beach all to hell, don't it?"

"Not really. I don't believe I'd trade Blackhawk Lake for this whole big ocean."

Clay rolled over on his back and peered up at the big sky. "I swear, I wouldn't mind living here someday."

Alma sat up and dusted sand off the tops of her legs. "Lord God, Clay, you're talking pure nonsense. There's no way you'd ever leave home. You wouldn't stay away from Easter and Dreama or Cake, or home, period."

"I don't guess I would," he said after a long pause. He dried off his fingers and felt around on the sand until he found his cigarettes.

"Ain't you the least bit homesick?" Alma asked. "We've been here over a week."

"Well, I miss everbody, but I'm not exactly dying to get home. I took ever bit of my three weeks' vacation. Ain't no use rushing home." Clay sat up and fired his Zippo, sucking in smoke. He patted her behind lightly and lay back down. She looked off down the beach.

"If you're wanting to go home, we'll load up right now and light out," he said. "I thought you was enjoying this."

"I am. I just don't want to blow every dime we have while we're down here," she lied.

"We won't go broke. Only reason I agreed to come here is so you could see the ocean," he said. "When you want to go home, you tell me."

I can't, she thought. For once in her life, Evangeline had apparently been right. It seemed like this place was reaching inside and stitching Clay back together. Alma didn't know if it was the distance or the time, but it had worked so far. He was becoming himself again, as if he had been covered in coal dust and she had rubbed it away to find him.

THAT NIGHT, ALMA went onto the balcony and looked out into the salty dark. The wind was hot and sticky, and her body was instantly drenched in a film of sweet dampness. She had never seen a place so lit up, and she wondered if maybe the people on the other side of the ocean could see the glow of this place on the horizon. The bright neon of the town destroyed any chance of studying the stars, which she was so used to doing back home. There was never a moon here, and she couldn't figure that out. In the movies, there was always a moon floating over the ocean, so big and yellow it looked ready to pop.

It was only ten o'clock, and the street below was strangely quiet. There always seemed to be a truckload of teenagers going by, their music thumping down the street. She had grown used to hearing people laughing and yelling softly to one another as they lay by the pool at night. Airplanes sometimes shook the earth as they flew just above the motel, heading for the air force base up the road. Tonight was silent and calm. The only sound was the incessant drone of the air conditioners that hung out of each front window of the building.

Clay had gone to the store to fetch them a cantaloupe, as she had been craving one all day. Her mouth watered at the prospect of cutting the firm melon apart, dousing the pieces in salt and sucking the meat down to the rind. She looked down the street, waiting to see him come up the sidewalk. She wanted to see if that same old feeling came to her gut when she laid eyes on him. She relied on this feeling to remind her of how much she loved him; she hated this place so much that she was beginning to blame him for bringing her here.

Alma took her fiddle from its case and began to play the last song she had written. The first bars were so slow that they almost numbed her arm. The slow and forceful notes were meant to stir up the image of a ship pressing through ocean water. The rhythm rose as the people in her song began to trod land, climb mountains, bend to drink from clear streams. The pace sped and curled as they cleared land, raised houses and children.

She closed her eyes and let the music lift her, carrying her out over the street, where she drifted up and down between block-shaped hotels and squat condominiums, rushing out over the surf, out into black air that swirled over black water. Finally, she was in the middle of the ocean, and the sky was so full of stars that it looked completely silver.

When she opened her eyes again, Clay was leaning against their door, holding a brown paper bag heavy with melons. Others had come out onto the balcony, too. There was a tiny old woman sitting in a plastic chair by her door, a leather-faced woman standing in the door of her own room with a child hanging onto her leg. There was a man shaped like a snowman—his body was a stack of round, fat balls. He watched Alma with a wide smile cut into his face. She could see every one of his teeth and his thick gums to match.

She took the bow from the fiddle and looked at the floor, embarrassed.

"Don't stop," the old woman said. "It's beautiful."

Alma started to play again, but she couldn't. When she looked at the people, she felt as if they were some sort of enemy. She found herself thinking, *These are not my people.*

"Play just a little more of it," Clay said proudly, but she wouldn't.

"Did you write that song yourself?" the old woman asked.

"Yes, it's about our ancestors."

The roundheaded man stepped up and leaned one elbow on the railing. "You sure can play that fiddle," he said. "You mountain people sure can play music, I'll say that much. Lot of musical talent comes out of those mountains. Why is that?"

"Us mountain people can do damn near everthing good," Alma said, and didn't move.

The man raised his eyebrows and looked at everyone nervously. "I didn't mean anything . . ."

Clay put his hand on Alma's arm, but she pulled away and bent down to lay her fiddle back in its case. The buckles snapped smartly on the humid air. She picked up the case and went inside, leaving the door open behind her.

"What was that all about?" Clay asked, closing the door. "That feller never meant nothing by that."

"Well, I guess I took him the wrong way, then," she said sarcastically. "It was insulting, calling us 'you mountain people.'"

Clay set the bag on the card table and took the melons out as gently as a man handling a newborn. He placed them in the refrigerator to chill and sat down beside Alma on the bed. His hands were big and hot on the small of her back.

"What is it?" he asked.

Alma felt like she was coming out of a trance. She felt as if she were waking up, like a sleepwalker coming to her senses. "Nothing. I feel like I got too much sun today, or something."

Clay peeled off his shirt and spread himself out across the bed with his head in Alma's lap. She put her hand in Clay's hair and stroked his head gently. He closed his eyes and didn't speak. It was cold in the room after being out in the humid night, and Alma shook with a chill. She reached over to the nightstand and took the Gideons Bible out of the drawer with one hand. She had always practiced what her daddy called Bible cracking. He had always taken the Bible in hand and let it fall open to whatever page it was willed to.

She held the stiff book in her hand for a moment and then let it fall open on Clay's back. His breathing raised the book up and down as she read, so that the Bible appeared to be a living thing, capable of lifting itself and floating around the room. She leaned over and let her eyes fall on whatever verse they came to first.

Jeremiah 12:7.

"I have forsaken My house, I have left My heritage; I have given the dearly beloved of My soul into the hand of her enemies," she read silently.

Clay was almost asleep when her hand became still in his hair. "That felt good," he said. "Why'd you quit?"

"I have forsaken my house," she said aloud. "I have left my heritage."

"What?" he asked, but she didn't answer. She interpreted what this verse might mean to her and took her hand out of Clay's hair. She lay it on her belly and grabbed a handful of her own flesh into her palm. She had left her homeland, said good-bye to everything she had known all of her life, and now there was life growing in her belly.

• 27 •

Cake drove slowly to Finley's Kwik-Mart, as he wanted to prolong his time with Dreama. She was looking out the window at the darkness and singing along with Martina McBride on the radio, as if he weren't even there, but he liked her riding along with him anyway. He liked looking in his rearview mirror and seeing Tristan falling to sleep in his car seat, his bottle hanging halfway out of his mouth and his little eyes squinting up every time they met a car's headlights. It was raining, a steady, easy rain too cold for spring, and fog swirled down over the road like the mountains were on fire, so this gave him a good excuse to drive slow.

He had started calling down to Dreama's every time he went out for anything, to ask if she needed to go to the store or anywhere. He liked having Dreama with him. The first time she had gone to the store with him, she had jumped in the car and said, "Good Lord, I'm so tired of setting in that old house that I'd take a ride with Bill Clinton," but now she seemed pleased to be going not just for the ride but because Cake was taking her.

Cake glanced from the road to her lap, where her hands beat along to the music, slapping softly against each knee. Pentecostal girls were not supposed to listen to anything besides gospel music, but Dreama saw no sense in this. Her hands were small and pale, her fingernails bitten right down into the quick, with no polish, and he could see the tiny wrinkles in her fingers' joints when a car passed and gave light to the interior of his Camaro. He wanted to reach over and grab them, but he was ashamed for her to feel his own hands, which were always so hot and clammy.

"Do your hands sweat when you're in a vehicle?" he asked, turning down the radio a notch.

"What?" she asked, looking at him quizzically. He repeated his question, and she laughed. "Yeah, they do."

"Mine do, too. Anytime I travel anywhere, they get clammy."

"I never knowed anybody done that but me," she said. "I've always been nervous in a car. I didn't figure you was a-tall."

"I ain't. My hands just get clammy." He pulled into Finley's parking lot, where a dozen cars were parked every which way. Three teenage boys stood under the overhang of the store, drinking root beers out of brown bottles. They acted cocky, like they were standing there drinking real beer and it made them look big. The windows were crowded with neon cigarette signs and placards advising everyone to buy lottery tickets. The wide plate-glass windows of the store were bright with white light from within and cast an eerie glow on Dreama's face.

"I'll set out here with Tristan," Cake offered.

"No, I'm getting him out. He needs to wake up," she said, opening the door. "Too late in the evening for him to be taking a nap. You want anything?"

"I'll just come in."

Inside Finley's, country music was pouring out of speakers mounted in each corner. The cashier watched them walk in and raised her eyebrows at Cake, wanting to know if he was going with Dreama now. She wore too much eyeliner and her blouse was unbuttoned low enough to expose a dark fold of flesh. A cigarette—its tip ringed by her lipstick—smoldered in the ashtray propped atop the cash register.

Dreama walked heavily in front of him with Tristan on her hip. She tried to get the baby not to lay his head back down on her shoulder and shook him playfully. "Wake up, now, baby. Look, you in a big ole store." She walked back to the milk cooler, rooting through her jacket pocket.

"Cake, you care to hold him a minute?" she asked, and handed the baby over before Cake even had a chance to respond. The baby put his forehead to Cake's and looked him straight in the eye. Cake spun around, holding the baby out in the air. Tristan giggled loudly, but Dreama didn't notice. She took a little green folder out of her pocket and studied a coupon she took out of it, then grabbed two gallons of milk.

"What is that?" Cake asked.

"My WIC vouchers. You get milk and eggs and things like that free when you have a child and don't have no money. Daddy'd die if he knowed I was on WIC, though. It's not like food stamps, but it's government money, so he'd die. Don't mention it to him." She bent down and got a carton of eggs, then moved past Cake and Tristan, hunting for the canned juice.

Cake went on up to the front of the store and looked for some candy for the baby. The cashier smiled a toothy grin and said, "Hey there, little man," to Tristan. She looked at Cake. "That yours?"

"Naw, it's Dreama's."

"I didn't think you had one." She sucked on the cigarette from the corner of her mouth. "He seems used to you, though."

Cake grabbed a handful of Smarties and laid them on the counter before Dreama could come up and make him let her pay for them. "Give me a pack of Marlboro Reds, too. In a box," he said.

The cashier rung up the candy and the cigarettes. As she handed him his change, she said, "Who you going with now?"

Before he could answer, he felt somebody standing very close to his back, as if they were staring right at the baby, who was looking over Cake's shoulder. He turned around and met Darry's eyes.

"Hey there, Cake," Darry said, and reached out to take hold of Tristan's little hand. "I seen you and Dreama pull in."

Dreama came around the corner with two gallons of milk dangling from her fingers and the eggs and juice piled up against her chest. She broke through Cake and Darry without looking up and let the groceries fall onto the counter. One of the juice cans rolled across the counter before the cashier caught it. Dreama slapped down the WIC voucher and turned to face Darry.

"What do you want?"

"I'd like to hold my baby," Darry said, trying to keep the smile on his face while he spoke. He put his hands out to Tristan. "Come on, buddy. I'm your daddy."

Tristan clung to Cake and let out a little whine. Darry put his hands on the baby's sides and tried to pry him away, but he wouldn't come.

"He's not much on strangers," Dreama said, and there was no trace of contempt in her voice. It seemed that she was speaking to a stranger, defending her baby's lack of cooperation. "He don't know you, Darry."

"Well, I hope to change all that."

"If you don't start before long, it'll be too late. I've give you ever chance there is. It's bad enough you missed two weeks of sending me child support, but you could at least come see him. You could go to town and buy him a little outfit ever once in a while."

"I don't want to fight, Dreama. You're the one wanted the divorce."

Dreama took Tristan from Cake and rubbed the back of the baby's head. "I don't want to fight with you either, Darry. I just want some consistency in this baby's life. Either you come see him on a regular basis, or don't come at all."

"That's what I plan on doing. I want us to go back to court. I want joint custody."

"You can forget that," she said. "There's not a judge in America would give it to you."

"A man's got rights nowadays, Dreama, and I intend to take advantage of them."

Dreama picked up the carton of eggs and collected her thoughts. "You're not taking advantage of this baby, though." She looked into Cake's eyes to let him know she wanted to go. He grabbed the rest of the groceries and followed her toward the door.

Darry sprinted past them and stopped in front of Dreama, blocking the door. He put his hands out as if he were going to receive a laundry basket. "Just let me hold my baby, Dreama."

"No!" she screamed. "I'm not making him go to you!"

Darry reached again, pulling at Tristan, and Dreama pulled back, her hand on Tristan's head, holding his face into the neck of her jacket. She was about to cry, right along with the baby.

Cake had seen enough. He threw down the groceries and grabbed the back of Darry's collar. "Leave em alone," he said, and shoved Darry back by his collar. Darry straightened his shirt and then pulled his arm back. His fist connected with Cake's chin. They crashed into the candy aisle, then knocked over a metal stand that held comic books and paperbacks. Cake threw Darry back against a long shelf, and chips and crackers fell to the floor. They fought all over the store, a blur of fists and wild eyes against a backdrop of cans and boxes that slid from the shelves.

Dreama held Tristan tightly to her breast while the cashier screamed over and over for them to stop.

"They're destroying this store!" the cashier yelled. "Make them quit!"

Dreama scooted back toward the door. "I can't do nothing with them," she said.

"I'll call the law if you all don't quit!" the cashier hollered, leaning over the counter.

They fought against the wall of glass-doored freezers along the back of the store and finally Cake knocked Darry down. Darry couldn't get back up. He put a hand to his nose, then looked up at Cake with nothing in his eyes. Cake walked back up through the store, wading through bags of pretzels and flattening boxes of cereal. He had a bad cut on his brow and put two fingers to it. He gathered up Dreama's gallons of milk and cans of juice and sliced through the air beside her, heading out the door.

Dreama ran out of the store like she was leaving the scene of a crime and jumped into the car without even putting Tristan in his car seat. "Let's go. That girl called the law on us."

Cake peeled out of the parking lot and calmed his engine when they got back out on the road. Blood stung his eye.

"You ought not have done that, Cake," Dreama said, her voice broken by tears.

"What'd you expect me to do, dammit? He was bout to push you down."

"I appreciate it, but you ought not have done it." She started sobbing, but the baby sat up on her lap and watched the road.

"You set there and cry over that sumbitch after how he's done you?" Cake felt like crying himself, he was so mad.

"I'm not crying over him. It's not on account of him. I just can't believe I had a child by somebody like him. I don't see how I could've been so stupid." She held Tristan to her for comfort and broke down in a steady heave of tears.

Cake pulled over to the side of the road and watched the windshield wipers flop across the glass. He felt the blood sinking into his eye, but he paid it no mind. He reached over and took Dreama's hand in his.

"Don't cry now," he said. "I never could stand to see you cry."

Dreama jerked her hand away. "Don't," she said. "You only want me for your friend now that Clay's gone."

"What's that supposed to mean?"

"With him gone, you don't have nobody else. Ever since he got married, you've clung to me."

"It's not like that, Dreama," Cake said. "I've loved you ever since I was a little child."

"Just take me home," Dreama said, as if he had not announced the secret he had carried for so long. She fell against the window, shaking with tears.

EASTER CALLED MYRTLE BEACH to tell Clay that Cake had been put in jail for assault and destruction of property, but Clay was gone. She told Alma, talking faster than she'd ever done before, and Alma listened attentively, only saying things like, "Lord have mercy," or "Yeah."

Finally, Easter stopped and the phone lines hummed between them. "Alma, are you all right? Where's Clay at?"

"He went for a walk on the beach. He loves the ocean." She glanced around the little room, smelled the salt air, and felt like vomiting. "I hate that over Cake, though. Will his daddy put bail up for him?"

"No, but Marguerite is. She got Gabe to take her to the jail. First time that woman's been to town in twenty year, as I know of. Cake'll have to serve time over it, though. Broke Darry's nose and three of his ribs. Destroyed that grocery store." Easter couldn't help laughing, even though it wasn't funny.

"Darry needed stomped over the way he's done Dreama," Alma said. "Ever dog gets his day."

"Well, how is everthing?" Easter asked. "How's Clay doing?"

"Best ever was. He's a sight better."

"Thank the Lord. You all will be home before long, then, won't you?"

"We'll be home real soon," Alma said.

THEY SAT ON the sand, which was still warm from the long day, and looked out at the black water, just as they had every other night they had spent here. Clay lit a cigarette and watched the smoke drift lazily toward the sky. There was not much of a breeze tonight, and the sound of the surf seemed louder than ever. They had walked past the long line of hotels, past the pier, and crossed a crude wooden fence that took them to a private beach. Here the beach was empty and they couldn't see a sign of life except for some flashlights down the shore, where people were out strolling and looking for seashells.

"You know I've been sick lately, don't you?" Alma asked.

"You've been awful tired. What's wrong?"

"There ain't a thing wrong with me." She took his hand and put it atop her belly. She pressed it firmly into her gut, hoping he might feel the life burning inside her. He looked at her with troubled eyes, and then the old familiar shine came back into them, and his mouth fell open. "I'm carrying our child."

"We've got to leave right now," he said, and jumped up. He dropped the cigarette onto the sand and ground it out with the toe of his shoe. "We've got to pack up tonight."

Alma laughed, and the sound carried far out over the ocean, dipping over black, rocking water. "We can't leave tonight," she said.

"I don't know why not," he said, taking her hand and pulling her up. "I won't be able to sleep noway."

He led her down into the surf, and their feet sank into the earth each time the receding waves sucked at the sand beneath them. He put both hands to the sides of her face and kissed her—not her lips, but her whole face. He kissed her eyelids and her forehead, her cheeks and her nose.

When they got back to the motel, Alma convinced him to stay the night, as she was too tired to set out on the road. Besides, she felt a celebration was in order, one that could not take place in a moving vehicle. She put a bluegrass tape into the stereo and pulled him onto the bed.

"If it's a girl, we'll name it Maggie, after this song," she said.

• 28 •

After daylight had lit the room with a white glow, making everything inside seem to have a light burning within, Clay slipped from the bed and dressed without making a sound. Alma lay as she always did this time of the morning: on her side with one slender hand under her heart-shaped face, her auburn hair spread out across the sheet behind her. He looked at her for a long time, then decided to let her rest. He pulled on his Levi's and sneaked outside.

A cool, light rain was falling. Steam rolled up the street and off the parking lot, reminding him of the thick mists that eased over the mountains in the evening. The rain had washed away the scent of salt that always seemed present here. He took inventory of every scent and sound that came to him and tried to capture them in his mind. He wanted to remember everything perfectly because he felt this was the first day of his life. This is where he would begin when his children asked him about his life.

He walked to the beach and stood in the needles of rain, looking out at the endless stretch of water. There were already people out walking along the shore: old people with their pant legs rolled up and their shoes hanging off the ends of their fingers, children skipping and running through the surf. He spoke to everybody, even those who didn't glance at him until he had done so, and would have told them all that he was going to be a father if they had taken the time to stop and talk to him a few minutes.

When he went back to their room, he eased in so as not to wake Alma, but she was already sitting up in the bed, rubbing her eyes.

"Let's go home," he said.

"I'm ready."

They didn't have much to pack, but Alma insisted on cleaning the room before they left, even though Clay assured her that was what the motel maids were paid to do. She tied up the garbage, stripped the beds, and even washed out the bathtub before she would leave.

Clay peeled out of the parking lot, leaving black marks. He pushed in the tape that Alma had made for them to travel by. All the way home, he played one side of the tape, then flipped it over to hear the other again. They already knew every word to every song and sang them all the way across five states. They passed through violent thunderstorms, with lightning crashing down on either side of them as they raced along the flat fields of swampy grass. Houses and vehicles in the distance appeared distorted in the haze of heat and gasoline. Directly, the sun broke through and burned the purple clouds away. They rolled down the windows and let their hands push on the racing wind.

Alma fell asleep just outside of Asheville. Clay turned the radio down and sang to himself as the landscape began to look more and more like home. When they crossed into Virginia and he was sure the mountains he saw rising in the distance were those of home, he shook her gently and she started, rising up in her seat as if she thought they were in a wreck.

"Look up yonder," he said. "That's Kentucky."

When Alma saw the signs announcing that they were about to enter Cumberland Gap Tunnel, her stomach was heavy with homesickness. She fast-forwarded the tape to play a Bill Monroe instrumental called "Scotland." It was a full-throttle mess of wild, twirling fiddles, clicking Dobros, and plucking mandolins. They entered the tunnel, and when they burst out the other side in their own home state, the song had reached its fever pitch.

Alma squalled and yelped, slapping her hands against the dashboard. She couldn't control herself anymore and put her knees on her seat so she could hang out the window. She leaned her waist against the door and held her hand above her head. "Home!" she hollered. Her hair slapped against her face and the top of the truck cab.

• 29 •

THE QUILTER DIED quietly on a spring morning.

Sophie got out of bed sleepily, shook Paul's shoulder, and hollered for him to get up, then pulled on her housecoat and went out onto the front porch to sneak her usual cigarette. She pulled the housecoat tightly about her. She couldn't remember a spring morning being so cold. A thick frost had fallen and crystallized on the ground, making the grass and rooftops look as if they were covered with a light dusting of fine, sugarlike snow. The petals on the dogwood and redbud looked caked with ice.

Inside, Paul still wasn't up, and this was the first time she could remember this happening in ages.

"Get up, old man!" she bellowed. "It's wintertime out!"

She walked toward the bedroom, undoing the tie on her housecoat so she could get dressed to start breakfast. As she entered the bedroom, the cold outside seemed to consume the house. It was as if the morning air were steaming under the cracks around the windows like dry ice. Paul lay on his side with his back to her, the covers pulled up to his chin. She fell atop him on the bed, knowing that he was gone from her forever. She lay there with him a long time, then got hold of herself, began to smooth down his hair, and tried to close his mouth. She went into the bathroom and filled a dishpan with warm, soapy water. She didn't cry as she washed his face, his arms, his legs.

After the funeral, everyone gathered at Sophie's house, which seemed even larger now, sitting near the mouth of the holler. Sophie sat small and straight-backed within a circle of people who figured plenty of conversation would keep her mind off the matter at hand. Easter and Dreama took over the kitchen, dipping out heaping plate lunches that were passed into the living room. Marguerite brought a German chocolate cake and asked if she could help them get the food ready for the crowd. Most of the men stood out in the yard, smoking and talking about what a good man Paul Sizemore had been. Cake raced around the yard, playing ball with Tristan and the rest of the children.

Clay couldn't stand being at the house without Paul there. He had barely made it through the funeral and had almost refused to be a pallbearer; he had been afraid he would break down while he was helping pack the casket to the grave. He had helped to lower his great-uncle's casket into the ground, but he couldn't stand being here now. He had even forced himself to sit up all night with Sophie and the rest of the family the night before the funeral, but he couldn't take any more. He decided to use the baby as an excuse to leave and parted through the people with Maggie on his hip and Alma holding his hand. He bent down in front of Aunt Sophie and reached Maggie out to her.

"Give Auntie some sugar," he told the baby. Maggie threw her arms out and laughed when Sophie tickled her belly. Sophie took the baby and pulled her close. She ran her hand down the side of Maggie's face and kissed her on the mouth.

"Look at that curly red hair," she told the women crowded around her. She handed Maggie back to Clay. "That's the friendliest little thing ever was."

"We're gonna have to go get her on home. She's wore out," Clay said. "If you need anything, you call me, all right? We love you."

"Love you all," Sophie said. "You all go on home now and get you some rest."

Clay and Alma pushed through the crowd, hollering goodbye to everybody they passed. They walked across the porch, where people sat eating, with plates in their laps, and across the yard, where Cake was playing tag with all of the children. They went out the gate and had started walking down the holler road toward their little house when they heard Sophie calling for them.

"Clay! Wait, honey!" she hollered from the porch. Easter was standing beside her, wiping her hands on a dishcloth and smiling as if she knew something that they did not. Sophie came rushing through the crowd with a bundle wrapped up in newspaper that rattled loudly.

"I bout forgot," she said, out of breath. "Paul made this for the baby. It's a Flying Bird quilt. It worried him a sight because he didn't have her a quilt made when she was born, but he was getting to where he barely could move his fingers to stitch. He got it done bout a month ago and was waiting for the baby's birthday to give it to you all."

"Lord, you don't know how much that means to me, to have this," Clay said, and turned quickly to go. He didn't want to cry in front of her.

"Wait," Sophie said, grabbing his arm. Her small hand held

him so tightly that he glanced down at it. "Paul got fooling around in the basement last summer and found a big trunk of Anneth's clothes. Some of them was dry-rotted, but he saved what he could and made that quilt from them. It's made from her clothes. He knowed how much you missed your mommy, I reckon."

Clay looked at Sophie for a long moment, then let the gate slam shut between them and ran down the holler road with Maggie bouncing on his hip. Alma ran at his heels, hollering for him to wait, but he didn't. He ran to their house, burst through the front door, and fell to the living room floor. He sat Maggie on the floor beside him and ripped off the newspaper wrapping.

When Alma rushed into the house, she stood in the doorway and didn't say a word. Clay was standing in the middle of the living room with the quilt pulled up to his face. He breathed in his mother's scent. It was probably long gone, since the clothes had sat in a musty basement for twenty-some years, but he could still catch a scent of her there. He smelled cigarettes and Tabu perfume, Teaberry chewing gum and the detergent in her dresses. He could smell her skin and her strawberry shampoo.

He snapped the quilt out onto the air and let it settle on the living room floor. Alma got right down on her knees and ran her fingers over the fine stitching. Clay smoothed one hand out over the quilt and wrapped his other one around Maggie's neck. She watched him as if she knew what was happening.

"This was my mother's," he told her.

THE NEXT MORNING, Clay awoke with Maggie pushed close to him. Alma lay on the other side of the child, sound asleep. He slipped out of bed quietly, taking the baby with him.

It was early, but full daylight, and when he came out of the house, he squinted in the new sun. He tried to wake Maggie, but she fell back into a thin sleep with her head on his shoulder. He put his face in her hair, which smelled of the bedcovers. He climbed the mountain easily, and it seemed he could hear the sun glistening on the branches of the trees that stood straight and tall, their limbs reaching toward Heaven. Easter had once told him that she thought the birds sang so beautifully early in the morning because they were giving thanks to God.

He moved along the steep mountain path effortlessly, feeling as if he were going to the top of the world. The sun fell in straight lines through the bright new leaves. Dew dripped out of the sarvis and dogwood.

He climbed over rocks and splashed through the narrow creek that made its way down the mountainside. The farther up he went, the thinner the morning mist became. It was slowly being eaten away by the spring sun. Halfway up the mountain, Maggie awoke, but she didn't take her head from Clay's shoulder.

At the summit, the sun washed out over the earth, so bright and yellow that he could see through the leaves fluttering on the trees. He walked across the top of the old mountain and looked out at the land below. There were no strip mines to be seen from here, no scars on the face of the earth, only mountains, pushing against the horizon in each direction, rising and falling as easily as a baby's chest.

He walked along, showing leaves and new buds to Maggie. When he looked up again, he stood in a small clearing that he had never noticed before. The trees here were thin saplings, so small that he couldn't understand how they withstood the heavy winds that sometimes blew at the top of the mountain. Clumps of bluebells grew at his feet, but that was all. There was no field of wildflowers. That place was lost forever, Clay figured. His mother had taken a piece of the world with her. There were no birds here, either, and it seemed like he could hear the world turning beneath his feet. A breeze, no stronger than a breath, danced through the treetops. It caused leaves to tremble and limbs to scratch together, and it sounded to him like the high, soft sound of a dulcimer. He held Maggie's arm out in front of her and twirled round and round, as though they were in the middle of a wild square dance.

SPECIAL THANKS FOR THE NEW EDITION

My gratitude to Lee Smith, who read the manuscript of a young unknown writer out of the goodness of her heart and encouraged me for years; to Sharyn McCrumb for being an early teacher who taught me so much; to Robert Morgan for his generosity of spirit; to Kathy Pories for being the first editor to believe in my work; to my aunt, Thelma "Sis" Smallwood, for buying me my first typewriter and my first guitar; to my parents for always supporting my dream of being a writer; to all of my friends at the Appalachian Writers' Workshop whose love and understanding nurtured me; to Sandra Stidham and Barbara Hussey, my elementary and college teachers, respectively, who gave me permission to love literature as much as they did; to Tyler Childers for taking the time to write a moving foreword at what was likely the busiest time of his life. I am very thankful to Lynn York and Robin Miura at Blair for their devoted work in bringing this novel to a new generation of readers in a beautiful new edition. And finally, to all of the independent booksellers and readers who have kept the characters in this novel alive over the years.